# NO GOOD DEED . . .

EMIL O. ERICKSON

# DEDICATION

As always, to Margaret: lovely, intelligent, and irresistible,

And also because she still laughs at my jokes after all these years.


And to Robin Demouth, a dear friend and a gentleman worth
emulating.

NO GOOD DEED . . .

"'No good deed goes unpunished.' That's something my sainted mother used to say a lot when I was a kid. Right now I've got to see a man about a dog, but I'll be back. If you order us another couple of shots and chasers, I'll share a little story from a while back that drives home that point like a ten-penny nail through a softwood plank."

## CHAPTER 1

The surface of the rough-graded, dirt and gravel parking lot felt like a plowed and furrowed field as I bounced my '33 Ford coupe to the far end through the darker than deep purple night. The light from my headlights and an almost full moon offered little aid in avoiding every depression and partially buried rock in the line of my slow progress. After advancing into the darkness as far as I dared in the absence of any visible markers to guide me, I stopped, pulled the hand break, turned off the ignition, and sat in the dark for twenty minutes, occasionally using a flashlight to check my wristwatch.

With the engine shutdown, dead silence surrounded me, and frigid night air relentlessly sucked what little heat there was from the car's interior. Time crept by so slowly that at one point I held my Bulova to my ear to make sure it was still ticking. It was an unnecessary move, I know, but it gave me something to do as I sat there, waiting. I was far from bored, but eager for any diversion that could keep my mind off the risk I was taking.

At exactly 11:30, as I'd been directed, I got out, left the car unlocked, and, looking straight ahead at my objective, slowly walked toward the entrance to Ray's Bar & Grill. I left my suit coat lying on the front seat of the car, also per the strict instructions I'd been given. The cold slammed through my thin cloth shirt like sudden death. It was too dark even to see my feet as I walked, and the uneven pressure of the rough ground against the soles of my shoes made the short trip seem more precarious than it likely was. In my right hand I gripped, tighter than necessary, the handle of a light-brown leather briefcase that held the cash.

I'd had no trouble finding the place; it was the only thing lit up and still open for business along that stretch of Ventura Blvd. It didn't look like much in the dark, the only exterior light a string of unshaded bulbs hanging over a painted, unartistic wooden sign that identified it as Ray's. Not as seedy-looking as I'd expected for a low-life cafe and lower-life roadhouse-style bar located so far out from anything that might be considered a town. It would no doubt look a lot worse in the light of day; I could only hope that after completing my night's task I would still be around to find out.

It was the tail end of a hot summer, the last full week of September, but the land cooled off quickly in the west end of the San Fernando Valley when the sun went down and some of the damp air from the coast near Malibu found its way through the twists and turns of Topanga Canyon. Still, those conditions didn't account for the cold sweat down the center of my back and on the palms of my hands, nor for the slight weakness I felt in my knees as I made my way to the door.

Parked near the front were a handful of unwashed jalopies, any one of which could have been a slightly older and a little worse for wear cousin of my heap. A bank of un-curtained windows lined the front of the single-story, wood-framed structure, providing a clear look into the interior of the cafe. I didn't pause to take advantage of that view as I didn't anticipate I would have to face the threat that I feared in the semi-crowded bar and grill. I just opened the door and strolled in, as if I were a tired traveler with nothing more on his mind than grabbing a cup of joe to help stay awake before continuing his late-night journey.

As I entered, I quickly scanned the single, well-lit, long rectangular room that comprised the public area of Ray's. Facing away from me, four medium-height, nondescript men wearing what looked to be dusty work clothes were huddled together at one end of a bar that stretched out along most of the back wall of the room. A bored-looking bartender stood at the other end of the counter polishing a single glass with a bar towel that looked as if it would add more grime to the tumbler than it would remove. To the left of the bar a single swinging-door with a porthole-shaped window led to what I assumed was the kitchen.

The dining section of the place consisted of wooden tables with chairs for two or four spaced out between the windows that lined the front wall and the bar. Only two of the tables were occupied: One by a young Mexican couple clearly more interested in each other than in me. The girl was dressed in a loose, frilly, low-cut white blouse; a wide, floral print skirt; and leather sandals. The boy was clad in a clean shirt and string tie, clearly spiffed-up and slicked-down for the occasion. The other table was surrounded by what looked to be four local ranchers dressed in dungarees and still wearing their straw cowboy hats even though the sun had set outside several hours earlier.

No one paid me any mind as I crossed the width of the room and took a seat at an empty table near the unoccupied end of the bar, facing away from the front windows. From where I was seated with the briefcase jammed between the back of my calves and the front legs of my chair, I would be clearly visible to someone looking in from the parking lot. But with the reflection of the interior lights shining off the windows, there would be no way that I could see such a someone, even if I'd broken the rules that had been laid down for me and turned to try to look out—I supposed that was the general idea.

I sat alone for several minutes, unattended. Eventually, a tired and worn, late-middle-aged waitress in an even more tired and worn, unadorned dress that passed for a uniform came out from the kitchen, poured me the cup of black coffee I requested, and dropped a scrawled paper check on the table before disappearing through a door into the kitchen, never to be seen again during the remainder of the half-hour that I sat there. The lack of refills was okay with me, as the last thing I needed was to tank-up on coffee ahead of whatever else awaited me for the remainder of the night.

At midnight, as determined by my frequently monitored wristwatch, I dropped a nickel on the table next to the check to pay for the coffee that I'd finished off ten minutes earlier, left another nickel as an undeserved tip, picked up the briefcase, and walked back out into the parking lot. The crisp night air again penetrated my shirt like a pelting rain of tiny ice picks and chilled me to my core before I was halfway across the lot on my way to my car.

On the driver's seat next to my jacket, instead of an expected note, I found a small package wrapped in brown paper. I picked it up, slid in behind the wheel, and leaned over to grab my flashlight. I cut the twine on the packet with a pocketknife and carefully unwrapped the paper with my fingertips, although I doubted there would be any prints on the package from which the police might ultimately gain any information. The package contained the anticipated note—which was a good thing—and a pair of handcuffs with no keys—which from what was written about them in the note was *not* such a good thing.

Following the written instructions, I drove on Mulholland Drive to Topanga Canyon, where I turned south toward Malibu for about three miles. Despite the moon, the canyon was as black as a coalminer's nose at quitting time. The asphalt of the narrow, winding two-lane road seem to absorb rather than reflect the beams from my headlights. When I reached the two and a half-mile mark per my odometer, I slowed to just above a walking pace, my attention split between keeping my tires on the curving road and looking for the burnt-out hulk of a car that the note assured me I'd find on the shoulder exactly one quarter of a mile before a no-name dirt road on which I was to make a right turn. As it was, in the darkness I still almost missed seeing both the car and the side road.

When I did locate the turnoff, I drove even more carefully along what seemed more a weather-worn, pothole-marred footpath than a road. The darkness and the mist clinging to the trees and shrubs that lined my progress were so intense that I couldn't distinguish the hills surrounding me from the sky above them. Finally, my high beams lit up the massive oak tree and the large, solitary, erratic bolder that had been promised in the note. I couldn't have missed them, as at that point the road seemed to dead-end.

I left the car running in neutral, its headlights shining on the tree and its stone companion, rolled down the window on the driver's side, opened the door, and got out, grabbing my jacket on the way. Standing beside the open car door, facing toward the tree, colder now than before, even with my jacket on, I knowingly and willingly did one of the most foolhardy things I've ever done in my life: I hand-cuffed my right wrist to the open door's window frame.

The oak loomed before me, its trunk and twisted limbs a misty grey lattice contrasted against a more caliginous background. As I stood there, I realized I'd been mistaken about this being the end of the road. Just before it reached the tree, the narrow dirt track took a sharp jag to the left and dropped out of sight into the darkness. Where it led, I would never know, nor care to find out.

My eyes traced fantastic patterns in the rough bark and branches of the tree. Whether my shivering during the ten or fifteen minutes I waited there, my back to the route I'd just driven, was caused by the chill or by my fear I couldn't say for sure, but my best guess still is that it was primarily the latter. Any second thoughts about having agreed to this ill-advised adventure were useless now. I'd known from the get-go that I had no choice; I had to do it. Now there was nothing for it but to wait and worry. Despite my trepidations, I couldn't help thinking that this escapade was starting to seem like some poorly thought-out Hollywood script. The whole thing would've been ludicrous if the stakes hadn't been so high.

Finally, I heard a car driving slowly up the dirt road, its tires cracking loudly as they rolled over loose gravel. It stopped well behind me, the beams from its headlights blending with those of mine, lighting the tree and boulder more intensely but doing nothing to dispel the darkness that surrounded them.

I continued to focus my attention on the damned tree and rock. It wasn't easy, even though I knew that if I'd glanced over my shoulders into the headlights behind me, I wouldn't have seen anything through the glare. At that point I was certain that no matter whatever I might try to do beyond the written instructions I'd been given would be an even bigger mistake than the one I was already making.

A car door slammed shut with what seemed the report of a touched off cannon in the relative silence of the canyon. Then there was the softer sound of footsteps coming up behind me, crunching on the loose ground. A gloved hand reached out and touched my left shoulder before sliding under my arm and patting the side of my jacket. Satisfied that I had no gun, my unseen visitor's hand slid back. I was starting to feel a bit better about things, relaxing a little; if he was going to shoot me, he'd have done it by then rather than waste time looking for a weapon.

Then it hit me—not like an idea, more like a brickbat. It felt as if a hole had been drilled into the back of my skull and someone was trying to cram every sharp object he could find into the opening. It lasted for only a split-second before everything went dark and quiet and the pain stopped, but it was long enough for me to realize I was going down for a full count. My life didn't exactly pass before my eyes, but there was going to be more than enough time for my subconscious to re-live the events that had led me to this unpleasantness.

## CHAPTER 2

The house, a sprawling, two-story Spanish-style structure, seemed to take on different facades to match the time of day. Its white-washed plaster walls, textured to look like adobe brick, blazed pink and orange in the late afternoon sun as I walked toward it up the broad, automobile-packed driveway. Despite my dark glasses, an intense glare from a large, arched, plate-glass window was painful to the eyes. A massive oak front door, stained the same dark tint as the window trim, stood at the top of eight broad tiled steps glazed the color of dried blood. The whole setting had a campfire-like glow, an end of days feeling. I wouldn't have been too surprised to hear 'taps' blowing softly in the distance.

Finding the front door unlocked as usual, I took a familiar route through the house, moving from the over-sized foyer along a hallway that passed the living room and a den-like private office, through a bank of French doors off the dining room, and into a backyard patio filled with mostly handsome men in open-necked silk shirts and light-weight slacks and mostly beautiful women in bright colored summer dresses, all standing around a swimming pool big enough to give Johnny Weissmuller a workout. A five-man ensemble tucked away in a corner at the far side of a patch of grass was playing soft background music—Cole Porter, not taps.

I removed my dark glasses and slipped them into the breast pocket of my lightweight sport coat, not so much to avoid being mistaken for one of the Hollywood notables scattered about the patio, but on the chance that one of the aspiring, unknown starlets wandering by might take note of my compelling hazel eyes. Many had remarked, lefthandedly, that my eyes were the one redeeming feature in my otherwise rugged-beyond-its-years face, which had stopped its progress somewhere just short of handsome. That was fine with me, as it tended to distinguish me in a town in which good-looking pans were a dime-a-dozen.

I'd just grabbed a sweating glass of scotch and soda off a tray carried by a house boy in a white linen jacket, and pressed it to my lips, when I heard just north of a Southern accent declare, "Marshall, you handsome devil, you. What are you doing here?" This from the cutest little blue-eyed blonde you'd ever hope to meet, certainly the cutest I'd ever met. She was wearing a low-cut, cornsilk-yellow dress and high heeled, open-toed sandals and standing, as usual, the sole woman in the middle of a group of tall, dark, and handsome men, none of whom I recognized. The woman, whom anyone would've recognized, was Joan Blondell.

"Hello, Joan," I replied, and nodded at the rest of the group—who looked a little put out by the arrival of another suitor for Joan's attention. They needn't have been concerned as, even if it had been a possibility, I had no designs on the way-out-of-my-league and recently happily married Joan. Besides, I'd just entered into a promising relationship of my own, on which I intended to focus my full attention for the foreseeable future—meandering starlets who might be taken with my alluring eyes notwithstanding.

"Hi, I'm William Marshall," I said and in turn shook the extended hands, hearing each of the men speak his name, and— despite my determination to break a bad habit—without exception forgetting each name before releasing my grip. I quickly forgave myself for my lapse by assuming without proof that they couldn't have recited my name either.

"Where have you been keeping yourself?" Joan asked. "I haven't seen you around the studio lately."

"I'm in the newspaper racket now," I explained.

"Really?" Her eyes opened wider than their usual distinctive diameter, as if she were impressed, which I'm sure she wasn't. Joan had a knack of giving men the feeling that under the right circumstance they'd have a good chance with her, while at the same time letting them know without actually saying so that those circumstances would never arise. I for one didn't mind, as the ride was worth it.

My big career change had been to take a job as a low-level crime reporter for the Los Angeles Examiner. I had no training in the newspaper business—not even on a bike as a paper-route kid. A couple of years toward an English lit degree at UCLA before I'd dropped out, and a stab at screenwriting, without success, while working for Warner Brothers in a variety of menial jobs, made up the extent of my writing experience. But, as it turned out, my reluctant involvement in helping to solve a couple of murders and in shooting it out with a low-level thug had given me something of a dubious and personally unwanted reputation that Carl Greenberg at the Examiner thought might sell some papers. Never mind that my solutions to the crimes were more luck than skill and more contrived than accurate, or that the one time I was on the controlling end of a gun, while it was an action taken in righteous self-defense, might better be described as a bushwhacking than a gunfight.

I'd caught Greenberg's attention when I gave testimony involving the affair that had led to the downfall of Vincent Fisher as a major movie star. Gary Holder, my boss at studio security, had predicted that even though Fisher might get off on the murder charge, his career would be trashed. Although I'd been instrumental in helping to clean things up to Warner Bros.' benefit, it was the second time I'd been peripherally connected to a murder that came close to involving the studio. None of it was my fault, and there had been no reason to fire me—just the opposite—but there certainly was a feeling that I was on some sort of a negative streak. As an amateur gambler I could understand and sympathize with the studio's feelings that, if not exactly unlucky myself, I was something of a 'cooler' from their point of view. Greenberg's offer gave both the studio and me a clean exit, allowing us to skirt the issue.

My new job consisted of spending a lot of nights hanging around police stations and the courthouse; drinking tepid, stale coffee; getting to know a lot of good and bad cops, reporters with a lot more experience than I, and other disreputable characters on a first name basis; and waiting for something newsworthy to happen, which seldom did. So far it hadn't proved to be much more interesting than the work I'd done for Warner Bros., although I had hopes.

But at that moment and in the current company, drinking and partying rather than work was what I had in mind.

"Where's Dick?" I asked, looking around the patio for Dick Powell, Joan's frequent co-star and recently attained second husband. Powell was an easy-going, likable guy, who always seemed to have the time for a little good-natured banter. I was hoping that I might get an opportunity to indulge in some of that with him when I was finished flirting with his bride.

"He's not here; birthday parties for five-year-olds are a little out of his line," Joan responded non-judgmentally. "I'm with this guy today," She grinned and took hold of the arm of a tall, better-than-nice-looking fellow with both of her hands, pulling herself playfully up close to him. "Meet Ronny Reagan; he's new in town, just off the boat from Illinois."

Reagan flashed me a smile that seemed to say, 'You're going to like me when you get to know me.' I couldn't help thinking he might be right about that. What he did say was, "Call me Dutch."

I grinned back at him and said, "Call me Marshall. I've never managed to land a suitable nickname."

"Ronny has just finished shooting his first picture at the studio. Maybe you could put something about him in your newspaper," Joan suggested and slipped me a sly wink to acknowledge between us that she was just teasing me. Her eyelash moved so quickly that I might have missed it if I hadn't been expecting it.

"Well, it's not exactly my newspaper, Joan . . . not yet anyway," I said, playing along. "I suppose I could drop a word to Parsons that you're showing Dutch around town. That might get her to mention it in her column."

Louella Parsons wouldn't give the time of day, let alone any printer's ink, to a new kid in town, "fresh off the boat" as Joan had aptly described him. But Joan was hot, liked by both the public and the press; Parsons might welcome the chance to perk up her column by mentioning Joan, even if it was only a passing, one-line reference.

"I'd appreciate that," Reagan said with what sounded like sincerity.

"I can't promise anything, but I'll try," I said with equal candor, hoping that he would understand or that Joan would fill him in later that there was little chance that anything would come of it. "The way I see it, you've only been in town for a couple of months, and you've already made one picture and got yourself invited to little Danny Fitzgerald's birthday party: that's a pretty good start. Can you ride a horse?"

"Well, as a matter of fact, I can," Reagan said with an amused grin.

"Then you've got nothing to worry about, Dutch. In my book, all of that makes you a shoo-in." I was overstating the case just to be nice about it. I'd grown up around Warner Bros.' back lot and knew there were no sure things for people trying to break into the movie business. Reagan appeared to have all of the necessary physical characteristics and the requisite charm to make it, but I couldn't help hoping he hadn't burnt any bridges on his way west, which he might need to re-cross on his way back to

Illinois if things didn't work out in Hollywood.

Hoping to change the topic, I turned my attention back to answering Joan's initial question about my being at the party by explaining that I had the pleasure of being a nominal uncle to Danny, the birthday boy in whose honor the party was being thrown, so my attendance was required. Joan topped that by disclosing she was Danny's godmother. When she said it, I recalled she'd been working with Danny's father on a picture he'd produced at Warner Bros. about the time Danny was born.

In 1937 Hollywood it wasn't unusual for an afternoon, adults-only birthday bash for a five-year-old to extend into a late evening cocktail party. The children's party, which I'd also attended earlier in the day in my unofficial avuncular capacity, had involved several unruly five- and six-year-olds—their mothers on hand wielding highballs and martinis, paying the children little or no attention—cake and ice cream, red-white-and-blue balloons, and a series of Loony Tunes cartoons that the studio had sent over. It wasn't too bad; I like cake, ice cream, and cartoons—balloons and a pack of out-of-control kids, not so much.

Both parties were hosted at the home of Stephen "Fitz" Fitzgerald and Pilar Fuertes, Fitz's wife of six years and mother of their only child, Danny. Fitz, formerly an associate producer at Warner Bros., had turned independent last year and recently produced a well-received picture starring Pilar. Word on the street was that Fitz had also recently acquired the rights to a popular novel that, if he could write, produce, and direct into a decent movie, as he planned—feats that no one doubted he could pull off—he'd be on easy street both professionally and financially, not that he wasn't already doing just fine in those categories.

Fitz and I had connected when we were both at the studio. As an established producer, Fitz traveled in more exalted company than a mere nobody such as I had been at that stage of my glacial-paced writing career. But once during a casual conversation when I was driving him to the train station, we learned that we both had spent our teenage years in the same neighborhood in Glendale and had attended the same high school. Fitz, who was several years older than I, had graduated and moved on long before my family bought a house in that area just before the start of my junior year.

The discovery of our common backgrounds had led to a nodding relationship and eventually to a friendship after a few highly successful, unpaid babysitting gigs on my part with Danny. It turned out that Fitz and I shared many interests, but I suspect one of the main reasons that our friendship had developed into something more than superficial was that I was one, if not the only one of Fitz's acquaintances in Hollywood who wasn't at the same time a business competitor or someone looking for a favor.

I think what really cemented my relationship with the Fitzgeralds was the rapport I'd developed with Danny. From the get-go I was "Uncle Marshall," always fun, always willing to bend the rules, if not actually break them. Danny would run up and hug my leg when I showed up at the door, and there was always a goodnight kiss for me on the cheek. For people who know me casually, it's hard for them to believe I like little kids, but the fact is little kids make me smile. And I particularly liked Danny, one of the sweetest, most even-tempered kids I'd ever known.

Just as I was about to launch into another contrived assault on Joan, I was hindered by the arrival of Annie Shannon, Fitz's shapely, dark haired, deep blue-eyed, knock-out good looking and extremely smart personal assistant. She was wearing a ruby-tinted, short, sleeveless cocktail dress, which showed her slender arms and enticing legs to great advantage. The smile on Annie's lips, which were an exact match to the color of her dress, conveyed an honest friendliness toward the group. She had the carriage of a fashion model when she walked, and when she spoke it was with the accent of a mid-westerner, which meant she had no accent at all. If I hadn't had firsthand knowledge that it was otherwise, I might have suspected that she was a wayward angel who worked part-time as a girl-Friday for a movie producer for pin money. Introductions were unnecessary as she knew everyone in the group, having worked for Fitz for the last two years and having handled all the invitations for the party. She knew me well enough, as we'd been seriously dating for the last two months.

My resolve to avoid significant romantic entanglements with women following my ill-fated affair with the now semi-famous Laura Serle had disappeared within the initial two minutes of my first date with Annie. Her numerous physical and intellectual virtues were factors, of course, but what really closed the deal for me was that she laughed at my jokes, not all of them—that would be asking too much—but enough. That has been an all too rare quality in most of the women I have known, so I would've been a fool to let this one get away. In an intense two-week campaign following our first outing, I managed to win her over with my boyish charm and in spite of my slightly less than camera-ready kisser. Two months into the relationship it was as if there had never been anyone else—and I suppose in a sense there never really had been.

"Joan, I see that you have managed as usual to corral all of the eligible bachelors," Annie joked.

"I know, I know, I think it's my big blue eyes," Joan responded, offering a sly, yet friendly smile that had to run a close second to—if not a dead heat with—her peepers in the sexual attraction field. "I'm glad you showed up; I can use all the help I can get."

"I'd be happy to help out," Annie said, bestowing a close match to one of Joan Blondell's false-promise smiles on the men. "But it looks to me as if you have everything under control. It's kind of like watching Clyde Beatty at work with a cage full of hungry lions. I should probably just observe and take notes."

Annie made small talk with the group for a few minutes, a good surrogate hostess, though, to my thinking, paying too much attention by half to Reagan, before asking, "Joan, can I borrow this guy for a few minutes?" inclining her head toward me, "Fitz wants to talk with him."

"Okay, but I hate to lose him," Joan lied sweetly.

"Don't worry, he'll be back, I'm sure," she said as she led me away, her soft hand gently, but resolutely, clasping my elbow as she directed me toward where she wanted me to go. Normally I might have resisted losing the opportunity to toss softball pitches at Joan, but to my way of thinking gaining some alone time with the lovely Annie Shannon was a fair tradeoff. Anyway, I had the feeling that I was just about to run out the string on my stable of witty repartees.

## CHAPTER 3

Fitz wants to see me?" I asked as we walked toward the house.

"Yes, he does, but not right now," Annie replied. "Later, after everyone is gone. I just wanted to get you away from that group."

"Jealous?"

"Don't kid yourself." She smiled wryly as she said it. "I thought I should get you out of there before you made a fool of yourself."

"Too late for that, I'm afraid," I joked. "I was going to come looking for you anyway; with so many leading men prowling around, I thought I'd better protect my interests."

"And give up your spot next to Joan? I doubt it." The hint of a smirk and a twinkle in her eye told me that she was aware as I of the innocuous nature of my bantering with Joan. "Anyway, the true reason for my pulling you away is that your presence has been requested by the birthday boy for a bedtime story."

"Ah . . . yes," I intoned with a delivery that would've done W. C. Fields proud. "We're in the middle of my rendition of <u>Treasure Island</u> for five-year-olds. I do an imitation of Wallace Beery as Long John Silver. It's not very good, but Danny likes it. Would you like to hear it?"

From the dry look she gave me, I could tell she had little

doubt about the veracity of both of my last two contentions. "No I wouldn't, but apparently Danny does, so get on with it. Besides, Mag wants to join the party."

'Mag' was Magdalena Ruiz, Danny's nineteen-year-old Mexican nanny, the shortest woman I'd ever met: four-foot-ten at best in shoes with a good-sized heel. She spoke almost no English and gave little indication that she had any interest in learning it. Not that she was lazy, she worked hard enough and took excellent care of Danny. But not learning to speak English probably allowed her to avoid many conversations that she would just as soon not be bothered with. And I expected she didn't so much want to join the party as to stand in the background and unobtrusively watch the movie stars from a respectful distance.

Having reached the intended destination, Annie released her gentle tether and cast me off at the patio entrance to the dining room. Then after bestowing a quick kiss on my cheek, she turned without further ado to look for a new group of partiers to chat up.

I retraced my earlier route through the house to the main staircase near the entrance and climbed the stairs. When I reached the landing to the second floor, I saw and heard Mag standing at the far end of the hallway at the door to Danny's room near the back of the house, arguing in a low but unmistakably aggravated tone with her brother, Javier. My Spanish is poor—about average for an Anglo born and raised in Southern California—so I made no effort to try to make out what their dispute entailed. But one didn't need to be a linguist to recognize that it was a heated, angry exchange—Mag was little, but given adequate provocation she could be fierce.

Javier was taller than his sister—who wasn't? —but not that tall by other standards, and a little younger. He was thin and wiry, and always seemed to be looking at something on your forehead when he talked with you, and unimpressed by whatever it was that he saw there. His seemingly perpetual scowl and usual surly manner gave him the look of a hood in the making. He didn't work for Fitz but delivered Mag to work each morning and picked her up in the evenings, so it wasn't unusual to see him around the place. It was, however, odd to see him on the second floor instead of in the backyard or the kitchen, and on the receiving end of a bawling-out in Spanish by his sister; my previous impression had been that he was the one of the pair who did most of the intimidating.

The arguing stopped abruptly as soon as they spotted me at the far end of the hallway. Javier, scowling but now silent, retreated rapidly down the back stairs, clearly having no desire to enter into a conversation with me, cordial or otherwise. He needn't have made so quick an exit; I had no idea what it was that they'd been barking at each other and wasn't particularly interested in finding out. If it hadn't been for the confrontational tone, I wouldn't've given their spat a second thought. I was naturally a little curious, but I didn't bother to ask Mag what the tiff had been about.

Mag smiled weakly at me, the emotional remnants of her truncated argument still apparent from the strained features that showed through the glow of light sweat on her face and the tight way she carried herself. "Good evening, Sẽnor Marshall. Danny waits . . ." Her English vocabulary tapped out; she extended her arm toward the door to Danny's bedroom as an invitation for me to enter.

Smiling back at her, hoping to relieve some of the embarrassment we both apparently felt, I remarked with forced casualness, "Hi, Mag. How's Danny holding up under all the birthday excitement?"

"Bueno . . . Good," was all she had to offer. Mag's arm remained extended toward Danny's room like a detour sign directing my traffic away from her, an unspoken indicator that she was finished trying to make useless conversation in any language and wanted me about my business. So, without further comment, I stepped past her into the bedroom.

Sitting up in bed with his powder blue cotton pajamas on, Danny, his straight light brown hair for some reason carefully brushed smooth before its nightly losing battle with his pillow, held <u>Treasure Island</u> in his small hands, thumbing ahead in its pages to preview the Wyeth illustrations, which I had to admit invariably proved much more exciting to Danny than my verbal renderings of the text. When he saw me, he dropped the book on the bed covers and reached out his arms inviting a hug. "Uncle Marshall!"

I lost no time in accepting the proffered embrace and the kiss on the cheek that went with it.

Annie had told me that Danny had made a brief, earlier appearance at the evening event to be tickled and ogled over by those women with maternal leanings, and generally avoided by most of the men. By the look that she'd described in his soulful pale blue eyes, Annie could tell that Danny hadn't much cared for having his hair mussed or for being call a "little fellow," but he'd taken it in a typically tolerant Danny-like style before his banishment to the nursery to get ready for bed.

I took up the book from where it lay on the blanket and began to look for the place where we'd left off a few nights before. My readings were always preceded by a synopsis of what had occurred in the story to the point where we'd previously stopped. These summaries were usually punctuated with numerous interruptions by Danny's asking questions and seeking clarifications. This time, however, we didn't even get that far.

"Wait! Wait!" Danny exclaimed before I had a chance to begin.

"What?" I asked, uncertain as to the reason for his mild exclamations.

Danny took the book back from me and began to flip rapidly through its pages until he found what he was looking for.

"Read me this."

He pointed to a colored illustration about two-thirds of the way into the text that showed Jim Hawkins near the top of a mast, silhouetted against a clean white cloud hanging in a Caribbean blue sky, his feet firmly pressed into the rigging, both hands pointing downward and holding pistols. Below him, Israel Hands leaning out, hung by one hand to the uppermost part of the ratlines, his billowing, dirty white shirt contrasted against a tan, gaff-rigged sail, the pirate's straight right arm extending downward, a formidable knife in his hand poised for throwing. The caption read, "One more step, Mr. Hands."

Given Danny's propensity for interruption and his tendency to quickly drop off to sleep while his questions were being answered, in my previous readings we'd proceeded no further than Jim still dutifully waiting tables at the Admiral Benbow and being harassed unmercifully by Capt'n Billy Bones. I immediately realized Danny's wisdom beyond his years in the suggestion of our jumping ahead into something more exciting. At the rate we were progressing, Danny would be a junior in college by the time we reached the scene in which he was now indicating interest. Without comment—or any attempt to explain how Jim Hawkins found himself in this dilemma—I turned to the beginning of the appropriate chapter and began to read. As it worked out, Danny was asleep long before I was anywhere near where Jim and Israel began their climb up the mast of the good ship *Hispaniola*.

Alerted to Danny's slumbering by his soft breathing, I closed the book, gently set it down on the nightstand, turned out the reading light, checked that the night light was on, and gave Danny a kiss of my own on his forehead before tiptoeing out and softly closing the door behind me.

# CHAPTER 4

Returning to the party, I was disappointed to learn that Joan Blondell had left for the evening. I grabbed a drink from another tray carried by what looked to be the same circulating, hired waiter I'd dealt with before—or his identical twin—and sought to console myself by joining a group of three non-celebrity males focusing their attentions on Pilar and Annie. While I had no doubt that the women both could hold their own in such situations, I felt my presence might, in Annie's case anyway, give them more incentive to do so. It didn't take me long to determine that the only real threat among the three men was Charles Stoke, Esq., Fitz and Pilar's attorney, whose target at the moment was clearly Pilar. I can't say that I blamed him.

Pilar Fuertes, a twenty-four-year-old with long, black hair, dark blue eyes, and an athletic dancer's body, was an exotic beauty—a sort of Hispanic Hedy Lamarr. Her studio biography claimed she was Spanish on her father's side and French on her mother's—the Spanish likely arriving via Mexico City and the French more Louisiana Creole than Parisian. All of which may have explained her fiery temper and the fact that she and Fitz occasionally engaged in loud, although never to my knowledge physical arguments. Fitz had met Pilar when she was an eighteen-year-old unknown, would-be actress; cast her in her first significant role; and, except for a brief hiatus when Danny was born, promoted her career through a series of increasingly better parts. In typical Hollywood tradition, Pilar had kept her unmarried stage name to perpetuate her available, Latin sex-symbol image.

My relationship with Pilar was friendly enough, but somewhat distant by design. Pilar was not the type to develop what one would call friendships, her sexuality too intense for any man to overlook. And she was too good looking for any woman to want to stand close to her for long, let alone to be a regular companion. As a healthy male the best I could manage was to lust after her quietly from a distance, and as Fitz's friend to keep my hands in my pockets when I was near her. I'm not the type to cheat with a friend's wife—or anyone else's wife for that matter—but I'm not above benignly fantasizing about it from time to time.

"Is my son asleep?" Pilar asked me, more as a way to acknowledge my joining the group than any true concern about Danny's sleeping habits. Not that Pilar was a bad mother by any account; she loved Danny above all things and was attentive and caring when she was with him. But when he was being attended to by the trusted Mag or was safely bedded down for the night, she felt free to concentrate on her other favorite topic: Pilar—or, more accurately, Pilar's movie career.

"Sleeping like a carefree five-year-old with a successful father and a beautiful mother—a consummation devoutly to be wished," I replied and smiled good-naturedly to show that my assessment was sincere on all accounts.

"William has a knack for putting people to sleep," Annie chided to gently put me back in my place and to attempt to refocus the conversation on Pilar, which was always a good idea when Pilar was in the mix. "I doubt we'll hear anything from Danny until breakfast tomorrow." Annie's comment induced a friendly smile from Pilar before she turned her attention, or more accurately her alluring face, back to the men paying court to her.

Annie and Pilar had a special relationship: They got along well, a rare thing considering that they were both exceptionally attractive women and one of them a movie star. But Annie, who had no interest in a screen career, wisely never upstaged Pilar in any social situation and tried to make a point of subtly promoting her by complimenting her on some aspect of her appearance: her dress, her shoes, her necklace or whatever, or by mentioning some new development in Pilar's career that she knew Pilar would like to shoehorn into the conversation. Pilar also knew that Annie's relationship with Fitz was strictly business, friendly, close in a way, but with no romantic over- or undertones. That all added up to Annie's being a woman, if not the only woman in Hollywood, that Pilar felt she could truly trust.

"Fitz tells me you've started a new career," Charlie Stoke said, breaking into my thoughts and directing his previously focused attention away from Pilar. Why my recent change of jobs would've been a topic of conversation between Stoke and Fitz was a little surprising but not worthy of much consideration.

Charlie Stoke was a guy in his late thirties, friendly, witty, and a lot easier going than most legal types I've known. You might call him debonair, a term that seems to have many different meanings depending on who it is you're trying to portray. In my book his approach toward establishing that sobriquet seemed a little forced, but then I wasn't the intended target of his charm. Stoke with his natural blond hair, clear light-gray eyes, and straight, abnormally white teeth reminiscent of the keys on a fresh concert piano—not like the yellowing ivories on the tired bar room uprights with which I was more familiar—was damned good looking. He had a reputation for being quite the ladies' man, which I could believe. I suspected that his being a well-connected Hollywood attorney to the stars also gave him an advantage when it came to catching the attention and favors of many a budding actress. I'd met Stoke a few times when he'd visited the house with papers for Fitz or Pilar to sign, and at a few parties such as this one, but I didn't know him well.

"It's true," I answered Charlie's question, "but I'm not sure that 'career' is the right word. I would think you'd have to already have a career to say that you're starting a new one." My job at 'The Brothers' certainly hadn't qualified as anything like a career, and, so far, I hadn't found my new one at the Examiner to be much loftier. "Being a crime reporter, even a low-level beginner, sounds interesting, but so far there hasn't been much crime to report."

"Maybe all the criminals have heard you're on the job and skipped town," Stoke quipped.

"'Skipped town,' look at you talking like a detective in the movies," I responded, borrowing a line that my friend Lt. Archer of the LAPD had dropped on me a few months earlier.

Stoke laughed at my small joke at his expense, which raised him a line on my score card. "Well, I'm sure it'll only be a matter of days before you hit the big-time. I saw you talking to Joan earlier, pick up any juicy items there?"

"Just Hollywood stuff. I don't think Joan dabbles much in criminal activities. For me, any movie news would be a sideline, unless some leading lady decided to rob a bank or shoot her co-star. You haven't got any interesting tidbits for me, have you, Charlie?"

"Sorry. I'm just a contract attorney; crime's a little out of my area of expertise. Besides, if one of my clients was breaking the law, you wouldn't hear about it from me."

That ended the discussion about my recent change of jobs, which was a good thing from my point of view as I was still a little self-conscious about my lack of credentials in my newly adopted career. Stoke refocused his attention on Pilar, who as usual when the discussion wasn't about her had turned her head to one side to look away from the group. I didn't catch what he said to her, but it must've been a weak effort as there was a noticeable beat before Pilar acknowledged his comment by turning her face back in his direction with a frowning expression of complete disinterest.

There were attempts by others to rekindle the conversation by remarking on the latest rumors in the movie business, but nothing caught fire or did anything to placate Pilar's building pique. I was no great hand at talking small and knew better than to try to improve on that failing in this situation. A look of concern on Annie's face showed that she was agonizingly trying to think of a way to get the conversation back on track.

Ken Menske—bless his heart—always good for a laugh, managed to toss in a couple of recent anecdotes that no one else had heard before, which lightened the mood and took the pressure off the rest of the group. Ken had a reputation for easygoing, clever, self-deprecating humor, particularly at parties when he was well into his cups. The epitome of a small-time Hollywood producer, Ken was a short, pudgy fellow with thinning brown hair circling halo-like around a bald pate that even in the dim glow of the party lights seemed to glisten. A ubiquitous, half-smoked but currently unlit, wet-at-the-end cigar was expertly wedged between two fat fingers. He wore a tan sport coat, which probably had fit at one time, but which he now wisely left unbuttoned over his cream-colored, open-collared, bulging-at-the-midriff, silk shirt. A scarlet-hued, satin scarf knotted around his neck was almost hidden below his doubled over double chin.

Ken's entertaining stories, however, had nothing to do with Pilar and, accordingly, did nothing to improve her attitude. Pilar was getting bored and increasingly annoyed at not being the center of attention. She didn't offer anything of her own to the discussion, again in frustration turning her gaze away from the group and looking off across the patio at nothing in particular. An image of a mishandled champagne bottle with its cork about to pop of its own accord and its contents to spew forth on the group came to mind.

Menske must've sensed the problem as well, and buoyed by the success of his efforts with the rest of the group, he asked, "Pilar, what have you got in the works these days?" The question, while well-intended, was an ill-conceived effort and a surprising one given that Menske, a long-term associate of Fitz's and something of a regular around the Fitzgerald household, should've known that Pilar had nothing "in the works"' and that she'd been aggressively pestering her husband for a leading role in the new movie he was preparing for production. Fitz, from what Annie had told me, hadn't been receptive to the idea. Consequently, the topic had become a bone of contention between Pilar and her husband.

"Nothing." Pilar's lightening response came like a bullet aimed at Menske's forehead.

A hasty spark in his normally lazy brown eyes, enhanced by the lenses of his horn-rimmed glasses, was an indication that Ken realized his error even before Pilar's icy reaction to his remark. His left-footed comment to Pilar was out of character, but still, it hadn't been that big a deal. The truth of it was that it was hard for anyone to hold a normal conversation with Pilar without her eventually finding something with which to take offense if she was of that mindset. It was Pilar's typical approach for shutting down any conversation that didn't meet with her approval. This time she used a stone-cold look directed at Ken rather than a flow of heated words to express her wrath. Ken froze in place almost as if the chill radiating from Pilar's eyes had penetrated its target. The rest of us felt it too, if not as directly, nor as deeply.

Dr. Appel, the third man in the group that I'd recently joined, lifted the awkward silence with his perturbingly unctuous voice. "Pilar, my dear, it has been a tiresome day for you. Perhaps you should lie down for a few minutes . . . to calm your nerves,"

I'd briefly met Doctor Johann Georg Appel once before at the house when he was ministering to Pilar. He was a short, stocky man in his late-fifties, well-preserved if somewhat out of shape. His wavy grey hair, white silk shirt, dark blue silk tie and carefully arranged matching silk pocket handkerchief, all of which coordinated well with his tailor-made hundred-dollar grey suit with an ever-so-subtle chalk line running through it, gave him an air of distinguished competence. Whether he deserved it or not, I couldn't say for certain, but I'd heard otherwise. What I *could* say was that he had a reputation for being quick with the pills and the needles, being Pilar's main source for the same. I was surprised that he was at the party, since Fitz at one time had threatened to beat on him and turn him over to the cops if he didn't stop feeding

Pilar's developing habit.

Pilar turned and held out her hand for the doctor to take in his, preparatory to leading her away. Her face eased from a tense semi-scowl to a calmer, more passive expression. I felt the tension abate, as I'm certain it must have for the others in the group; it looked like the champagne cork was going to stay wired on to the bottle.

I'm certain that Dr. Appel's reference to Pilar's "nerves" was intended to protect him from any negative reaction to his comment. In those days it was an all-too-common ailment for actresses, and even some actors, who for some reason thought a nervous condition to be concomitant with—almost a necessary condition of—creative talent. It was something of an epidemic, which seemed to infect only star level performers and to cause no end of disruptions on movie sets. Unfortunately, an "attack of nerves" had become a convenient excuse for all sorts of immature, anti-social behavior. In Pilar's case it was only one of many of the gadgets that she kept in her emotional toolbox.

As a friend to both Pilar and Fitz, I was tempted to interject myself into what I saw was about to happen but realized it would be to no effective purpose and in all probability cause a crack in my otherwise unblemished relationship with Pilar. Charlie Stoke apparently had no such qualms. "There's nothing wrong with Pilar's nerves, Appel," Stoke remarked sternly. "You're a little too quick with the sedatives if you ask me, Doctor."

"No one asked you," a suddenly storm-cloud-faced Pilar said as she turned, detached her hand from Dr. Appel's, and swiftly stalked away from the group and into the house. Appel, after nodding furtively to the group, scurried away to follow her inside.

"That son-of-a-bitch," Stoke remarked at Appel's retreating back, loudly enough that the doctor would easily have heard him. "I ought to kick his ass down the driveway and out onto the street."

It would've been something interesting to watch, and no

doubt an even greater pleasure in which to participate, but it wasn't to be. With a couple of more hours of drinking, we might be lit up enough to try it, but as of then Charlie and I were both still well on the sober side of reason.

While I was onboard with Stoke's obvious disdain for Appel, I couldn't help thinking that his verbal reactions had exceeded those to be expected from a family solicitor or even those of a close friend, such as myself. Perhaps there was more to the rumors I'd heard of a romantic relationship between Stoke and Pilar than I'd previously given credence to, at least from Stoke's perspective.

Ken and Annie had remained silent during Stoke's comments and Pilar's exit. In the uncomfortable moments that followed, the four of us stood there without speaking: Stoke staring at the door through which Pilar and the doctor had entered the house, Ken and I looking down at our feet, and Annie surveying the pool area to see if there had been any reaction to our scene from the other guests. After that awkward, self-conscious, but short pause in the conversation, the group broke up and wandered away in different directions.

Annie, assuming the role of hostess, as often happened with the sudden disappearance of Pilar at such events, wrapped an arm around one of mine and directed us toward another group of partiers, one far enough away from where we'd been standing not to have heard Stoke's remarks directed at Dr. Appel. It was a smart move on her part, avoiding the need for disingenuous explanations to curious observers. By the time we would circle back to anyone who had been close enough to observe the excitement, they probably would've forgotten all about it.

But I wasn't about to forget it. "What do you make of what just happened back there?" I asked Annie before we reached the new group that she'd targeted.

"Nothing," was her quick, firm reply.

"Come on, you know what I'm talking about. Is there anything going on between Pilar and Stoke?"

Annie stopped and turned to face me straight on as she replied directly. "I don't know, but I wouldn't tell you if I did. What I will tell you is something that you probably already know or suspect; Pilar has three priorities: Danny, her career, and her marriage, in that order."

"So you think there's nothing to it."

"I didn't say that. What you probably don't know, and as a man probably won't understand, is that Pilar to some degree looks on sex as a tool. She would be quite capable of using it if she thought it would promote her career, while at the same time not letting it have any impact on her feelings for Fitz."

"Wow!" I replied, more than a little taken back by Annie's remark. She was at least partially right in assuming that I wouldn't fully grasp Pilar's ability to segregate, to wall off sex and personal relationships to suit her needs, but I sensed that Annie's assessment of it was on target.

# CHAPTER 5

The evening wore on, and I was wearing out. By the time Annie and I had completed our circuit of the guests, and now under the influence of several stiff drinks downed over a period of not enough hours, my attention span for social banter, never extensive, had contracted considerably. Annie had dutifully fulfilled her assumed role of hostess in Pilar's absence, and we were now headed toward one isolated group of four men huddled together at the far end of the pool. This less-than-sinister-looking cabal was headed up by our host Stephen Fitzgerald, waving a drink as he emoted to make a point, as if he were an evangelist enthusiastically directing his small congregation toward the collection box. From the way his body swayed with slight jerks, it was clear that the partially filled glass of liquor in his hand was only one of many he'd packed away over the course of the evening. He appeared to be in a heated discussion with Ken Menske, who for some reason seemed hellbent on 'stepping in it' that evening. This time, emboldened by several more drinks of his own, Ken appeared to be less reticent in expressing his heartfelt views on whatever the subject of their clearly confrontational conversation.

Standing close by was an uncomfortable looking Dick Melvin, a tall, thin, underweight, B-movie type with slicked-back, black hair, who clearly was intent on not being part of the current debate.

The fourth man, Jack Willis, Fitz's full-time chauffeur and some-time bodyguard, stood a little back from the others, more a careful observer of the action than a participant. I'd been told that Willis was ex-army, a statement reinforced by his fixed frown, close-cropped brown hair, and ramrod-straight stature. A man of average height, his muscularity made him seem shorter, almost stocky, built like a barroom bouncer and, although I'd never had an occasion to find out, looked to be twice, maybe three times as tough. Why Willis was at the party was beyond me; Fitz wasn't in any danger that I knew of that required a bodyguard—certainly not at an evening cocktail party from an overweight, out of shape, inebriated Ken Menske.

As we approached, Annie, realizing the contentious nature of the discussion between Fitz and Menske, paused and pulled back on my arm, briefly displaying a natural instinct not to interfere, before concluding that the better approach was for her to try to defuse the situation—apparently with my help. She whispered to me, "You take Fitz; I'll handle Kenny." There was no time to express my reluctance to get involved, which would've been a waste of words anyway, falling as they would've on lovely but deaf ears. Once decided on a course of action, Annie wasn't one to waste time debating it.

While Annie and I had been in close proximity to him from time to time when chatting with the other guests at the party, this was the first time that evening I'd been with or spoken to Fitz directly, previously just nodding or waving from across the yard. At some point, just about the same time that the sun had dropped below the treetops, Fitz had disappeared inside the house to switch from light wool slacks and a colorful, open-collared silk shirt into a white dinner jacket and black bow tie, which, as was his wont, made him standout compared to the casually dressed party guests. Not that his six-foot tall, carefully maintained athletic build; pale green eyes contrasted against a ruggedly masculine face; and an Irishman's smile—which seemed to silently say 'trust me'— weren't enough to do the trick. I don't know how much trust his smile engendered, but it rarely failed to make people meeting him for the first time take a liking to him, a liking that through constant reinforcement tended to linger for years. It'd certainly had that effect on me.

Knowing that Fitz's arguments, while loud and animated, rarely contained rancor, I decided to approach him as if nothing were amiss. "Stephen, my man, congratulations on siring such a fine young lad. But what, if anything, have you accomplished in the last five years to come close to matching that achievement?"

Fitz abruptly halted his diatribe directed at Menske, turned toward me, and smiled broadly. "William, it's about time you got around to spending some time with your host," Fitz said, reaching out and grabbing my shoulder, kneading it gently with his free hand in a friendly gesture. The other hand held his now nearly empty drink. After gazing warmly at me for a moment, he responded to my question, "Nothing even close, I'm afraid."

Fitz had adopted a convention of calling me 'William' to my face rather than 'Marshall' like everyone else. I countered by calling him 'Stephen' when speaking with him directly, rather than 'Fitz.' It was a compromise we'd reached, arising out of Fitz having once, early in our developing relationship, referred to me as 'Willie,' to which I'd responded by calling him 'Stevie.' That had been enough to get my point across. The fact that we spoke to each other using our given names gave me a feeling that our friendship, despite the differences in our ages and social standings, was a closer one than we had with most other people.

Whatever the immediate verbal dispute with Menske had been about, my casual reference to Danny, Fitz's favorite topic, was enough to divert him. "Have you been entertaining him? I wondered where you were."

"Of course, I've been entertaining him . . . or more accurately, he's been entertaining me," I countered. "When we finally got to the main event, he was hanging on my every word— all five of them before he fell asleep."

"Yeah, I know you often have that effect on people," Fitz kidded and good naturedly slapped me gently on my shoulder. It was the same bad joke Annie had dropped earlier in the evening; I was beginning to wonder if there wasn't something to it.

"Not true, Stephen," I replied in a lighthearted attempt to salvage my self-image. "That far into a conversation with me most adults don't usually fall asleep, they just want to take a swing at me.

"Besides, why would I want to spend time with you when I could spend it with your son or your wife; he's a lot more fun, and they're both a lot better looking."

"True on all counts, I must admit," Fitz replied, reigniting his warm Irish smile. "Well, at least you've found some time to spare for me now."

I knew that I'd scored points with Annie by diverting Fitz's attention and ending his confrontation with Menske without getting directly involved in it. Ken, on the other hand, clearly would've liked to continue the discussion if he could have figured a way to get it started again, but all he could manage in his less than sober state was a hangdog frown. He looked down at his feet and rocked slowly, uncertainly on them in a remarkably erratic, slightly rotating pattern.

Annie, who'd positioned herself slightly in front of Menske with her side to him while she pretended to listen to my banter with Fitz, sensed this too and opted to take charge of Ken before one of his swings from side to side or forward and back reached a tipping point. "Kenny, let's go inside and get you some coffee while I call a cab to take you home." She took his arm and deftly led him away. For his part, Ken wasn't so far gone as not to understand that being taken in hand to be tended to by the lovely Annie was a far, far better outcome than he would've achieved by rekindling a drunken argument he had no chance of winning. They left the group and walked toward the house without providing any of the standard departing salutations.

As soon as Menske was gone, it was as if he'd never been

there.

"William, you know this bum, Dick Melvin, don't you?" Fitz asked. "Dick was just explaining to me, for the umpteenth time, what a great actor he is, and I was agreeing with him of course. You got here just in time; we're both running out of superlatives. Being a writer and all, William, I figure you might be able to pick up the slack."

"Sure, Dick and I know each other," I responded, although I really didn't know him well. "How's it going?"

Up to that point Melvin had been lying back, doing a credible impression of a garden plant badly in need of a dousing of Spring rain, while Fitz and Menske had been having at it. With Ken gone, Dick now seemed to have relaxed. Grinning and reaching out he grabbed my hand with a none-too-firm grip. Then he picked up on my lead, mugged a sad face, and answered, "Okay, but I've got nothing going right now. I'm trying to get Fitz to find me a part in *Watcher*. Maybe you could put in a good word?"

Watcher on the Wall was the popular novel for which Fitz had recently bought the screen rights and was in the process of writing a script. To steal an overworked expression from my new profession, he'd 'scooped' the studios by anticipating the popularity of the book and recognizing its movie potential before the major studios caught on and snapped it up. Word was that his preemptive offer had cost him a lot of money. But if he could pull it off as writer, producer and, as some expected, director—and turn it into the hit it could easily be—he'd establish himself as a major player in the trade. Even badly written, poor productions of movies from popular novels were frequently box office successes, and Fitz was neither a bad writer nor a bad producer-director. Fitz had never struck out on a movie, which put him in good stead when he was at Warner Bros., but neither had he hit one out of the park; *Watcher* seemed as close to a sweet pitch as he would be likely to find.

"You wouldn't want that, Dick," I replied to Melvin's plea. "Stephen knows I'm no expert in the movie business. If he took any notice of my recommendations at all, he'd be more likely to do just the opposite of what I advise. Best I can do for you is to keep my mouth shut."

"That's okay," Fitz interjected. "Dick has already convinced me. I have some ideas."

"I appreciate that, Fitz." The sincerity and relief in Melvin's voice came through like a bright light through cut crystal.

For a while Fitz and Melvin reminisced about films they'd worked on together. Most of the stories were interesting and usually funny. This was the first time that I could remember interacting with Dick to any extent, and as I listened to him swapping yarns with Fitz, I was starting to cotton to him.

At some point, the shadowy Willis must've wandered away without a word, unnoticed, perhaps to assist Annie in her efforts to see the drunken Menske off on his way home.

We must've talked for longer than I realized, as the party was starting to wind down to those holdouts who wouldn't leave until the booze was gone—which would never happen at Fitz's place—or until the host saw them politely but resolutely escorted down the steps to waiting cabs to take them home to sleep it off or to some all-night club to continue the partying. There were never any hard feelings about getting a gentle bum's rush to the door; in fact, at that point, the evictees probably had little or no feelings at all.

It was about one o'clock when Fitz said he wanted to talk with me alone in his study. He asked Annie, who had rejoined us, to begin the process of closing down what was left of the party. Melvin, still remarkably sober given the number of drinks he'd put away, said his good nights and walked off into the night, a happy man having achieved his goal.

## CHAPTER 6

Fitz poured double shots of cognac into two massive crystal snifters and handed one to me as I sat leaning back into the soft Corinthian leather of the couch in his study. After easing himself into one of two matching chairs across from me, he said, "Here's looking at you pal," as he leaned forward and clinked his glass against mine. He held the glass up to the light for a second to admire the bronze-tinted liquid before pulling it back, resting his nose over the top of the snifter, and inhaling deeply, but not drinking—not just yet. From experience I knew he'd repeat this viewing and sniffing ritual at least five times before he'd actually take a sip from the glass cradled in his hand. As always on such occasions, I followed his lead, inhaling the potent fumes and waiting to drink until he did; after all, it was his VSOP, so I let him set the pace.

After the second sniff, he pulled his face away, gestured at me with the highly polished glass, and smiled—apparently, the auspices were good. Maybe, with any luck, this time he'd start drinking after the third incantation. He gave me the serious look he took on whenever he had something important to impart. It worried me a little, although I don't know why, since I knew he'd never ask me to commit a felony or do anything that was too immoral by my admittedly easy-going standards.

"William, I want you to do something for me, and I hope you'll say yes," he said, his face as serious as I'd seen it in all the time that I'd known him.

"I expect I will, but I can't say for sure until you tell me what it is," I responded, smiling an 'of-course-I-will smile.' "Who' do you want me to rub out?"

"Always the wise guy," he quietly chuckled. "Good, I like that about you. But this is serious stuff, so I need for you to can the smart mouth for a few minutes. Okay?"

I knew that Fitz wasn't admonishing me; he was just making sure that he had my attention. "Okay," I echoed, working up a serious face of my own, hoping that it didn't look forced, and taking a drink out of sequence, more because I could get away with it than any real need to steady my nerves—although I do hate the 'serious stuff.'

"I'm setting up a trust fund for Danny in case anything happens to me. I want you to be the trustee." Fitz flashed me one of his disarming smiles to make sure that he had me hooked and onboard with his request.

I didn't know exactly what that term meant in this situation, but I did know what the word 'trust' meant to regular guys like me. What Fitz was proposing didn't sound onerous and, given enough time, I was fairly certain I could figure it out, "Of course. I'd be honored," I answered truthfully.

"Great. But that's not all. I also want you to serve as the executor of my estate," he added, taking a drink of his own ahead of his normal routine. I followed suit to buy time to think on this new proposal and to stay one shot ahead of him.

"Stephen, I don't know anything about being an executor. Wouldn't an attorney like Charlie Stoke be better for something like that?" I suggested.

"No." His tone was emphatic. "You I trust. I don't totally trust Charlie. He's a good attorney—even honest, as far as that goes—but he's not a friend." He paused, deciding whether to tell me more. "You know there's a rumor going around that he's having an affair with Pilar. She's been seen having lunch with him a couple of times. And there are too many people in my business who can't wait to make certain that one hears about these things. No one likes to have that sort of crap flying around, if you know what I mean. I'm sure there's nothing to it, but it doesn't make me any more comfortable with him."

I tried my best to show no reaction to his revelation. "I imagine not," I said in a non-committal tone.

"I can see from your face you've heard the rumor," he said. I didn't reply, just made a mental note never to play poker with Fitz if he could read me that well despite my best efforts at presenting a blank expression.

"Pilar's got nothing happening right now, and no work always makes actors Nervous Nellies," Fitz added. "There's no right part for her in *Watcher*, and I'm not going to be able to start up anything new for her until that's finished. So she's been making the rounds trying to scrounge up something on her own, getting together with every producer and director she can get ahold of. Given his connections, that's probably why she was having lunch with Charlie Stoke."

Fitz took another pull on his drink. "There's probably nothing to it," he repeated, sounding tentative. I hoped that he was right but couldn't help thinking that it sounded more as if he was just trying to talk himself into it.

"In fact, I'm sure it's not true," Fitz added, coming across as even less certain. "But such rumors don't exactly buildup my trust in him. An 'honest lawyer,' that alone ought to make you suspicious," he quipped, breaking his own rule about not cracking wise. "You could use him to help you with the legal stuff on the estate if you want, but I need you to make sure things are handled properly.

"Except for Danny's trust fund, I'm leaving everything I have to Pilar, but that's not as much as you might expect. If this new film comes off as I think it will, I'll be sitting pretty; but right now, I've hocked everything I have to get the project going. Worst case, I figure I'll at least get my money back.

"If anything were to happen to both Pilar and me, everything will go to Danny's trust. In that case, I'd like you to be his guardian as well as the trustee. It's a lot to ask, I know, but frankly I can't think of anyone better for the job."

"Okay, I'm in," I replied.

For a normally carefree guy, the potential responsibilities were piling up on me fast, which gave me pause. But there was no way I'd turn Fitz down where Danny's interests were involved, and he knew it. "Well, here's hoping it never comes to that," I said.

"Great." We touched glasses again and drank to seal the deal.

"You'll probably never have to tap into Danny's trust. Pilar's career is going well . . . but you never know with actresses." Fitz paused and considered his next comment with a serious, almost troubled expression. "She's a hot item now, but next week she could be poison. Who knows? My best guess is that with a couple more hit roles, she'll be set. She's a terrific actress, you know."

"So I've heard . . . and not just from her," I counter, smiling wryly.

"Yeah, she's not shy about blowing her own horn, but you gotta do it in this business if you don't want to get stuck in traffic." Fitz's face was almost beaming now; whatever the dark cloud that had been casting its shadow on his thoughts had scudded away. "It's too bad that I can't give her the part she wants in *Watcher*, but I'd have to re-write the key female character too much. I can't take that chance. I want to keep it as close to the book as I can. Have you read it? There's no fit for a Latina volcano like Pilar."

"Sorry, not my kind of reading material," I allowed.

Fitz wasn't fazed or, knowing me, surprised by my lack of knowledge of contemporary romantic literature.

"This is my big chance and I'm not going to blow it," Fitz continued in a somewhat more measured tone. "If I can pull it off, I'll be able to write my own ticket. I'll be able to choose pictures and roles for Pilar that'll be perfect. Her nose is a little out of joint right now, but she'll come around and see that I'm right."

"Her nose looks pretty good to me," I joked. If Fitz was going to start with the wise cracks, I figured I could as well.

Fitz smiled, picking up quickly on my attempt to lighten things up. "Pilar's not the only one after me. It seems like everyone in town wants a piece of the action. Kenny Menske has been pestering me to let him co-produce. That's what we were arguing about tonight. But I'm the one who's putting everything on the line for this. It's my baby, and I'm not sure I want to share it with anyone."

Fitz was obviously conflicted, not wanting to let down a long-time friend and associate, but afraid to let go of any part of his big score. I could understand that but thought he was making way too much of it. "Stephen, everyone knows you're the brains and the talent of the outfit," I observed. "It seems to me that you're going to have your hands full with writing the screen play and directing the picture. As I see it, you could use some help with the nuts and bolts on the production side. You've told me before that Ken's done decent work for you; I don't think you'd lose anything by letting him share in the action."

Fitz's shoulders lifted, his eyes widened, and I could see by the expression starting to appear on his face that I'd scored the point. "Yeah, you're right. You're always the good guy, William. I'll let Kenny in on it. He'll do a good job. But I'm not going to tell him right away; let him stew awhile. I'm still a little pissed off," Fitz said, laughing to show he wasn't pissed off at all, and added,

"He's been such a pain in the ass about it."

Why was it people were always calling me a "good guy," and somehow making it sound like an insult rather than a complement? Rather than further ponder the imponderable, I decided, 'to hell with it, and them,' and moved on to more important matters, such as enjoying Fitz's excellent cognac.

As Fitz poured us another round, Annie, as if on cue, joined us, toting a folder containing the trust documents. Apparently and not surprisingly, Fitz had had little doubt that I would acquiesce to his requests. Annie neatly laid out the papers on a small, round table in the corner of the room and witnessed our signatures as we inked them in on the appropriate lines, making certain they were reasonably legible. That task completed, Annie turned down the drink Fitz offered her, pointed out that she'd stopped drinking two hours earlier, and allowed as how one of the three of us should stay sober. She did offer, however, that she'd be happy to sit with us while we finished our drinks.

"So, is everything buttoned up?" Fitz asked.

"Yes," Annie replied. "I sent Viola and Dotty home hours ago."

Viola Newhouse was the Fitzgerald's housekeeper and Dotty Hanson was the cook. I hadn't seen either of them while the party was in full swing, but the little meatballs in a creamy gravy and mini open faced gravlax sandwiches with a sweet dill mustard sauce—on which I'd dined heavily—had been a dead giveaway that Dotty had been plying her trade that evening.

"The caterers have finished cleaning up," Annie added in a weary voice that made me wonder if she hadn't done half of the 'cleaning up' work herself—knowing Annie she probably had. "And everyone else has gone home, unless there's someone I missed asleep in the bushes."

"It's been known to happen," Fitz responded playfully.

"How's my wife?"

"She's sound asleep; has been for a while."

"Yeah, thanks to that damn' doctor and his needles. Somebody should shoot that guy," Fitz said, and took a hard swallow of his drink. My thoughts went back to the earlier incident with the doctor and Charlie Stoke's almost violent reaction toward him. It made me wonder again about just how close the *business relationship* was between Stoke and Pilar; thoughts that I concluded were best left unexplored.

Fitz was still focused on Appel. "That son-of-a-bitch, I told him to back off. Maybe I should have Jack talk with him."

I couldn't imagine anyone, even a big guy like me, enjoying such a chat with Jack Willis; for a little guy like Appel it would be terrifying.

"As long as it's just talk," I advised. "Willis impresses me as the type who might get carried away, who might run out of words and exceed his charge in such a situation."

"Yeah, that would be a shame," Fitz remarked in a way that seemed as if he thought the opposite were true.

Annie brought us both back to reality. "Stephen, you know that you're going to do no such thing. I'm surprised you're even talking like that. Besides, even if you got Appel to back off, there are plenty of others just like him in this town ready to step in to fill the gap. What you need to do is find something for Pilar to do; when she's busy working, there's no problem. Right now, she has too much time on her hands and too much nervous energy to go with it."

Fitz, realizing the wisdom of Annie's remarks, nodded silent agreement.

The shutting down of Fitz's liquor-driven, pugnacious

strategies toward Dr. Appel accomplished, Annie pointed out that it was time we all stopped drinking and made our way to bed. She wisely demanded and took my car keys from me, announced to Fitz that she wouldn't be into work before "noon tomorrow," and drove me to my house in Glendale.

## CHAPTER 7

For the next three weeks I was busy plying, or, to be more accurate, learning the basics of my trade: interviews with grumpy cops and grumpier freshman assistant district attorneys as green as I and even less enthusiastic about the mundane cases they had been assigned to handle; one- or two-line rewrites of cryptic police press reports into something an average reader, a target audience with a fifth-grader's vocabulary and grasp of sentence structure, could understand; and endless *urgent* errands with no discernable purpose assigned by end-of-career night editors with not nearly enough to keep them busy. No time for me to even think about making social visits or to give much thought to good friends like Fitz. I did see Annie on my days off for sleepover dates if she had the time and I was in luck. Those pleasant diversions were at my place, and on those occasions the Fitzgeralds were not a topic of conversation.

That tiresome routine changed radically one evening with a distress call from Fitz. "Marshall, I need you. Come over right away," he demanded rather than requested in an obviously anguished voice that left no room for discussion.

"What's wrong?" I asked automatically, although I had a feeling that no coherent explanation would be offered at that moment.

"Not now. I'll talk to you when you get here. Come as fast as you can."

"On my way!" I got in just before he hung up. I wasn't even sure he heard me.

I rushed into the living room; retrieved, replaced, and retied the shoes that I'd kicked off a few minutes earlier when I'd arrived home from work; grabbed my suit coat and hat from where I'd thrown them on the couch; and was out the door within minutes.

There was no easy route from Glendale to West L.A. The quickest would be to take Los Feliz to Western, skirting downtown, and then head west on Sunset. I pushed my tired Ford to a new speed record and broke more than a few traffic laws in my haste to cover the 25 miles. I was worried and frustrated by the fact that I didn't know what it was I should be worried and frustrated about. To compensate for my lack of information and to avoid dreaming up an array of dire scenarios that had no basis in fact, I directed my attention to driving along the dimly lit roads at greater than safe speeds.

It was just about 9:00 pm when I reached Fitz's estate, raced up the driveway through the open gate, braked to a stop and parked at an oblique angle just next to a black sedan that I didn't recognize.

As I began to run up the steps, Dr. Appel exited the front door, a somber frown on his face. He passed me without any sort of greeting, almost as if he didn't see me right in front of him, marched down the steps, opened the rear door of the big car without waiting for his driver to assist him, and got in.

For no apparent reason the driver, his face barely visible through the car's window in a faint light from the interior, flashed me a hard smile as the sedan made the loop and drove away. I wouldn't have given it a second thought if it hadn't been for the incongruity of it. But there was no time to ponder that, as Annie met me at the door with a frantic, tearful expression on her face, which immediately scared the hell out of me and trumped any considerations of sinister smiles directed at me by people I didn't know. She offered no explanation for her obvious distress or the reason for my being summoned but led me instead directly into Fitz's office.

The look on Annie's face had been one of near panic; Fitz's was one of anger. He was seated behind his desk with an open green quart bottle on it, a half-empty iceless glass of scotch in his hand, and a tan leather briefcase standing upright in front of him. He stared up at me but didn't say anything right away. His hard, quizzical expression was as if he didn't quite recognize me or, if he did, wasn't exactly certain as to why I was there. It was a look for Fitz that was alien to me, and it didn't suit him.

Not waiting to be invited, I sat across from him and asked, "What the hell's going on, Stephen?"

He still didn't answer right away. It was a simple question, one that deserved a short, straight, simple answer, but apparently one that needed some extended thought on his part. When finally he did speak, it was in the tormented voice I'd heard over the telephone, but this time laced with more anger. "It's Danny. They've taken Danny. Damn them to hell!"

As I stared at him, his face and body seemed to sag. "What am I going to do, Marshall? What am I going to do?" Fitz's anger had turned to despair.

I didn't respond, my own thoughts now a carbon copy of the look on Fitz's face. I probably wouldn't have said anything coherent if I'd tried. I could feel the adrenalin beginning to pump into my system. I wanted to jump up and shout, but my legs and lungs had other ideas. Then a chill ran through me, as if the temperature of my blood had suddenly dropped several degrees. For me the anger and despair were giving way to a personal resolve to do whatever was necessary to get Danny back.

Fitz haltingly spelled some of it out in short, abrupt half sentences: "Last night . . . We were asleep . . . Didn't know until Mag showed up this morning . . . Got in somehow . . . Should've heard him . . . Can't figure it."

Annie, standing behind me broke in, "They left a note in Danny's room and then called around 9:00 am this morning. A man's voice demanded $15,000 and said it had to be delivered tonight. They gave us very detailed instructions and said that we should follow them to the letter. I took them down as Stephen repeated them to me. Here." Annie handed me a scrap of paper with her handwritten notes.

"Stephen got the money from the bank this afternoon." She continued and pointed towards the briefcase in front of him.

Fitz's expression was still despondent, but his voice was now a little more controlled. "I need you to make the delivery, Marshall." That he again called me 'Marshall' as he had on the telephone, not 'William', drove home the gravity of what we were discussing. If his purpose, conscious or subconscious, was to emphasize the seriousness of the situation, it was unnecessary; I was already there, in spades.

I had a million questions bouncing around in my head, but I could tell from the way that Fitz had already uttered his barely coherent comments he wasn't about to slow down now to explain everything to me: his only concern right then was doing what needed to be done to get Danny back.

"Sure, sure I will," I responded without hesitation. Then after a little semi-rational thought added, "But what about Willis? Wouldn't he be better at something like this?"

"Jack's out of town, not back until Friday," Fitz replied, giving a quick summary of reasoning that he'd apparently already worked his way through. "Anyway, I couldn't trust him not to take a gun. The kidnappers said no cops and no guns. I can't take that chance. You're the only one I trust. You're the only guy I know with balls enough to do what needs to be done without carrying a gun."

If we'd been talking about anybody but Danny, I'm not sure my balls would've measured up to the task. Handing off $15,000—a hell of a lot of money in the throes of the Depression—alone and unarmed in the middle of the night to someone mean enough to kidnap a five-year-old, didn't sound like an ideal plan. I wasn't thrilled with the setup, but knew I had to see it through. Danny was in danger, and I *needed* to be a part of the solution.

The instructions from the kidnappers that Annie had written down were that someone—they were adamant that it not be Fitz—should drive with the ransom to a bar called Ray's, located at a remote spot in the west end of the Valley off of Van Nuys Blvd. At exactly 11:30 that person was to leave his car unlocked at the far end of the parking lot, leave his jacket in the car, go inside the bar, sit at a table with his back to the windows, and order a cup of coffee. At midnight he was to pay the bill and go back to his car. If the kidnappers were satisfied that he was alone and unarmed, there would be a note in the car telling him what to do next.

It was all pretty straightforward. I didn't know anything about the place called Ray's, but I was familiar with the general location and anticipated no trouble finding it. I glanced at my watch. "I'd better get going if I'm going to get there in time."

I left Fitz sitting behind his desk, his fist wrapped tightly around his still half full tumbler of scotch. Annie walked with me out to my car.

"I don't like this, William," Annie said as we stood momentarily on the top step of the front porch, a symbolic pause that drove home the feeling that she'd just expressed aloud.

"I don't like it either, but I don't see that we have much choice," I responded with a stoicism I didn't feel. Then I asked her one of the questions that I'd been reluctant to put to Fitz. "Why did he wait so long to call me?"

"He didn't want to put you at risk. He kept saying he would

do it himself," Annie explained. Then she added, looking a little guilty, "I'm afraid I was the one who convinced him that it would be safest to follow the kidnappers' instructions. I'm sorry."

"Don't be, Sweetheart; feeling that I can be part of the solution is the closest thing to a bright spot in this whole mess. I'll be fine. I don't plan to be any kind of a hero; I just want Danny back safe."

She kissed me on my cheek, and I was on my way with a briefcase full of cash in tow. Any feeling that I was a hero, a knight-errant being seen off by his lady-fair on his way to slay a dragon, subsided quickly as I concentrated on navigating a dark, twisting Sepulveda Blvd. through the Santa Monica Mountains and into the Valley, and later disappeared totally when my own lights went out in an even darker Topanga Canyon.

## CHAPTER 8

It was well after sunrise and the mist from the prior night had all but burned off by the time I came to face down beside the car, my mouth partially filled with dirt and small bits of rock. My right wrist, no longer handcuffed, ached from where I'd hung from the car door after being slugged, but that was nothing compared to the throbbing pain in the back of my head. Trying to get up, I found that I couldn't put weight on my sprained right hand. On the third attempt and using only my left arm, I was able to get to my knees and lean against the car's running board. I paused and waited for the pain to ebb before attempting my next feat: standing somewhat close to upright. That may not sound like much, but considering my condition I would equate my efforts to those of an aerialist doing a triple summersault without a net before an unappreciative crowd.

The car was no longer running, the head lights were turned off, and the door I'd been cuffed to was closed. I grabbed the door handle with my left hand and managed to pull myself fully upright. The key in the ignition was visible through the window. The briefcase that had been in the back seat was now replaced by a child-sized object wrapped in a blanket. The bundle was not moving, as still as death.

Suddenly the ache in my head and pain in my wrist no longer seemed to be of much importance. I pulled the door open, scrambled in, leaned over the back of the driver's seat, and pulled the blanket back just enough to be sure that it was Danny and that he was alright. He was warm to the touch, breathing with a soft and regular rhythm, and apparently uninjured. The child didn't stir much when I patted him gently. He might have been drugged, or maybe he was just a tired Jim Hawkins in the middle of a big adventure. I resisted an almost overwhelming urge to take him in my arms and hold him close; with any luck, he'd stay asleep until I got him home.

Once I was satisfied that Danny was okay, the pain in my head again took center ring. Reaching back, I cautiously touched the knot on my head, which felt to be the size of a softball. I've had my bell rung once or twice in the past, but the after effect of those knocks was nothing compared to this. My focus on Danny's condition and safety now turned to anger aimed at the unknown scumbag who'd knocked me out unnecessarily. I resolved that as soon as I got Danny safely home, I would make it my life's work to find and repay the bastard—and with interest. Granted, I had no idea how to accomplish that, but hopefully when my head stopped throbbing, something would come to me.

The motor kicked over without a problem when I turned the key and pressed the starter; at least my assailant hadn't left us with an empty gas tank or a dead battery. Driving south through Topanga Canyon, I picked up the Coast Road just east of Malibu and turned toward Santa Monica, stopping at a payphone at the first gas station along the route to call Fitz; I could only imagine how frantic he must have become when I hadn't returned with Danny as expected.

The phone was answered on the first ring by a raspy, man's voice that I didn't recognize.

"Who're you?" I asked, surprised and confused that it was not Fitz on the other end of the line.

"You Marshall?" he responded with a question of his own rather than his identity.

"Yeah," I answered, figuring that if I let him win the first round, we might be able to stop the questions short of twenty. "So, who are you?"

"Just a sec." I heard him set the phone down . . . then a sound of muffled voices in the background before the receiver was picked-up again. "Hello, Marshall," a familiar voice said. "This is Lt. Archer. You got the kid?"

Archer? Fitz must have called the police when I didn't show up with Danny as expected.

"Yeah, I've got him. He's okay."

"Where have you been?"

"The bastard sapped me at the pick-up spot. I came to just a half hour ago," I replied, spontaneously reaching back and gently stroking the back of my head with my free hand.

"Where are you now?"

"I'm just outside Santa Monica at a filling station payphone."

"You okay to drive?" Archer asked. "I can send somebody."

A fair question and a reasonable suggestion, which I rejected without much consideration. "No, don't send anyone. I'm okay. I just want to get Danny home before he wakes-up."

"Alright, get here as soon as you can."

"What's up?" I asked without much hope of getting an answer.

"Just get here. We'll talk then."


It took a little less than half an hour to get to the house, turning east on San Vincente at Santa Monica headed toward West L.A., plenty of time to think things over even with an aching busted head. That Fitz would get worried and call the cops when I didn't turn up or call in made sense. But what I couldn't figure was why Fitz hadn't answered the phone himself. And why, when I hadn't returned with Danny the previous night, they expected it to be me on the line rather than the kidnappers? And the biggest question of all: Why was Lt. John Archer, the nearest thing I had to a friend in the LAPD, there? Archer didn't handle kidnappings; he was a homicide detective.

My concerns grew when I turned onto Fitz's street, where several squad cars lined both curbs near the house, way more manpower than necessary to handle a kidnapping. Even more unsettling, an ambulance was backed into the driveway, blocking it. I double parked next to one of the squad cars, near where Lt. Archer, Annie, and a couple of uniformed police were waiting to meet me.

Archer looked the same as always: medium height, medium athletic build, and middle aged; a crumpled brown suit that matched the color of his disheveled brown hair; and the stub of a smoldering cigarette in his nicotine-tinted fingers. The only noticeable difference in his usual appearance was the absence of any of his expressive smiles—an absence that didn't do anything to allay my fears.

Archer took charge. "Miss Shannon, would you please take the boy inside? Have one of the ambulance guys take a look at him, and have his nanny put him to bed. Better take him in through the back in case he wakes up."

Annie, her face flushed and eyes reddened by what must've been a recent stream of tears, nodded and with my help lifted Danny out of the backseat. She gave me a silent, sad, vacant frown and again looked as if she might break down. But she didn't; instead, she cradled the still sleeping child in her arms and carried him away.

"One of you guys move his car," Archer said to the two cops. I reacted by handing over my keys to one of them.

"Marshall, you come with me."

He led me past the ambulance and up the palm-lined drive toward the front of the house. The relaxed hacienda atmosphere I'd experienced on the night of Danny's birthday party was replaced in the pre-noon sunlight by a well-lit, shadow-less façade reminiscent of a movie set—too clean, too perfect to be real.

Archer stopped abruptly at the top of the steps before we entered, touching my arm to be certain he had my attention and to set me up for what he was about to relate. "Fitzgerald's dead," he said in a sad voice, two levels softer than his normal even tone. "Sorry to break it to you like this, but the body's still in there. They're just getting ready to move it."

Staring at Archer, with the expression and feelings of someone who'd just been gut punched, I said nothing. I was too confused by what I was hearing to unleash any of the emotions I could feel building below the surface, emotions that were likely to erupt soon. I was mentally numb, trance-like, and the pain in my head was again beginning its tom-tom-beat with a frenzy.

"You don't seem surprised," Archer continued, his expression switching to inquisitive from dour. I realized later that, like any good detective, Archer had been closely watching for my reaction when he'd dropped the hard news on me with little preamble.

"I suppose I'm not," I replied dully. "I knew that something was wrong when it was you and Annie rather than Fitz on the street to meet me; no way Fitz wouldn't be there himself to take Danny. I suspected something might have happened to him when I phoned from Malibu and he didn't answer, but I didn't want to admit it to myself."

I stared at Archer for a few seconds trying to get some

control over my scattered thoughts before I asked the obvious question, "What happened?"

Cops always wait to be asked. For them, someone not asking is a damned good indication that the person already knows the answer. And knowing the answers to such questions when you shouldn't know them was a sure way to move to the front ranks in the parade of suspects.

"We're not sure yet," Archer answered. "It happened early this morning. One shot to the chest. Miss Shannon was asleep in the guest room.  She says the shot woke her, but by the time she got downstairs, the shooter was gone, and Fitzgerald was dead on the floor in his office."

Archer's curt comments had evoked a stack of blurry pictures that I tried, despite or maybe because of my whirling emotions, to organize and bring into focus by verbalizing them. "So, someone comes by in the middle of the night, finds Fitz sitting alone in his study, and shoots him? Why? It makes no sense."

"Let's hold off on talking about Fitzgerald for now," Archer said, putting me off. "Miss Shannon has already filled me in on the details of the kidnapping at this end. What I want to know now is what happened to you last night?"

Two guys in white cotton coats, matching loose pants, scuffed-up black leather shoes, and small-billed, kepi-like caps, were removing Fitz's sheet covered body on a stretcher as we walked into the house. They faced straight to the front as they moved past us, scrupulously avoiding looking directly at us, for which I was grateful; no man likes for other men to see even a hint of tears in his eyes, and I'm no exception. I'd seen violent deaths before—more in the last four months as a crime reporter than in my previous twenty-three years—but not like this, never a friend. A chill ran through me. If I thought that I was prepared for this scene, I wasn't. Turning away, I stepped quickly through the front door of the house and at Archer's direction into the living room before my emotions could overtake me.

## CHAPTER 9

Lieutenant Archer and his partner, Sergeant David Buller, a short, stocky, ill-tempered type with a military haircut, who could've been mistaken for Jack Willis's less warm and cuddly kid brother, followed me into the living room. I now realized it'd been Buller with whom I'd first spoken on the telephone when I called in to say that I had Danny and that he was alright. Buller and I had crossed paths a few times since I'd started my new job as a reporter, and, for no reason I could put my finger on, he'd developed a dislike for me. Maybe he resented the fact that over the last year I'd built a strong friendship with Lt. Archer, his boss, or maybe he was just an unfriendly type. Before this I'd never given his attitude much thought; it hadn't been important, but now I had an unsettling feeling that that might change.

A stern, unwelcoming-faced Buller pointed at a couch, which I took to be an unspoken command for me to take a seat, and with which I complied also without comment. Archer and Buller planted themselves on another couch facing me across a polished wood coffee table. They were making themselves—if not me—comfortable; I had a bad feeling that this was going to be a long and unpleasant session.

From where I was seated, I could see a two-way flow of police moving in the hallway between Fitz's office and the front of the house, some carrying things, some empty-handed but on what looked to be an important mission, while others seemed to have no apparent purpose to their wandering by. Glancing from time-to-time at their movements gave me an excuse to look away from Archer or Buller as we spoke. For some indefinable reason, occasionally avoiding looking directly into the detectives' eyes seemed to help me control my emotions. I could feel that my hands were starting to tremble slightly. Embarrassed, I tried to hide this by pressing the palms of my hands down firmly on my knees as I sat leaning forward on the couch as if concentrating on what the detectives were saying.

When they asked what I knew about the events of the previous evening, I told Archer and Buller everything I'd been told about the kidnapping, which I realized as I spoke amounted to next to nothing, and the details of what had happened to me in Topanga Canyon, which were almost as painful to recount as they had been to experience.

"So, you have no idea who took the kid and hit you?" Archer summed up the extent of my ignorance nicely, adding a feeling of uselessness to my anger and grief. "And I suppose like everyone else you don't know of anyone who had a grudge against Fitzgerald?"

"No. Fitz could be a hard-ass at times, but never to the point anyone would want to kill him," I offered, more as an observation to myself than to the two men staring at me as I spoke.

"You'd be surprised how little it takes for an ordinary Joe to decide to murder someone," Archer said.

"What can you tell me about what happened?" I was angling for information with little hope of getting any, but apparently Archer, tuned in to my frustration, decided to give a little.

"I'm not sure I can tell you much until I'm ready to release it to all of the papers, seeing as you're a reporter now, and also a witness of sorts," Archer commented.

"And a suspect of sorts too, I suppose," I reluctantly

pointed out. "I guess lying unconscious all night on a dirt road in Topanga Canyon, alone except for a sleeping five-year-old in the back seat of my car, isn't much of an alibi."

"I don't know; that lump on the back of your head speaks for you. No one would do that to themselves; I'm not even sure they could." Archer leaned back, folded his arms across his chest, stared at me blank faced, and finally said, "I know you, Marshall. I trust you . . . somewhat. So here's the deal: I'll fill you in on what we know, if you promise not to print anything that I haven't okayed and given to the rest of the press."

"Alright," I said, "I can live with that." It was no problem for me; all I wanted at that point was to understand what had happened to my friend and to find his killer. My editor would push me to write the inside angle, but I figured I could put him off until the story was complete. Buller didn't seem any too happy with the arrangement, but as usual he deferred to his boss.

As it turned out, Archer didn't know much more than I would've learned from Annie later: Just about the time that I was getting blackjacked in Topanga Canyon, Annie, dead on her feet from being up and under extreme emotional pressure for eighteen hours straight, went upstairs to lie down in the guest bedroom, leaving Fitz alone in his office. Pilar was still out from a sedative Dr. Appel had given her just before I'd arrived on the scene that evening and seen him making his exit.

"Like I told you, a little after one-thirty, the sound of a gunshot woke Miss Shannon," Archer explained. "She'd been sleeping on top of the blankets with her clothes on, so, even allowing for a few seconds to shake off her grogginess and to realize what was going on, she got downstairs quickly. But not soon enough to see anyone. She found Fitzgerald dead, his body face down on the floor next to the desk in his office. The coroner said he'd been shot once in the chest. From the location of the entry wound, the bullet must have passed through his heart. He was almost certainly dead before he hit the floor.

"There were no signs of a struggle. The French doors leading from the office to the backyard patio were closed but not locked; the same was true of the front and back doors to the house, so the killer could have come in and left by any of those ways. The door to the wall safe in Fitzgerald's office was wide open, with nothing in there except a few business papers."

Archer paused for a few seconds in his narration, probably to gauge my reaction to what he'd been telling me. He stubbed out the butt end of his cigarette in an ashtray and began the process of taking another from a pack and lighting it. I considered turning away to give myself a mental break, to pretend again to find something about the activity in the hallway suddenly interesting, but I thought that that might do less to ease my tension than it would serve to make me look guilty—of what I wasn't sure. Instead I just sat there stiffly upright on the couch and returned Archer's atypical blank expression.

"Miss Shannon tells us that Fitzgerald put the ransom money in the safe in his office when he brought it from the bank," Archer continued, "then transferred it to a briefcase just before giving it to you. She isn't absolutely certain but doesn't think he normally kept anything else of value in the safe.

"When she discovered Fitzgerald's body on the floor, Miss Shannon tells us that her first instinct, despite a natural shock that might have frozen the average person, had been to kneel beside him and check the body for life. She realized right away that he was dead, but her first call was for an ambulance anyway. Then she called the police. She said it wasn't until she'd hung up with us that it occurred to her the killer might still be in the house and she might be in danger. That's when she'd vaguely recalled—possibly only imagined—that she'd heard the sound of a car starting and driving away as she'd hurried down the stairs. Even so, she grabbed a poker from the hearth of the fireplace to take with her when she when back upstairs to check on the still sleeping Miss Fuertes." For the first time Archer allowed himself a sly smile. Knowing that nothing bad had come of it, his expression was no doubt triggered by his mental image of Annie armed with only a thin iron rod sallying forth possibly to face a pistol packing murderer. I can't say that I shared his amusement at that moment, although I could understand it.

"It sounds to me like *your* Miss Shannon is a pretty cool customer in a pinch," Archer pointed out. From the way that Archer referred to her as "*your* Miss Shannon," it was clear that he was wise to my personal attachment to her.

"Yeah, maybe a little too cool," Buller interjected. I didn't like what his comment seemed to imply, but let it pass, chalking it up to Buller being his normal unpleasant self.

When the police had arrived, they closed off Fitz's office, searched the rest of the house, and interviewed Annie and Pilar. Annie had explained the broken windowpane in the backdoor when she told them about the kidnapping from the night before. From the police's examination of Pilar's bedroom and a discussion with her, it was learned that some relatively inexpensive costume jewelry she kept in a box on a dressing table in her room was missing. Pilar remembered that the jewelry had been there before Dr. Appel had given her the sedative that had calmed her and put her out. So apparently, the stuff had been nicked on the night that Fitz was murdered. There was no sign that the wall safe behind an oil painting in her bedroom where she kept her better jewelry had been touched. When Pilar had opened the safe for the police, they found that her valuable pieces were still there.

"The killer must have known something of the layout of the place," Buller offered. "My read is that he came in through the door at the rear of the house, took the back stairs to the second floor, and headed straight for Miss Fuertes room; there's no sign that he disturbed anything else upstairs. He found the cheap stuff but must not have known anything about the good pieces in the safe, otherwise he'd have rousted the woman and forced her to open it."

"The way I see it," Buller continued, "he was frustrated with just the cheap junk, saw that Fitzgerald was still up, confronted him, and when Fitzgerald wouldn't come through, he shot him."

Lt. Archer didn't say anything while Sgt. Buller presented his theory, but his lack of reaction seemed to mirror my own thoughts. It didn't sound much like the work of any typical cat burglar that I'd ever heard of; the whole idea is to get in and out without coming face to face with anyone. The fact that the lights were still on in the front of the house and in Fitz's study would most likely have put off any competent second-story man. And a professional would've expected there to be a safe for the expensive stuff. For a pro, no doubt someone adept at picking locks and locating and opening safes by listening for the sound of tumblers falling into place, there would've been too much risk involved in disturbing the sleeping Pilar or in confronting a wide-awake Fitz in his study.

I didn't bother to share my speculation with the sergeant, figuring that Archer would set him straight later. Instead, I asked, "Is it possible that Pilar is wrong? Could the jewelry have been taken the previous night by the same people who took Danny?"

Archer answered, "Could be, but Miss Fuertes was adamant that the jewelry was there when she went to bed last night . . . Still, she could be mistaken. Considering the amount of juice that had been pumped into her by the doctor after her boy had been grabbed, it's hard to consider her a credible witness to anything; the sneakthief could have tucked her in and given her a 'nighty-night' kiss, and she wouldn't have known the difference."

"Say, where is Pilar?" I'd realized while Archer was speaking that Pilar had been absent since I'd arrived back to the house with Danny. "Is she okay?"

"She's fine, plenty shaken up but nothing wrong physically. Apparently, she slept through the whole damn' thing," Archer commented with just a hint of suspicion in his voice. "Miss Shannon waited until we got here to wake her. Whatever that doctor gave her was powerful stuff. When she finally did wake up, she was out of control for a while, but Miss Shannon was able to calm her down. She refused to take another sedative until we found out what was happening with the kid. After you called, she took something; she's sleeping again now."

"Good," I said, relieved that there wouldn't be an irrational or irate Pilar for Annie and me to deal with once the cops were gone.

"How were things between them?" Buller asked, directing the conversation back to things that were more interesting to him than Pilar's wellbeing.

"Fitz and Pilar? Good, I think." I paused for a second to decide whether to fill them in on the rest. Concluding that they were going to hear it anyway, I figured they might as well hear it from me sooner rather than later from someone less objective. "You're going to hear a rumor that she and her attorney, Charles Stoke, were playing around, but I doubt it's true. Fitz didn't believe it either."

"How do you know that?" Buller asked.

"He told me so."

"Fitzgerald told you that? You *were* good friends," Buller remarked sarcastically.

"The best," I replied, giving him a cold stare.

"On the chance that there is something there, do you think either Miss Fuertes or her friend Stoke could have done this?" Archer asked. "Miss Fuertes seemed genuinely distraught when we talked to her, but she was one of only two people who we know for certain were in the house when it happened. If she was faking being drugged, she could have slipped downstairs, shot him, hid until Miss Shannon was calling us, and then slipped back upstairs."

"Yeah, she's a good enough actress to pull it off. But I don't see her killing anyone in cold blood," I responded. "Hot blood—Frankie and Johnny stuff—maybe, but cold blood, sneaking around, up and down stairs, I don't see it. And she sure as hell wouldn't have done it while she was worried about Danny's being missing."

"What about this Stoke guy?" Buller broke in again.

I gave it some consideration before I replied, "Stoke? No, I don't see Stoke as a killer. My guess would be that if he wanted to kill somebody, he'd hire it out, not do it himself. I could see him cuckolding a client, but not killing one. And, if he and Pilar had something going and wanted to take it to another level, why kill Fitz? Divorces are two for a dollar in Hollywood; she could've just hightailed it to Reno to get one. And come to think of it, Fitz was worth more to both of them alive than dead: he was a lucrative client for Stoke and he was a major promoter of Pilar. Why would either of them want to kill him?"

"What about the kidnapping? How does that fit in?" Archer asked. "It's hard to believe the two things are a coincidence, but I don't see a connection."

"Neither do I. If someone wanted to get Fitz alone so they could kill him, they would've had him deliver the ransom himself instead of me. It would be a lot easier and safer to shoot him out in the canyon where they slugged me than in his own house with other people around.

"There is one thing about it though," I added, "the whole kidnapping set-up seemed way too complex, too orchestrated."

"Professional-like?" Buller asked, sitting up in his seat, suddenly more attentive.

"No, just the opposite, too staged. I'd think that someone

who knew what they were doing would've come up with a simpler plan. This was like a movie script, with the meeting in the middle of nowhere and the handcuffs and all."

"What about the Shannon woman? Anything going on between her and Fitzgerald?" By the way Buller asked the question, I could tell that he too already knew about my relationship with Annie and was trying to goad me.

"I hope not," I replied glibly, but with a look that let Buller know that his low blow of a remark hadn't gone unnoticed. I wasn't about to fall for his obvious attempt to get a rise out of me, but neither did I want him to think that he was putting one over on me.

The exchange between Buller and me was starting to get personal and wouldn't add anything helpful to Archer, so he broke into our verbal sparring in a way that took it down a notch. "Miss Shannon told us that you are a couple," he said, confirming my earlier speculation.

"Really? That's good to hear. I was afraid she might just be toying with my affections," I responded caustically. I shot Buller another look to let him know that I owed him one and to make him think that I was someone who always found a way to repay such debts—although I'm not really. Either way, I doubted that Buller was going to lose any sleep over my animosity.

"There's one more question," Archer continued. "Miss Shannon says she thinks that Fitzgerald may have kept a gun in his safe, but she isn't absolutely sure about it. There's no gun in there now. Did he give it to you to take with you on the drop-off?"

"No. The deal was no guns. That's why he sent me. I remember that the safe was open when I left with the cash, but I don't recall seeing a gun. Still, I could've missed it; I was focused on other things at the time."

As Archer asked me more about it, I realized that things

had happened fast after Fitz finally relented and called me in to deliver the ransom; the focus then was on getting Danny back, not on how they had snatched him. I appreciated as Archer spoke that I was learning much more about what had happened than I was offering in return.

Archer filled in the gaps as to how it appeared that the kidnapping had gone down, "The nanny was alarmed when she arrived for work to discover a broken windowpane in the kitchen door at the back of the house and the door unlocked. She rushed upstairs and found the boy missing. She told us that normally she was the first to see the kid in the morning to get him up, dressed and fed a hot breakfast before either Fitzgerald or his wife stirred. When she saw that the boy was gone, she ran down the hall and woke Fitzgerald first, and then they both rousted the wife. When they all went into the boy's room, they found a note on the pillow of the unmade bed."

Lt. Archer handed me a plain sheet of typing paper on which a message had been pasted in words apparently cut from magazines. Black powder smudges with no discernable patterns on the paper and the fact Archer handed it to me were indications that the note had already been dusted for fingerprints, apparently with no success. The note read, "THE BOY IS OKAY. NO COPS. WAIT FOR A CALL."

"A call came in from the kidnappers about nine o'clock in the morning," Archer explained. "That's when Fitzgerald got the detailed instructions. Then he called the bank right away to arrange for the money and went there around one o'clock to pick it up.

"We got all this from Miss Shannon, but she only heard Fitzgerald's side of the telephone conversation with the kidnappers. Your name as the guy to make the drop came up as soon as the call ended. Miss Shannon said she suggested Fitzgerald contact you right away, but he told her he wanted to think about it. She says he was considering ignoring the kidnappers' instructions and delivering the ransom himself, but finally decided that it was safer to follow their instructions."

"That's what she told me, and it sounds like Fitz. It would've been just like him to take all of the risk himself," I commented. "Still, I'm surprised Fitz didn't reach out to me a lot earlier, when the kidnapping had first been discovered. Not that I would've necessarily come up with a better plan than the one that got me slugged and Fitz killed, but I wish he'd given me the chance."

"Yeah, but his reaction sounds like most anybody who's had his kid snatched," Archer countered. "Anyway, that's all we know about it until you answered the call to deliver the ransom. After that you know more about it than we do, and, as you've pointed out, that's damn' little."

"What the sergeant said about the thief knowing the layout of the house is probably true of the kidnapper as well," I pointed out, purposely referring to Buller in the third person, as if he weren't physically there sitting with us. It was an ill-mannered slight on my part to get back some for his earlier comments about Annie. It was probably too subtle for him to catch, but it made me feel better.

"There are lots of ways to get into the house," I pointed out, "but someone not familiar with the household routine wouldn't have known about those. On the other hand, someone who did know it would also know that Pilar and Fitz sleep in separate bedrooms near the front of the house. Fitz is a light sleeper; he almost certainly would've been expected to hear something if the kidnapper had come up the front stairs. And it's no secret that Annie lives in the guest cottage near the back of the property. If they'd all been tucked in for the night, as a kidnapper would've expected, there'd be little chance that anyone would've seen or heard the kidnapper if he came across the yard."

"And none of them would've heard the kidnapper break the glass pane in the back door near the kitchen, if that's what happened," Archer added. "We're told that the hired help had left for the night by the time the child was taken. The housekeeper and the cook learned of the boy's kidnapping when they arrived at work the next day. Your girlfriend says they both reacted pretty emotionally when they were told about it."

Archer reached out, took the notepad from Buller's hand, leaving the sergeant's pencil poised in the air above a now empty palm. He flipped back a few pages to find the names he wanted. "Miss Newhouse and Mrs. Hanson were told about the kidnapping when they arrive for work yesterday, then were sent home and told to stay away until called. Miss Ruiz, the nanny, was sent home as well, but was asked to come back this morning in the hope that they would get the boy back last night.

"Miss Ruiz showed up for work a couple of hours ago. When she was told of Fitzgerald's death, she took it hard and has been in too worked-up an emotional state for us to talk to her yet." Archer handed the notebook back to Buller and looked at him as he spoke. "After he's finished up here, I'm going to send Dave out to talk to the other two, to check their alibis for last night before they find out what's up."

The Fitzgerald's domestic staff normally worked only days, so it made sense that they would've been out of the house when Danny had been taken and again when Fitz was shot. In my eyes, none of them represented even remote possibilities as suspects in Danny's kidnapping or Fitz's murder. However, they all had their own keys to the back door and knew that Fitz, always the last one up at night, tended to be inconsistent as to whether he bothered to check that the front door and the French doors off the dining room and his study that faced out onto the back yard were locked before he headed for bed. So, for them, breaking a pane in the door to get in on the night of the kidnapping would've been unnecessary. But I didn't mention that fact to Archer, as I supposed that even the ineptest amateur would've realized the need to make a show of a forced entry for the night Danny was taken.

Annie joined us in the living room and sat down next to me on the couch. Tired and disheveled, she looked like she was ready to collapse under the emotional weight of everything that had been dropped on her in the last couple of days. She made no effort to hide our personal relationship, sitting close to me, grabbing my arm, and pulling her body tightly toward mine.

"How's the boy?" Archer asked.

Annie's head snapped around to face Archer, as if she'd been called to attention by a drill sergeant. I felt her body stiffen. "The ambulance medic says he's unharmed physically, but he's been drugged with something, not too much, just lightly—thank God." Annie gave out an audible sigh that combined her sense of relief with an indication of her mental exhaustion. "He's still asleep, will be for several hours yet."

Archer's diverting Annie's thoughts to Danny and the fact that he was unharmed seemed to ease her burden. For a moment she rested her head on my shoulder, which I took as another indication of her rapidly approaching mental fatigue, but then she popped up again and launched into a stream of questions directed at me, not pausing to allow for my response: "Where were you last night? What happened to you? They told me you were hit on the head, knocked out. Are you okay?"

It dawned on me as Annie spoke that Fitz had been shot before Danny and I would've been expected back at the house. With her being awoken by the shooting and then discovering the body, Annie would've had little time to think about the fact that I hadn't returned with Danny. It probably would've been when she began to explain to the police about the kidnapping that she'd realized that Danny and I were long overdue. My heart sank as I thought about Annie's concern for Danny and me increasing the emotional burden of finding Fitz murdered and dealing with a distraught Pilar. With the pace of her rapid-fire questions, I sensed that she might be spinning toward a bout of nervous exhaustion. I wasn't sure how to handle that.

Once again Archer appeared to grasp the situation and came to the rescue. "Miss Shannon, the boy and Marshall are okay; that's the important thing. No need for you to worry about them now. There'll be plenty of time for Marshall to fill you in on the details after you've had some rest. We'll talk again later. Marshall, you tend to her and see that she gets some sleep."

The more that I saw of Lt. Archer in action and got to know him, the more I liked him.

## CHAPTER 10

Fitz's funeral was a low-key affair by Hollywood standards, but then, he was a producer, not a star. Annie had handled the arrangements for Pilar, who had wanted to keep it small. Even so, several big-name actors, actresses, and studio types showed up at the church service to pay their respects, which said a lot about their feelings toward Fitz. Of the six pallbearers, mine and Ken Menske's were probably the only names that wouldn't have been recognized by even the most casual of movie goers.

While Fitz hadn't been particularly religious, his checkbook had kept him in the good graces of the Catholic Church. The presiding priest made a proper show of it. While I have little Latin, the pace of his delivery and his tone of voice spoke to me clearly, evoking emotions like a well-sung Italian aria.

Following the mass, at Pilar's request Annie and I rode from the church to the graveside with Danny and her in the leading black limousine. Pilar was remarkably composed considering that, per Annie, she'd stayed well clear of Dr. Appel and his palliative ministrations since Fitz's murder. That reinforced my faintly thought-out theory that Pilar's frequent minor emotional breakdowns at small frustrations or perceived social slights were more an act to perpetuate her image, a learned mannerism, which even she'd grown to expect of herself. I supposed she realized, consciously or otherwise, that Fitz's death called for a more reasoned response.

Danny was too young to completely understand what it was all about, but seeming to sense the gravity of the situation, he kept uncharacteristically silent and inactive. He asked no questions; perhaps, at some five-year-old level of understanding, he realized that he wouldn't like the answers. Instead he clung to his mother's arm, and later, after the service, to my hand.

Once I had assisted with moving the casket from the hearse to the grave, I took up a position standing next to the seated Pilar and Annie and watched as the sextons lowered the coffin with straps into the ground. The priest, after droning a few incantations and wielding a silver aspergillum to sprinkle holy water over the casket, switched to English for his final reading. "The virtuous man, though he die before his time, will find rest. Length of days is not what makes age honorable, nor number of years the true measure of life . . ." For the second time—the first having been upon seeing Fitz's sheet-covered body being carried out of the house—I found it hard to keep control over my grief.

Fewer people, those with a more personal than professional attachment to Fitz, attended the short graveside service. Charlie Stoke stood on the far side of the grave, directly across from Pilar, his eyes seemingly never straying from her. From where I stood, I couldn't see whether her eyes, covered by a full black mesh veil, linked up with his, but her body seem to stiffen slightly the one time I noticed her lifting her head in Stoke's direction. It was an almost imperceptible movement, barely enough to catch my attention, and I supposed that it could have just been my imagination making more of it than there was.

Ken Menske, apparently having as much if not more trouble controlling his grief than I, stood next to Charlie. Ken held a neatly folded white handkerchief to his forehead, periodically appearing to wipe non-existent sweat from his brow before lowering it quickly to the side of his nose just below his glasses, no doubt to stifle an actual tear before it could form.

Viola and Dotty had been at the church for the mass, but

following it they'd gone back to the house to finalize preparations for the gathering that would follow later in the day. From my point of view that was a good thing, as their tearful presence at the grave probably would've been all it would've taken to breach the weak emotional barriers that Ken and I had constructed and were fighting to defend.

Jack Willis was there, standing alone at a distance, back from the crowd, scowling maybe a little more than usual. He didn't come forward to offer his condolences to Pilar as she sat by the grave receiving them from others, and he left before I got a chance to talk with him. He hadn't contacted Pilar on his return to town. I supposed that he assumed correctly that she no longer required—nor desired—his services. I don't think she blamed him for Fitz's death, but his being the bodyguard who wasn't there when needed hadn't improved her already disdainful opinion of him.

Lt. Archer and Sgt. Buller, also standing back from the mourners, watched the crowd. As it was later explained to me by Archer, this was standard police practice when an unsolved homicide was involved. A useless exercise it seemed to me; the killer, if he was there, was hardly going to break down and confess on the spot. But when we discussed it, Archer had countered my opinion by saying that sometimes a sharp detective could learn a lot by observing the mourners' reactions, or lack thereof. Archer was as keen a detective as any I'd ever met—though admittedly I'd only known a few, and many of those not the best of the breed—so I didn't discount the wisdom of his tactic.

I'd seen the detectives approach Jack Willis shortly before he left, but nothing much had seemed to come of it. Their brief discussion hadn't appeared to be confrontational, but I'd sensed from his body movements and the way he'd shaken his head as he walked away that Willis was taking advantage of Archer and Buller's reluctance to create a scene at the service to put them off. They hadn't followed Jack out of the cemetery, so I assumed they were satisfied that whatever they had to ask him could wait for a better opportunity.

I don't know whether Archer and Buller learned anything important, but scanning the faces of the people at the graveside didn't tell me anything. It was just as in a scene from a movie: The men stood stiff and straight, their hands folded in front of them, their faces stern and resolved. The women, some standing and some sitting on white linen-draped folding chairs near the open grave, displayed various states of grief, dabbing away tears with wrinkled handkerchiefs. It seemed almost too normal. If the killer was among the group, he wasn't giving himself away to me.

With Fitz having been a true Irishman of the old school, there was of course a wake. It was a subdued affair by Gaelic standards, a substantial number of the attendees not being of that persuasion. Most of the big names who'd been at the funeral, having done their duty and paid their respects, had dropped off, probably not seeing any reason to mingle further with the hoi polloi. Two notable exceptions were Victor McLaglen and John Ford, both of whom had served with Ken and me in carrying Fitz's coffin. Though I knew that they were long-time associates and friends to Fitz, I'd never met either of them. Aside from shaking hands at the funeral and sharing a few remarks at the house, nothing of note passed between Ford and me. McLaglen, on the other hand, was in his element at the wake. His gregarious style and oversized, toothy grin did much to lighten the mood for me and everyone else in attendance.

"Marshall? Marshall? Sounds suspiciously English to me," McLaglen said with a friendly laugh that showed there was no real malice in his questioning of my antecedents.

"Some maybe, but mostly Scot on my father's side," I responded with a friendly grin of my own.

"Ah, good then. Your people make a fine whisky, I'll say that for them," McLaglen commented and held up his glass of the same to emphasize his point.

"True enough. Though I've tasted some mighty fine Irish whisky in my time," I said, holding up my own glass in a like salute and thinking back to my late-night drinking bouts with the recently fallen, unlamented Vincent Fisher.

"Aye. But I wouldn't be embarrassing you by further discussing the relative merits of each," McLaglen lightheartedly chided.

I was grateful that McLaglen opted not to get into a discussion of our linked heritages, as my limited knowledge of Scottish lore was even less than that of my mother's Eastern European Jewish roots. Instead, we enjoyed the next half hour swapping anecdotes of our individual good times with our mutual friend Fitz. I supposed that sharing warm and happy memories of the departed was what wakes were all about.

Charlie Stoke was being his normal charming self, his charismatic flare, a talent necessary in a high-price lawyer to the stars, on full display. His interactions with Pilar were appropriate and solicitous, and maybe a little more formal than necessary. I also noticed that, while he didn't hover over her as some were doing as she sat on a couch in the living room stretching a single glass of wine over the entire event, Stoke hardly ever took his eyes off of her. But probably only I, and maybe Annie, given our general awareness of the dynamics of their nebulous relationship, would've noticed it.

At some point as I'd expected he would, Stoke pulled me aside to briefly discuss business. "We need to set up a time for you to come into my office to go over your responsibilities as executor of the estate," he informed me.

"Okay. When?"

Stoke reached into a pocket of his suit for a business card and handed it to me. "Call my secretary to set up a time that is convenient for you. Let's try to pick a date when we can get together for lunch after we wade through the paperwork. There isn't much to it; it shouldn't take more than half an hour in the office."

"That sounds good to me," I responded. I didn't punch a time clock on my new job as a crime reporter; a certain flexibility in how I spent my day, including the perk of an occasional long lunch, balanced out the long hours spent hanging around night courts and police stations.

Ken Menske came to the wake, but we didn't interact aside from nodding a hello and raising our glasses in a silent salute from across the room. We'd exchanged a short, somber greeting at the church prior to serving as pallbearers. I considered that it would be good to avoid getting cornered into a one-on-one conversation with him, as I suspected he knew that I'd been tapped as Fitz's executor and might try to bend my ear about the plans for the *Watcher* script. Pilar had alerted me that Ken, when he'd called to offer his condolences, had suggested that he could take over the production on her behalf. At that point, I hadn't given it any thought and wasn't in the mood to talk business. The fact that he didn't approach me I took as an indication that he shared my feelings.

I made a point of finding an opportunity to talk alone with Dr. Appel. Doing my best to emulate Charlie Stoke's style, keeping the tone of the conversation friendly, while still getting my point across clearly, I said, "You know, Doctor, you and your tending to Pilar were a major topic of conversation the last time that I was alone with Fitz."

I paused to let the doctor consider the tenor of my comments. The slightly troubled expression that drifted onto his face and his lack of response I took as indications he understood where our conversation was headed.

"Fitz indicated to me that he wasn't entirely satisfied that your treatments were having the effect he would like to see for Pilar," I continued in a quiet but slightly more edged tone. I mentally congratulated myself for carefully choosing words that would make my point and attitude clear to the doctor while avoiding directly referring to him as a slimy, drug-pushing quack. "It seems to me Pilar has been doing pretty well for the last few days without your assistance. I'm thinking she should continue down that road for a while to see how it goes.

"Of course, I'm only a friend of the family, and Pilar is a grown woman, so what she does is her business, not mine. On the other hand, she's Danny's mother, and Danny's a special kid in my book, so I take a particular interest in his mother's wellbeing . . . you understand. Maybe it's a bit presumptuous of me, but I'm something of an artless slob who doesn't really give a damn about such niceties. I'm sure that if Fitz were alive, he'd find a more sensitive, subtle, and diplomatic solution to this problem. My approach to such things often tends to be heavy handed . . . physical even." My calm even tone was intentionally much less ominous than my words. I admit that, as I spoke, I was beginning to tap into my darker, more primitive self. "I hope I am making myself clear here."

"I . . .," he started to respond but thought better of it. Apparently, I'd made my point. An icy-cold, blank-faced Dr. Appel turned and walked away without raising objection or contributing anything to our admittedly one-sided conversation. Within a few minutes of our discussion, I noticed that the *good doctor* was no longer at the party.

Later that evening after the guests had left, Pilar, Annie, and I sat together at a table in the backyard near the pool. The ladies polished off a bottle of cold white wine, while I downed a couple of beers. Pilar seemed more relaxed than she'd been over the past several days when the three of us had been busy making funeral arrangements, fielding a variety of questions from the police— none of which seemed to indicate that they were any closer to solving the mystery of Fitz's murder—and keeping a close watch on an understandably less easygoing than normal Danny. Pilar had masked her grief when we were together, although there were telltale signs of redness around her eyes and a drawn pallidness to her cheeks that makeup couldn't hide, which indicated that her stoicism might not be as solid when she was alone in the night.

Watching Pilar in action had driven home Annie's observation about Pilar's ability to focus her attention and energy on what was most important to her at the moment and to the exclusion of almost everything else. Now that the immediate tasks for which she had responsibility were handled or at least settling down, both Annie and I had expressed our concern to each other that Pilar might be ripe for a real emotional breakdown. Pilar with too much time on her hands and no immediate prospects for an acting gig might easily fall back under Dr. Appel's sway and into her old habits.

So I was surprised and somewhat relieved when Pilar started off our conversation in a firm, almost businesslike manner, listing the new set of tasks that she saw before her and outlining how she would like our help with them. She'd previously arranged with Annie to stay on for a while to provide support for Pilar while she focused on finding a new project. Pilar also felt that Annie's being there would add some stability to the household from Danny's perspective. A few days earlier when I mentioned that I'd been tapped as the executor of Fitz's estate, Pilar had said that Charlie Stoke had already told her that and that she was the sole heir. She didn't seem to have any problem with my role, in fact seemed relieved that she would not have to deal with the legal and financial details.

Not surprisingly knowing Pilar, the topics that she most wanted to discuss, as we sat in the shade of a massive elm sipping wine and swallowing beer, were of a more personal nature. "William, I would appreciate it if you would arrange to spend as much time as you can with Danny. He seems to be coping, but who knows with such a young child. With him it is often difficult to know how that he is feeling. He must be having concerns that he is not showing, concerns that he is not expressing. I am certain that your being with him would be a great help. He loves you so."

That last comment melted my heart and certainly would've melted resistance to her request had there been any. "Of course I will. I'm glad you asked. I intended to even if you hadn't."

"That is good to hear. Thank you, William," she said and graced me with another heart-melter of a smile. "Perhaps you could move in here for a while? That would be good."

"Sure, I can do that," I replied, again without hesitation. I suspected that Annie had prompted Pilar's additional request, as I'd already broached the idea with Annie separately. While being at the house every evening after work would allow me to have more quality time with Danny, I had another motive for wanting to take up residence there. The police would drop their tight nightly surveillance of the house following Fitz's funeral. While I doubted that there was much danger, I still wasn't comfortable with the idea of Pilar, Annie, and Danny being alone in the place.

"I have another request of you, William." Having effortlessly succeeded in getting me to go along with her first two appeals, Pilar lost no time in making her third, more problematic one. "I want you to find out who did these things to us, William. I want them to suffer. I want them to pay for what they have done."

While I had already personally resolved to do what she was asking, Pilar's words drove home my feeling of inadequacy to fulfill the task she was asking of me. "I know Lt. Archer, he's a good man. I'm sure he'll do the job," I said, weakly trying to avoid committing to a promise that I had little hope of keeping.

Pilar's smile had switched from heart-thawing to knowing. It was clear to me that she understood the reason for my reluctance to commit to her request and wasn't having it. "You I know. You I trust. It is you who must do this for me."

That settled it, once again I had no way out—and wasn't really looking for one.

## CHAPTER 11

Annie moved into a guestroom to be closer to Pilar and Danny and to have another adult in the main house as additional security. As was agreed, I replaced Annie as the fulltime resident of the guest cottage so that I could keep a watch on the back of the house during the night. In addition to some of my clothes and personal effects, I augmented the furnishings of the cottage with a large flashlight and my Colt .38 Special revolver, which I kept locked in a drawer in the bedroom during the day and out on a table next to an overstuffed leather chair in the living room at night. I doubted that there was much chance the kidnappers or Fitz's killer would return to the scene, but like everyone else I was still uptight and not interested in taking any chances.

In the evenings after work, I'd show up at the house, eat dinner with Annie and Danny if they had not already eaten—Pilar being invariably out and about in the evenings—play with Danny until his bedtime, read a few more lines of <u>Treasure Island</u>, and, after bestowing the requisite, gentle kiss on his forehead when he dropped off, quietly leave the room. Later, I would work for a few hours in Fitz's office on the things I needed to get up to speed on as his executor. Then I would enjoy a nightcap with Annie before kissing her goodnight, double checking that all of the doors to the house were secure, and retiring alone to the cottage.

I would settle into the chair in the front room of the bungalow, my self-assigned post for night watch, with my coat and shoes off but still dressed in my slacks and shirt, a blanket draped over my chest and legs. A couple of low-wattage lights were kept burning through the night over the patio area at the back of the house to discourage any would-be intruders and to allow me a reasonable if obscured view over the yard and pool area through the window of the cottage. I set my alarm to wake me periodically, but it was rarely necessary as at best I was only clocking twenty or thirty minutes at a stretch. I wasn't getting much sleep, but that wasn't why I was there. Besides, I had a lot on my mind that wasn't compatible with a sound night's sleep.

I was frustrated that I wasn't accomplishing anything meaningful in the search for Fitz's killer or Danny's kidnappers. Other than a fruitless return with the police to the isolated spot in Topanga Canyon where I'd been slugged, and pestering Lt. Archer by telephone a couple of times a day for information as to the status of his investigation, to my thinking I was contributing next to nothing to the effort. The lieutenant was sympathetic with my concerns and patient about my frequent calls, but there was nothing he could or, considering my status as a crime reporter, would tell me that I didn't already know.

After I moved onto the estate, I found opportunities in the evenings to chat with Dotty and Viola. While it was beyond imagining that either of them could have had anything to do with Danny's kidnapping or Fitz's murder, I decided to begin my own investigation by talking to them on the off chance that they may know or have seen something that, while in itself seemingly inconsequential, might at least get me pointed in the right direction. I knew that Sgt. Buller had already formally interviewed them soon after Fitz's death and before they'd come back to work. I calculated that if I was going to get anything more out of them than what they had already told the sergeant, the best plan would be for me to approach them with a soft sell; anything too blunt would probably set them off again emotionally and end up producing nothing of value.

Approaching Dotty was easy: I had a history of wandering into the kitchen uninvited, sticking my finger in the dumplings or whatever else was on the menu, and getting in good-natured trouble with the cook. It was a technique I'd developed when waiting tables at the fraternity house during my all too brief and always hungry college days. Dotty would scold, then rap me gently with a wooden spoon, before dishing me up small samples.

Dotty Hanson worked Tuesday through Sunday, coming in midmornings and staying until the cups and dishes were washed, dried, and stowed in the cupboards. She was a big, middle aged, dark-blonde Swedish woman. Although a none too recent emigrant, Dotty had not made much effort to lose a thick, lilting accent, which in those days in L.A. was of a type rarely heard beyond an athletic club massage table. Dotty was friendly enough in her way but not much of one for witty repartee. I would often sit at the kitchen table enjoying my illicit treats, while Dotty would share with me the trials and tribulations of her day.

When I approached Dotty there was no trouble raising the topic of the crimes, as she brought them up. It was almost as if she was intent on solving the mysteries herself. As her enquiries continued in a steadily increasing intensity, it soon became apparent that it was just her natural curiosity working its way up to top speed. Still, the questions that she asked, and which I tried to answer as straightforwardly as I felt that I could, did most of my work for me. It was clear that she had little new information of her own to offer, and I became even more convinced that she could not have been involved in the crimes in anyway.

Over time I'd developed a knack for mentally converting her 'w' sounds back into 'v's. With that skill and a few innocuous questions of my own it didn't take me long to learn without asking for the information directly that Dotty seldom left the kitchen and to her recollection had never been on the second floor of the house. She of course knew that there were back stairs, as they were located near the kitchen.

Tormund, Dotty's husband, also an imported Swede, was a seaman on a freighter that ran a regular route between L.A. and

Hawaii. From the way she'd often described him, he was bigger than I was and just about as clumsy—certainly not cat burglar material. When I asked casually how he was, Dotty offered that he was fine as far as she knew since he'd been away at sea for the last three weeks. That easily verifiable alibi would take him out of the picture for the nights when the crimes had gone down. As I summarized it later for Annie, I gained nothing beneficial from my efforts with Dotty, except a slice of excellent apple tart and a cup of Scandinavian-strong black coffee.

Viola Newhouse, with her pug nose and usual tomboy grin, was a dead ringer for Patsy Kelly, the popular comic actress. She performed her housekeeping duties weekdays, nine-to-five, and the occasional weekend for extended hours if there was a *do* to arrange and monitor. Her similarity to Kelly didn't stop with her physical appearance; her irreverent, wise-cracking approach made us kindred spirits of sorts, perfect foils for each other's simi-witty, droll remarks. She seemed to genuinely like everyone she met, Annie and I being no exceptions—although I couldn't help thinking that her affinity for Annie might extend a little beyond what most people would've considered appropriate in those days. And while she was never dour or uncordial, she was serious about her household responsibilities, giving everyone—not just me—the feeling they might have forgotten to wipe their shoes off on the doormat before they entered the house.

I knew that I'd have to be more careful when approaching Viola; she'd be more likely to pick up on what I was up to. But knowing something doesn't always mean you can do anything about it. I'd hardly started in with her before she cut me off with, "Why don't you just ask me what you want to know, Marshall: 'Do I know anything more about the kidnapping or Mr. Fitz's murder than I've already told that police detective'?"

I adopted a sheepish grin much like that of a chocolate-smeared kid who's just been discovered hiding in a closet with a box of Christmas candy. That look on my part apparently was enough of a confirmation for Viola as she continued to speak without waiting for a verbal affirmation from me. "The answer to your question is, 'Of course not.' I've told the police everything I can think of, which is next to nothing, as far as I can figure. I live alone, so I don't have an alibi for either of those nights. But that doesn't mean I had anything to do with any of it . . . because I didn't."

Her clipped remarks and sly smile marked a full return to Viola's normal mocking style, which, while recently absent, had been slowly re-emerging since the days following Danny's kidnapping and Fitz's murder.

"I doubt anyone thinks that you did; I certainly don't," I countered her defensive remark, looking to rekindle the cordial relationship we'd developed over the last few years. "But you may know more than you realize. For instance, can you think of anyone, other than Annie, me, and yourself, who would know the layout of the house? Anyone who would know where Danny's and Pilar's rooms were located?"

Viola didn't have to think about it for long. "Willis. Jack Willis knows those things as well as anyone."

Unlike my less than positive assessment of him, Viola's distaste for Willis was an active loathing. She resented his being around the house and rarely spoke to him unless it was absolutely necessary. I'd never heard of any specific reason for her uncharacteristic aversion toward him, so I assumed that her often stated opinion that he was "a lowlife" was the cause.

"Yes, I suppose that he would," I commented. "And he's a strange one, I'll give you that. But my impression has always been that Jack took his bodyguarding duties seriously and was damn' loyal to Fitz, way beyond what his paycheck required."

"Maybe not so much as you might think." Viola folded her arms across her chest and frowned in an obvious attempt to add significance to her comment. "He travels with a pretty hard crowd: crooks and underworld types."

"How do you know that?"

"I'm no snoop . . . well maybe just a little now and then," she allowed. "Anyway, I see things and I hear things: whispered telephone conversations and meetings afterhours at the front gate with tough looking thugs in big black sedans. A couple of weeks ago, not too long before Mr. Fitzgerald was murdered, I saw Willis in a heated conversation with Dr. Appel's chauffeur—another one cut from the same bolt as Willis if you ask me. You can bet they were up to something; they broke off talking as soon as they saw me."

My first thought was to dismiss what she was telling me as unimportant, assuming that Jack was just repeating to Appel's driver Fitz's message to the doctor about backing off on his supplying Pilar's habit.

"Did you tell that to the police?" I asked.

"You bet I did."

Given Viola's obvious distain for Willis, it was difficult to decide what to make of her comments. Willis's connections and ability to deal with society's bottom tiers were parts of the reason Fitz had employed him, so I didn't see it as a reason to consider him as any more suspect than I already did. Viola had shared her thoughts on Willis with Buller, and I felt confident that the sergeant would've already followed up on it in his usual heavy-handed style. It would've been a confrontation that I'd have enjoyed watching from a safe distance, as I doubted that Jack Willis would be quite as easygoing in his reaction to Buller's approach as I'd been.

Having learned little from my light-touch approaches to Dotty and

Viola, I redirected my efforts to going through Fitz's papers in the evenings. The police had been through Fitz's things already, but Archer had encouraged me to take a fresh look. He thought that given my close relationship with Fitz something might stand out to me that they'd missed. But so far nothing had. To a non-business, non-numbers type such as myself, Fitz's books, records, calendars, letters, and other papers all seemed fairly mundane. However, after some torturous and no doubt deficient analysis on my part, I was able to assess that Fitz's financial situation, while not rosy, was not as dire as I'd been led to believe. There was enough money still left in the bank to cover Pilar's expenses for at least the next six months to a year, even without much cutting back on her lifestyle. That should give her plenty of time to cash out on the *Watcher* screen rights and to locate a starring role in another movie. The only unusual recent transaction of any kind that I saw was the $15,000 in cash Fitz had withdrawn from his bank account to cover Danny's ransom.

For the most part, everything in Fitz's appointment calendar for the last few months looked routine: meetings and lunches with studio executives and a few actors, social events, golf dates, a couple of doctors' appointments, and one trip to his dentist. The lone anomaly was a penciled-in meeting a couple of months past with Paul Logan, a mob-connected bookie with whom Fitz was known to place the occasional bet. Fitz liked to play the ponies—another thing we had in common—betting amounts others might think excessive. But I never heard that he'd ever gotten himself in deeper than he could handle. I knew of Logan from my early days in the Boyle Heights neighborhood; from time-to-time my father would place bets with Logan, who, in those days, was a low-level runner for one of the local bookies. It probably amounted to nothing, still it was something I thought I should point out to Lt. Archer. When I called him about it, he told me that they'd already picked up on it.

"We talked to Logan. He said he didn't know anything about a meeting and had never even met Fitzgerald in person. Apparently, Fitzgerald's guy Willis was the contact man with

Logan. When we questioned Willis, he claimed to know nothing about any meeting."

"You buy that?" I asked.

"Logan is probably lying about something—it's in his nature, especially when talking to us—but what that might be, I don't know," Archer replied. "You should talk to him. If, as you say, Logan knew your father, maybe he'll remember your dad having a snot-nosed kid in tow with him. If he liked your dad, he might be willing to open up to you for old time's sake." I could almost sense one of Archer's signature grins beaming unseen at me across the phone line.

"Maybe, but don't count on it," I countered if for no other reason than to let Archer know that I was wise that he was sending me on a wild goose chase. The fact that Logan knew my father from several years back and might remember me as a kid whom my dad would've had with him on occasion, didn't mean he'd tell me bupkis about his business with Fitz just for "old time's sake."

"By the way, you should know that Willis's alibi checked out," Archer added. "We confirmed that he was with his sister in Bakersfield the nights of the kidnapping and the shooting. I wouldn't necessarily trust the sister's word for it, but they did a lot of socializing with old friends while he was there. We had the local guys talk to them. He was there alright.

"Our own chat with Mr. Willis didn't go all that well. I don't think that he likes my sergeant." My mental picture of Archer's smiling face grew even sharper as he spoke. "It damn' near came to blows. Anyway, we got nothing useful out of him. Have you talked with him lately?"

"No, I haven't spoken to him yet. But I'm going to; Pilar has asked me to settle up with him. I doubt he's involved. My impression is that he was extremely loyal to Fitz. On the other hand, he'd be the one most likely to know if someone had a reason to want Fitz dead. But if he didn't tell you anything, maybe he doesn't know anything."

"Maybe. Or maybe he wants to handle it himself," Archer commented ominously.

"Yeah, that sounds more like Willis," I agreed. It was a lot easier for me to picture Willis seeking his own revenge against someone who'd killed the person that he was charged with protecting than his being a participant in shooting him. "I'll drop by his place as soon as I can to see if I can get anything more out of him."

But before visiting with Willis, I had to attend to a couple of more mundane matters. I called Ken Menske and explained my idea to peddle *Watcher* with his help to one of the major studios. Not surprisingly, Menske's initial reaction was negative. That was until it dawned on him that it might well be his last, best hope for salvaging anything out of the project for himself. We agreed to meet the coming Saturday at his place to discuss it further.

The next call was to Charlie Stoke to arrange the meeting he'd suggested to discuss exactly what my responsibilities would be as executor of Fitz's estate and as trustee for Danny. We arranged to meet at his offices later that morning and head out to lunch after we'd gone over the paperwork.

As a low paid rookie reporter, I was always up for a free lunch, but my real reason for agreeing to break bread with Stoke was to press him with some questions not involving the estate that I felt needed answering and would be better asked on neutral ground rather than in his chambers where he would have a psychological edge.

## CHAPTER 12

Charlie Stoke's office occupied a suite on the top floor of a three-story, granite-faced building on Wilshire Blvd. near downtown L.A. His secretary, a cute young lass who looked as if she might be playing hooky from high school, ushered me into an office almost as large as that of a top-tier studio executive. Stoke sat statue-like behind an equally massive desk, his back to a bank of windows that looked out onto the boulevard below. The late-morning light spilling through the south-facing windows, bright enough to partially blind me, gave Stoke in his high-backed black leather chair the appearance of a silhouette cutout.

He stood up and came around from behind his desk to greet me and indicated with a gesture that we should move to a small conference table with four comfortable-looking, fabric-covered chairs in a corner of the room. Someone had already neatly laid out on the table all of the documents that we would need to review. Stoke took me through each one in order, explaining its purpose and having me sign any that I hadn't already inked a month earlier in Fitz's study. I'm no lawyer by a long shot, but Stoke's explanations were clear and straight forward enough for me to follow along—that was until we got to the particulars of Danny's trust.

"Fitz took out an insurance policy to fund the trust," Stoke explained.

"Yes, he told me about that when he asked me to be the

trustee."

"Did he tell you that the policy was for $50,000?"

"No. That's a lot of money." As a newspaperman, I've a talent for succinctly stating the obvious. I'd seen a payment for a hefty insurance premium when I was going through Fitz's check book, but having never bought insurance myself, I hadn't given it much thought at the time.

"Yes, it is. But that's only the half of it . . . literally," Stoke commented. "Fitz was murdered, so the double indemnity clause applies. If everything works out, the actual payout will be $100,000."

"My God, that's a fortune!" I sat stunned for a minute trying unsuccessfully to come to grips with the concept of that kind of money; it proved beyond the capacity of a young guy, who thought that he'd pulled a fast one by landing a $20-per-week job as a first-year reporter, so I stopped trying. Instead I asked, "What do you mean by, 'If everything works out'?"

"Well, with a payout this large and with a murder involved, I imagine the insurance company's investigators are going to want to take a hard look at the circumstances of Fitz's death before they payoff on the policy. It could be some time before you see any of the money."

"That's no problem," I commented. "I doubt Danny will need the money anytime soon, if ever."

"And Danny's only five years old, so despite being the indirect beneficiary, I doubt they will look at him as a suspect for his father's murder," Stoke commented.

"True," I said, thinking that Stoke uncharacteristically was making a tasteless joke.

Stoke gave me a long, enigmatic look, then said, "On the

other hand, once the money is paid into the trust, it will be under your sole control as trustee.  There's nothing to prevent you from absconding with it all."

"'Absconding'? I'm not even sure I know how to spell 'absconding,'" I quipped before the significance of what he was inferring had penetrated my thicker than I would like to admit skull and reached the more rational areas of my brain. In fairness, I was still reeling mentally from trying to grasp the concept of $100,000 cash in one lump sum in the middle of an economic depression.  In a less jovial manner I said, "So I take it you're saying that makes me a first-class suspect for Fitz's murder." I didn't like the logic but couldn't refute it.

"I'm afraid so," Stoke said and added, "It's not my job to point it out to the insurance company or the police, and I won't, but I doubt it will escape their notice."

"This just gets better and better," I said, trying to sound less concerned than I actually was. 'All the more reason to find the real killer quickly,' I thought once my mind started to function again at a somewhat near normal pace. Solving the mystery was a great idea, but an outcome toward which neither the police nor I seemed to be making much progress.

Our business completed, Stoke and I walked to lunch at the hat-shaped Brown Derby, which was just a little over a block away from his offices. As luck would have it, Joan Blondell was there lunching with a small group of admirers. When she spotted us walking into the restaurant, she waved to us from across the room and graced us with one of her inviting smiles. We waved back, politely showing with friendly, mock frowns our dismay at not being a part of her entourage. I considered how much nicer it would've been to be trading one-liners with Joan than sitting at a table with Charlie Stoke, trying to enjoy my lunch while worrying about whether I might have a future date with the hangman for a murder I didn't commit, and wondering how I should best approach the next sensitive topic I intended to discuss with Stoke.

It has been pointed out on more than one occasion that diplomacy is not my strong suit, so I decided to go with what was: bluntness. "Charlie, normally I try to keep my nose out of other people's business, particularly their personal relationships, but circumstances aren't normal, and it doesn't look like they're going to be for a while," I started in. "So I'm going to ask it straight out: What is going on between you and Pilar?"

Stoke's face showed that his first impulse was to be angry at my admittedly impertinent question, but he changed his mind, probably realizing that anger would just make me more certain there was something between them. After a brief reflection and an astute calculation, Stoke came up with, "I guess what I dropped on you back at the office gives you a special need to know some things that would otherwise be none of your damned business. Gentlemen generally don't talk about such things, as you know; we lawyers call it being discrete."

"You can call it whatever you want just as long as I get an answer." I wasn't at all interested in playing word games with advocate Stoke—a game I would certainly lose—nor at the moment was I concerned about either of us maintaining our bona fides as gentlemen.

Stoke caught my drift like it was a lazy, high fly ball dropping square into his mitt. "Okay, okay," Stoke responded with just a hint of lingering irritation. "When I tell you what you want to know and you realize that it has nothing to do with Fitz's murder, I am going to rely on your discretion to keep it to yourself."

Stoke had smoothly switched to a "no hard feelings' smile that wasn't totally convincing, but my doubts could've just been due to my less than trusting nature. I aped his expression, thinking, 'What the hell, I might as well keep it friendly, at least until I hear what he has to say.'

"Pilar came to me looking to see if there might be some sort of legal angle that she could use to force Fitz to give her the part she wanted in the film Fitz was producing," Stoke continued in an even monotone that sounded almost as if it was rehearsed. "She came on strong over lunch, pretending she had come to me because of a personal affinity that she had for me—and I let her pretend. She made it clear that she was prepared to pay me for my efforts in a currency that could only be had through the 'Bank of Pilar.'"

Stoke paused and stared at me, waiting for a reaction, which I, with no small effort, refused to provide. When I didn't react, he continued. "Look, I know sleeping with a client's wife is not good practice, but there's nothing in the Bar Association's Code of Ethics that covers it, and Pilar is a very beautiful woman." Stoke made it all sound like it was just business as usual—maybe it was for him.

What Stoke told me didn't surprise or shock me—several years of living and working around Hollywood types had inured me to what people were capable of in the arena of sexual pleasures—but I will admit to a certain amount of disillusionment in this case.

"Anyway, nothing came of it," Stoke continued, showing clear disappointment by the way he said it. "Pilar and I had lunch here a week later to discuss it again; she didn't want me calling the house. I told her the only plan that might have a slim chance would be for her to divorce Fitz and to try to get some control over the rights to the production in the settlement. When she heard that, she dropped the whole thing . . . and any further thought of an intimate liaison with me. I've seen her a few times since, and it's as if the matter had never been broached, as if nothing had passed between us.

"Look, I admit that one of the benefits of being a well-connected attorney in this town is that there is no shortage of young starlets willing to trade their favors for help with their careers. And I have helped out more than one or two along the way. But I never initiated anything or promised anything," Stoke was quick to add.

"And it's often worked out well for them. I'm the appreciative type." A sly, knock-their-bloomers-off smile crossed his handsome face, a one-two combination I'm certain couldn't help but add to the success of his endeavors. 'A true gentleman of the old school,' I thought to myself sarcastically.

"Of course, Pilar's a different matter," Stoke continued. "She knows her way around. She wasn't about to go for it unless she was certain that I could make something happen. When I couldn't, she dropped it, cold. I admit in Pilar's case my hopes that something would come of it were much higher than hers."

Stoke's explanation had a ring of truth to it. Annie's assessment of Pilar's priorities apparently had been spot-on: Pilar might've given Stoke the tumble he was angling for if he could deliver the goods for her, but not otherwise. Her false start with Stoke might explain Pilar's subtle reaction toward him at Fitz's funeral. Still, it didn't explain the intensity of Stoke's aggressive reaction toward Dr. Appel at Danny's party when Stoke thought that Pilar's *best interests* were at risk from the doctor's ministrations. Maybe, just maybe, Charlie Stoke's interest in Pilar wasn't quite as cavalier as it had been in his numerous other romantic conquests.

Stoke surprised me by offering, "The police must have heard the same rumors you did. They've already been by to talk to me. I told them that I was home alone in bed on the night when Fitz was shot. I suppose I don't have any real alibi, but they didn't push it, so I assume they're satisfied."

In light of what Stoke had just told me, I had no qualms about being the one who'd pointed the police in his direction. "What did you tell the police about why you were meeting with Pilar? I'm guessing that you didn't share with them your considerations of the special rewards that might be involved in helping her cause."

"No . . . no I didn't. I only told the police that our lunches together involved business matters, which made them subject to attorney-client privilege, and, despite the fanciful gossip, nothing sexual had transpired, which is true—albeit a lawyer's type of truth, I'll admit."

For some reason, I was starting to like Charlie more, despite his illicit designs on my dead friend's wife; maybe it was his candor. And while I wasn't necessarily buying everything he was selling, I still didn't see him as a murderer. Even if he was lying about whether he was having a transaction-based affair with Pilar, it didn't seem like much of a reason for either of them to kill Fitz. Unless something more came my way, I felt I could relegate them to the inactive category of my efforts at investigation.

My discussion with Stoke may have to some extent eliminated a couple of unlikely suspects, but it had come up with another one, *me*—not exactly the result I'd been looking for.

## CHAPTER 13

I didn't go directly back to work as I'd intended after my lunch meeting with Charlie Stoke, which, surprisingly, considering my ham-handed approach to the subject of his relationship—or lack thereof—with Pilar, had settled into a cordial conversation over a couple of tasty Brown Derby Salads. Instead, after walking Stoke back and saying a friendly goodbye on the sidewalk in front of his office, I drove downtown to police headquarters to tell Lt. Archer what I'd just learned about the size of Danny's trust fund, and that he should pencil-in and perhaps consider double-underlining my name on his roster of suspects. I figured that hearing about the insurance payout and its implications from me would go over better with the police than their finding out about it later from the insurance company. Luckily, Archer was at his desk; not so luckily, Buller was with him.

A slyly smiling Archer told me that my name was already on the short-list of suspects but congratulated me on moving it up to near the top. Unfortunately, with this new information, I was now the only one, other than the unidentified burglar, who could be seen as having anything like a strong motive to kill Fitz. A stenographer took down my short statement and even shorter answers to the few questions Archer and Buller asked me.

While the interview was being typed for my signature, Buller, his brain apparently spinning at revolutions well into the red, decided to unload on me for no apparent reason other than his not wanting to miss the opportunity. "The way I see it, you're the guy, Marshall," he said with undisguised malice as he stood, leaning forward, his fists pushing down on the table between us, his face about six inches from mine. "You knew about the insurance, you snatched the kid so that you could arrange to get Fitzgerald alone, doubled back, and shot him. Then you show up with the kid bright and early the next morning, coming on like some big hero."

Some guys never learn. I hadn't melted under Buller's blowtorch-like, tough guy routine the first time he'd pulled it on me when I'd been reeling from the news of Fitz's murder and nursing an aching head, so I didn't know why he thought that it would get him anywhere now.

"I suppose I sapped myself on the back of the head too," I said in a calm voice, curbing my emotions and the urge to pop him one in the jaw. I was beginning to think the ape who hit me that night might have done me a big favor, though not a big enough one for me to forgive him for the pain I still felt whenever I absentmindedly touched the back of my head or happened to pull my hat down a little too firmly. If the payoff had gone as we hoped that it would, I might have returned to the house in time to prevent Fitz's murder. Or more likely, I would've arrived back, unsuspecting and unarmed, in time to have been shot along with my friend. On balance and with all things considered, despite his unintended good turn, whoever hit me was still definitely in my limited but selective catalog of bad guys.

"Your girlfriend could have done that for you," Buller commented, still trying to get a rise out of me. That comment almost did the trick.

But by then, I'd worked around cops like Buller long enough to understand that he was just trying to bait me. Giving in to the urge to belt him, as satisfying as it might be in the short-term, would certainly have resulted in my being thrown in the can. I suppose that was what Buller was hoping for; it was unlikely he really believed his convoluted theory about my involvement.

"It's a thought," I commented, still managing to maintain my outward easygoing attitude, "but not a very good one. If you really believed it or had anything like proof, you'd have already arrested me. You know I didn't do it, so why are you wasting your time trying to pin it on me?"

"We'll get the proof." His face was turning red, and a bead of sweat had formed and was precariously hanging from the end of his nose. He was working himself up into a snit. I momentarily considered pulling his chain a little to see if he might take a swing at me. Ready for it, I knew that I could easily avoid a punch thrown by him in anger. That would give me an excuse to strike back. Still, while it might have made me feel better, it wouldn't have helped my cause and would probably have taken a toll on my good relationship with Lt. Archer.

Archer had been standing by, noncommittally watching the little drama between Buller and me unfold and showing no inclination to curb it.

"I'm not worried about that," I said in a more confident tone than I really felt, "because it didn't happen. You're wasting your time, Buller. You keep working yourself up like this over nothing, you'll keel over in a fit."

Despite what seemed to be my relatively benign comments, Buller still looked like he might come across the table at me. I pushed back in my chair preparing to rise to meet him, if necessary, fist clenched. But Archer's well-timed placing of his hand on Buller's arm, and a firm yet calming comment, "Okay, let's all take it easy," had an immediate soothing effect. Buller sat down, scowling but saying nothing, and I relaxed my hands.

That was the end of my short but emotion-packed interview with the detectives. After I signed my statement, Archer walked with me to my car. He didn't say anything one way or the other about the near miss with Buller, which didn't surprise me, but the fact that he walked out with me made me believe he was still on my side; I sure hoped he was.

It was late in the day but still light by the time I arrived at what I was only just beginning to think of as 'Pilar's house' and my new, temporary residence. The drive from downtown to West L.A. had given me time to settle down some from the initial shock of finding out that I was a serious suspect for Fitz's murder and Danny's kidnapping, even if an unlikely one. It also allowed me to cool off from the emotional fervor of my admittedly inconsequential, yet heated run-in with Sgt. Buller. Archer's relaxed and apparently still friendly attitude had gone a long way toward easing my mind, but I suspected that I wasn't going to fully be my old, carefree self again until the underlying mysteries were resolved, and I was back in the clear.

Annie informed me that Pilar was out—where and with whom unknown—and not expected home until late. Annie, Mag, and I ate an early dinner sitting at the kitchen table with Danny. He was still somewhat subdued, but there were signs he was starting to revert to his normal self. After the meal Annie and I sat at the table and played Uncle Wiggily with him; reading the cards for him, mispronouncing the ridiculous names, and helping him to count out the steps along the twisting paths; until it was time for Mag to put him to bed. Later that evening, Annie told me that Danny tended to perk up, smile, and laugh more when I showed up at the house after work. That made me feel better; at least I was making some progress toward one of my key objectives.

Mag had been as nervous as a tick in a flea powder factory since she'd been told of Fitz's murder, a condition I put down to a personal and cultural aversion to being in a house where someone had died violently, a mindset with which we all could empathize. She left, without her normal words of goodbye to anyone, as soon as Danny was down for the night, scurrying out to her brother Javier's car, which, uncharacteristically early, was waiting on the street by the front gate, its motor running. As soon as Mag was inside the vehicle, it sped away as if it were the getaway car for a bank job rather than the nanny's regular ride home.

Alone at last, with everyone away or down for the night, Annie and I sat together in the living room exchanging kisses and caresses with the enthusiasm of a couple still in the early stages of what was looking to be more than a casual romantic relationship. That went a lot further toward righting the world for me than had either Archer's reassuring smiles or even Danny's laughter.

Coming up for air and a pause in our pleasant physical activities, I filled Annie in on the events and revelations of my busy day. When I told her about it, Annie was even more astonished by the amount of Danny's trust fund than I had been. "I had no idea. Fitz handled the insurance himself. I knew about the trust, of course, but I thought it was limited to the initial $5,000 that he'd set aside in his will to fund it."

"I suppose with so much tied up in *Watcher*, Fitz thought that insurance would be the best way to fund the trust," I considered aloud, trying to satisfy my own questions about the size of the insurance proceeds. "Taking $50,000 out of the estate if it became necessary to fund the trust before the film was finished could have been tough. And, while Pilar loves Danny, I doubt that she would've seen any wisdom in segregating that much cash and putting it under someone else's control. As Stoke explained it to me, the insurance pays directly into the trust and doesn't impact the rest of the estate, so the issue will never come up."

"Stephen had a good head for business," Annie remarked, "but this plan seems beyond his expertise."

"Maybe it was Stoke's idea," I suggested. "I didn't think to ask him about it. I suppose I was too shocked by the dollar amount and the implications for me to think it through."

I explained how my control over the trust fund would give me a theoretical motive to do away with Fitz. I also told Annie about my subsequent meeting and conversation with Archer and

Buller.

"They can't really think you could've had anything to do with this?" she said in a semi-incredulous tone, indicating that, while she was sure I wasn't involved with the kidnapping or the murder, she was equally certain the police might well think just that. I appreciated her kind words and said so, even if they offered little in the way of comfort or real reassurance.

"I don't think they do, but I have to admit, in light of the amount of dough we're talking about, it's a reasonable theory," I said. "It's a good thing Archer and I have some history. He knows me well enough to know I'm not one to go around shooting friends. Although, I have to admit that for a hundred grand I might be willing to knock off an acquaintance or two." I smiled at my own poor joke to make up for the one missing from Annie's face.

My attempt to make light of the matter a failure, I continued in a more serious vein. "I don't really think Buller believes that I killed Fitz, but he may still think that I'm somehow involved in Danny's kidnapping plot. Archer says, 'it's just his way.' I know a lot of cops use that heavy-handed, tough guy approach on suspects whether they have anything on them or not. Archer isn't going to look at me for any of this, or let Buller come after me, unless he sees some hard evidence of my guilt. Since I didn't do either of the deeds, there can't be anything out there that proves I did."

"Still . . ." Annie clearly wasn't ready to move on.

"Yeah, there's always 'still' isn't there. But I say there's no sense in worrying about the 'still' until it gets here. I will say that all of this has given me a renewed incentive to find out who killed Fitz."

I moved on, relating to Annie some of what I'd found out about the rumored relationship between Pilar and Stoke. "Apparently, Pilar approached Stoke to see if he could help her find a way to get Fitz to change his mind about writing in a starring role for her in the *Watcher* script. That's why they were seen having lunch together. When Stoke told her that there was nothing to be done, she dropped it."

"That sounds right," Annie remarked. "That may be when Pilar finally came to grips with the fact that she wasn't right for the part."

"Maybe so, but I can't recall ever hearing of an actress admitting that she wasn't right for a part," I joked.

I didn't mention Stoke's allegation that Pilar had dangled sexual favors in exchange for his help in influencing Fitz because I wasn't certain I believed everything Stoke had told me, including the parts about Pilar having made the offer or that she hadn't actually delivered on it. Annie had been way ahead of me about that possibility, so she wouldn't have been all that surprised at Stoke's revelations. But I'd all but eliminated any idea of Stoke's relationship with Pilar—whatever it may have gotten up to physically—having anything to do with Fitz's murder, so unless that changed, I saw no reason to discuss it further. Even though Annie had no illusions about Pilar's unique personal philosophy toward life or her core character, the two women had developed a working relationship and a friendship of sorts, so I didn't want to say anything at this point that might impact their rapport.

Annie moved on to a new topic. "Pilar again mentioned to me that she'd like you to settle up with Jack Willis. Pay him whatever he's due, whatever you think is fair. She doesn't want him around. She drives her own car most of the time and can hire a new chauffeur if she finds she needs one. She never liked him. I think she blames him for not being around the one time that Fitz needed his protection."

"Okay, I'll handle that," I said. "Archer wants me to talk with him, which is what I was planning to do anyway. It's strange that it all went down the one time that Jack wasn't here, almost as if whoever was involved was waiting for him to leave the scene.

According to Archer, Willis's alibi for the nights involved is solid, which takes him out of the frame for any direct involvement in either the kidnapping or Fitz's murder.

"I can't picture him as having anything to do with Fitz's death," I continued, "but I suppose that he could've supplied the necessary information about the routine and layout of the house to the kidnappers and then conveniently arranged to be out of town when it happened. His taking days off in the middle of the week to visit a sister, who' as far as anyone can recall he never mentioned before, has a distinct smell of three-day-old fish, if you ask me. And he didn't offer anything to the police when they talked to him.

"The way I look at it, if there's anyone who has an idea of why someone would want to kill Fitz, that anyone would be Jack Willis."

## CHAPTER 14

The Friday evening traffic was a killer. It was nearing seven o'clock by the time I'd left the Examiner offices in downtown L.A. and driven out on a clogged Olympic Boulevard to Jack Willis's place in Culver City. The apartment building, a not-too-rundown, eight-unit walk-up stacked on two levels, was located on a side street not too far from the MGM studios and near the Helm's Bakery facilities. The area didn't look like much, but it sure smelled good when the bakery ovens were fired-up, as they were then.

There was no interior hallway to the apartment house, all of the doors facing out toward the street. Willis occupied a middle unit on the second floor, its door conveniently identified with a capital "B" just above the spot where my knuckles came in contact with it.

Willis opened the door a crack on the first knock and peered out at me before opening it all the way. I hadn't expected that Jack would be particularly glad to see me, as the taciturn bodyguard never seemed glad to see anybody. Even so, his cold look and lack of comment on finding me at his door seemed overplayed. His quick and cautious reaction to my being there made me wonder if he'd been expecting someone else, someone with whom he wasn't all that eager to meet. Or it may have just been his way. I expected Jack's life experiences had brought him in contact with many people whom he wouldn't be all that happy to link up with again. I had no reason to believe that I was one of those persons, so I grinned and sounded off with a cheery, "Hi, Jack. How's tricks?"

Dressed in a loose-fitting off-the-rack charcoal grey suit, a white cotton shirt, and a tie so dark that you couldn't pick out whether it had any pattern to it, he might have just arrived home from a day of pounding the pavement looking for a new job. But I discarded that idea as soon as I noted the two-day old beard covering his squared off jaw. Even though I'd never seen him wearing anything much different in all the time he'd worked for Fitz, there was something about the way he looked and carried himself that made him seem incongruous answering the door to his apartment in a suit and tie.

"What do you want?" he asked as he turned his back on me and walked back into the apartment, leaving the door open, which I took as an indication that it was okay for me to enter. So I did.

"I have something for you," I replied. "Pilar asked me to give this to you." I handed him a check for a month's salary, which may or may not have been due him, as well as an extra month's pay by way of severance. Pilar had said I should use my own judgement in settling up with him. That he hadn't shown up at the house since Fitz's death I took as an indication that he realized his services were no longer desired. I supposed that, as he'd walked away from his job, he wasn't due any severance, but Fitz had liked him, so I'd decided to be generous with what was now Pilar's money.

Willis took the check and the unspoken fact he was no longer employed without comment. He dropped the check on a nearby coffee table and looked at me narrowly through his blue-grey eyes, his legs slightly bent at the knees in a fighter's stance, and an expression just short of ferocity on his face. It was Jack's normal look, so it didn't cause me to have any particular concerns for my safety. It wasn't that he was actually angry about anything; it was just as if he was always prepared to be and considering whether he ought to do something about it.

He didn't offer me a seat, so I asked my first question standing in the middle of his small living room. "What the hell happened, Jack?"

He didn't answer. There was no reaction and no change in his expression. It was as if he hadn't heard my question, as if I hadn't said anything.

It was obvious that Willis had no intention of answering my open-ended question and was prepared to stand there silently glaring at me for a lot longer than I was willing to do the same, so I decided to try a softer, more personal approach.

"Look, Jack, I've seen enough to know that you took your job of protecting Fitz seriously. You liked and respected him; you couldn't have done the job for as long as you did if you didn't. I'm sure that you want to see that whoever killed him gets what's coming to him.

"You have to know that Fitz and I were close, and that I have a special feeling toward Danny. I intend to find out who did this if I can. We want the same thing here, Jack. If you know anything about any of this, I need you to tell me about it."

"I don't know anything." His response was too quick, almost as if he wanted me to know that he wasn't being truthful with me. But I saw no point in calling him on it; Willis wasn't the type to show his hand once he'd decided how to play it.

"Okay, maybe you don't know anything for sure, but you must have some ideas," I said to see if an indirect approach might give him a way to share information that for some reason he didn't want to state outright. "You, more than anyone else, knew what was going on with Fitz. You must at least have some ideas about who might want to harm him."

After a pause with a look as if he might actually be giving it some consideration, Willis shook his head slowly and came up empty. "No . . . nothing."

My new approach hadn't produced anything meaningful from Willis, but at least it had elicited a response. I gave him another verbal nudge to see if anything more would be forthcoming. "As I see it, Danny's being snatched one night, and Fitz being shot the next almost certainly has to be connected. And your being gone at the same time just seems too much to swallow. It stands to reason that whoever took Danny and whoever shot Fitz had to know that you were out of town. Who would've known you'd be gone?"

Seeing that he wasn't going to be rid of me by ignoring my questions, Willis relented a crack. "Fitz, Pilar, your girlfriend, that's it unless one of them passed it on to someone else," he answered without hesitation as if he'd already thought through the list a few times himself before I asked. "Anyway, I was only at the house during the days, not at night. They could have grabbed the kid any night. I wouldn't have been there. Anybody who knew my routine would know that."

"Yeah, but if you hadn't been out of town, you sure as hell would've been there the next night after the kidnapping when Fitz was shot," I pointed out. "If the same people who took Danny intended to kill Fitz the next night, they would've wanted you out of the way so that you wouldn't throw a monkey wrench into the plan."

"What makes you so sure it was the same guys who took the kid and then killed Fitz?" Willis was opening up a bit but not offering much. I had a feeling that what he was telling me was a subtle attempt to send me in the wrong direction.

"I can't be for sure, but it stands to reason," I replied. "The two things were too close together. Too much of a coincidence."

"Maybe." Willis shrugged his shoulders dismissively and frowned but said nothing more. His terse, uninformative response combined with the fact he offered nothing and asked no questions of his own convinced me more and more that he knew things that for some reason he had no intention of sharing.

"Any specific reason that you picked those dates to be out of town," I asked, trying to make my question not sound accusatory, but not succeeding well.

If Jack found my question too pointed, he hid it well and answered straightforwardly. "Nah, my sister in Bakersfield had been after me to pay her a visit. Nothing was happening with Fitz, so I took a few days off. No special reason for the dates."

The idea that Willis came from a close-knit family in which the siblings were pressing for a reunion was a big stretch for the imagination, but I had no actual basis to call him on it. And even if I had, pressing him would likely have just caused him to clam-up even tighter.

I'd run out of ideas and approaches for trying to wheedle information out of the recalcitrant Jack. As I prepared to leave, I decided on one last, innocuous threat: "I'm going to find out who did this, Jack. If you're not telling me something I need to know, I'll remember that."

Ironically, that parting comment triggered the most revealing response that I got from Willis. "Stay out of it, Marshall," Jack grumbled in a menacing tone aimed at my back as I walked out the still open door of the apartment, "You've got no idea what you're dealing with. I'll take care of it."

I turned sharply and faced him, my temper approaching the flash point. "You'll 'take care of it.' What the hell is that supposed to mean? How are you going to take care of it? Are you telling me that you know who did this?"

"It means that I will take care of it." With that unhelpful, closeout comment, Willis shut the door in my face.

## CHAPTER 15

Ken Menske lived on the knife-edge of Beverly Hills, a short block away from the raucous traffic of West Pico Blvd. It was a nice-but-nothing-special house that could be seen from the street—without having to peek over a tall fence as was the case with many of the other, higher-end homes in that town—and with an un-presupposing front door in a small archway that could be reached without much effort via a cement walk bordered on each side by a well-trimmed, mostly crab-grass-free lawn.

His place was nowhere near as grand as Fitz and Pilar's, but still impressive by my admittedly pedestrian standards. 'Acting as second or third banana to successful producers such as Fitz must pay well,' I mused, as Annie and I covered the short walk from my car to the door.

We were anticipated. Ken, rather than Caroline, his dour, equine-faced housekeeper, met us at the door even before we knocked. Menske was unmarried at the time, although, like many Hollywood producers of his ilk, he had a history of a few short-lived, failed marriages to lesser-known starlets. I suspected that over the years Ken had learned that paying the salary of a part-time, not so alluring, chief cook and bottle washer was a lot easier on his pocketbook than funding the would-be lavish lifestyle of attractive women half his age with double his libido.

That he greeted us himself with ebullient charm I took as an indication of Ken's eagerness to discuss the disposition of the *Watcher* rights and the potential for his involvement in the future production. After a brief exchange of pleasantries, he ushered us into a sitting room set up to double as a home office, a shrunk-down, almost mirror image of Fitz's study. The couch Annie and I sat on was fabric covered rather than done up in soft leather, as was the matching chair Ken occupied across a low, unadorned table from us. He offered us coffee or tea rather than a shot of cognac as Fitz was wont to do, which at one o'clock on a Saturday afternoon was probably a better choice. When Caroline came in to take our orders, Annie chose tea while I opted for black coffee, although I would've preferred a cold beer had it been offered. I didn't suggest it, assuming that Annie would be more impressed with my all-businessman-like facade if I refrained from imbibing while important matters were being discussed.

"I've thought a lot about what you proposed over the phone, and think that you should reconsider my initial idea," Menske started in. He was wasting no time in getting right down to the matter at hand and his desired outcome. "As I understand it, Fitz had pretty well finished the script, so there isn't much to do there. I'm sure I could find investors to put up the money for production and a good director to see it through. A successful production is bound to be a better payoff for Pilar than any straight buyout of the rights to *Watcher* that you might broker with a studio. I'm also sure that we could write in a major role for Pilar without breaking too much from the basic plot."

Menske's taking another pass at trying to get his hooks into producing *Watcher* didn't surprise me, and his points had some merit, especially the part about the greater potential payoff for Pilar. I was prepared to counter it, but Annie beat me off the mark. "We understand your point Kenny, and it's an option to consider, but we also need to think about Pilar and Danny's immediate needs. William, as executor of the estate, would have a better feeling for it, but I'm not sure it would be wise for Pilar to take on any financial risks just now."

I was relieved that Annie had taken the lead in responding to Ken's proposal. Despite what she'd said, she was just as well informed about the financial condition of Fitz's estate as I was, if not more so. And having worked as Fitz's personal assistant for the last few years she certainly had a better idea about the risks that would be involved in letting Menske take over as the lead producer on *Watcher*. She'd stated the case much better than I would've been able to do it.

Menske didn't respond right away to Annie's comments. I could see he wasn't happy but must've realized that nothing would be gained by arguing the issue. I had the feeling that if I'd made the same points to him in the same words, he would've continued to push back, citing his greater experience in the movie industry. He well knew that my own was limited. While Menske had more years in the trade than Annie and I put together, he couldn't credibly play a greater insight card on Annie, who had worked so closely with Fitz and was more aware of Fitz's intentions and hopes for *Watcher* than anyone else.

Still, Menske's help would be valuable in peddling *Watcher*, so I didn't want him to turn his back on our plan. "Ken, we'll keep your option in the mix for sure, but I think we should at least see what the studios are willing to offer before making a decision. Your help in getting to the right people at the studios and in negotiating and evaluating their proposals will be immensely helpful. That is if you can do it with an open mind. I promise not to make any final commitment until we have all discussed every offer that winds up on the table and you've had a chance to make your own pitch based on what we find out. Fitz told me that he intended to have you work with him on *Watcher*, so I know that he valued your expertise as a producer."

A shadow of sadness fell across Ken's face. "I know," he said in a slow, soft voice. "I know. . . He told me, but we never got the chance to discuss it in detail." Menske removed his glasses and wiped them clean with a handkerchief. There was a hint of tears in his eyes, and I recognized again, as I had at the graveside, that Ken's grief at losing his friend and colleague of many years was as great, if not greater, than mine.

"Of course I'll help in any way I can," he said, replacing his glasses and returning to business matters as a way to recover his composure. "I give you my word that I'll do my damnedest to promote the best offers I can get from the studios."

"Good; we knew you would, Kenny," Annie said with a warm smile directed at Menske that had to go a long way toward strengthening his resolve to help us.

"Ken, I think you should take the lead on our pitches to the studios," I suggested. "But all three of us—and Pilar if she wants—should be involved in any substantive discussions." I turned toward Annie as I said, "Annie tells me the studios will probably make it a requirement that they can put their own guy in as the credited producer." I looked back, straight into Menske's eyes, and averred truthfully, "But I will promise you this: I won't agree to any deal that doesn't give you at least as good a position in the production as Fitz would've arranged for you."

"Thanks, Marshall. I really appreciate that," Menske responded with warm sincerity.

Apparently now firmly on board with the plan, Menske rattled off the names of several bigwigs at the major studios and his ideas for how they should be approached. Annie took notes and offered several seemingly sound suggestions that Ken quickly picked up on, agreeing, amending, or shooting down each idea in short order. They were both in their element now, happy as two kids playing with their food when mother wasn't watching. More than half the time I had little or no idea whom or what they were talking about, so I just sat there quietly, listening and, to a small extent, learning something.

Once an action plan for beginning the marketing of *Watcher* had been blocked out, Ken turned the conversation to something that I suspected had been lurking in his not-so-subconscious, itching to get out. "I know that you're a big-time crime reporter these days, Marshall," Ken started in, abruptly changing the subject. He sounded more his normal relaxed and jovial self now that his involvement with *Watcher* had been established. "Have you heard anything new about Fitz?"

'. . . about Fitz?' Ken couldn't bring himself to use the words, 'Fitz's murder.' I knew just how he felt.

"Not much. The police are working on a theory that he may have been shot by a burglar." I assumed that Menske was unaware of Danny's kidnapping, as the police had kept it out of the papers, and I saw no reason that I should share that information with anyone.

"I guess that makes sense," Ken commented. "No one else would've had a reason to kill Fitz. None that I know of anyway."

"Pilar has asked me to keep tabs on the investigation and help out where I can," I added. "The first part is easy enough to do, given that my editor wants me to stay on top of the story. And I have some history with the lead detective on the case, so he'll at least make sure I know as much as he's willing to share with the rest of the press. But I'm not sure that there is much I can add to the effort. Have the police been by to talk with you yet?"

"The police? Why would the police want to talk to me?" Ken seemed genuinely surprised by my comment.

"You knew Fitz as well as anyone. The police would figure that you'd probably know if there was someone with a major grievance against him. Are you sure that you don't have any ideas?"

Ken thought about it and answered, "No . . . no one. There have been some incidents from time to time on sets, but nothing recent and nothing big. Fitz's guy . . . what's his name, Willis? . . . was always there to keep things from getting out of hand. And Fitz usually found a way to eventually smooth things over. He was good at that."

"Well, the police are bound to talk with you soon," I commented. "You and Fitz were going at it pretty hot and heavy on the night of Danny's birthday party. They're going to want to know about that."

"At Danny's party? I was pretty drunk. I don't remember much. Does that mean I'm a suspect?" Ken's reaction was the same as everyone's when they suddenly realize that the police are nowhere near as certain of their innocence as they are themselves. I could empathize with Ken; I knew the feeling well.

"Everyone's a suspect at this point," I said, playing it like Lt. Archer. "The good news for you, Ken, is that anyone who saw the spat, Annie and I included, would say it was a fairly innocuous verbal dispute between two well-less-than-sober individuals. I don't think that Willis even saw you as any kind of threat.

"The other bright spot from your point of view is that you fall into the category of suspects who were better off with Fitz alive than dead." I didn't see any reason to tell Ken that, so far, I alone made up the population of the opposite group.

"Come to think of it, there is one thing," Ken interjected, apparently satisfied with my reasoning that took the spotlight off him.

"What's that?"

"You know Fitz was plenty steamed at that guy, Dr. Appel?"

"Yeah, I sure do."

"Well, the last time we spoke Fitz indicated that he'd picked up some information that he could use to get the doctor in Dutch with the cops, if need be."

"Do you know what it was?" I asked, my attention now fully roused.

"I don't. Fitz wouldn't say. You know how he could be, how he liked to play things close."

"Yeah, I do." A picture of Fitz's cunning look, the one he pulled when he thought he knew something no one else did and couldn't resist teasing everyone about it, came to mind. "Well, it's something to think about. I'll mention it to the cops, and you should as well when they get around to you."

With a despondent, sorrowful expression, Ken nodded his agreement with my recommendation but said nothing more.

## CHAPTER 16

After our meeting with Ken Menske, Annie drafted me to be her personal chauffeur for the next several hours to help her run a series of mundane errands. It was nearly six o'clock by the time we got back to the house. Viola was on her way home, pausing at the front door with coat and hat in hand long enough to inform us that Pilar was "out" and not expected back "any time soon." Viola didn't volunteer any information about Pilar's whereabouts. Her apparent lack of knowledge of Pilar's liaisons was reasonable, as Pilar, true to form, probably hadn't shared that data with her.

Annie, Mag, and I ate an early spaghetti dinner with Danny—his all-time favorite meal, and much appreciated by me as I'd missed lunch altogether—and played with him for about an hour before putting him to bed. I managed to get through three entire lines of <u>Treasure Island</u>—still well short of Israel Hand's demise—before my ersatz Jim Hawkins fell asleep.

Annie let Dottie go home early, saying that if Pilar showed up hungry, she'd fix her an omelet. There wasn't much risk of that, as Pilar, extremely careful about maintaining her figure, rarely ate anything in the evening unless at a formal dinner, and then only picked at whatever food was served and drank sparingly.

As soon as Danny was down for the night and Mag had left, I poured Annie and me a couple of stiff drinks, and we settled in side-by-side on the same big leather couch in Fitz's study that I'd occupied on the night of Danny's birthday party. The police had finished their extensive examination of the room within a couple of days of Fitz's death and had freed it up for our use.

In dealing with the estate it had been necessary for me to spend several unexciting and minimally productive hours in the evenings at the desk in Fitz's office to go through his papers and to get a handle on his finances. Even though the police had removed the blood-stained throw rug on which Fitz had fallen after being shot, and there were now no visible indications that a crime had been committed in the room, I admit to a certain ill-defined queasiness when I'd first re-entered Fitz's study and sat in his chair behind his sprawling oak desk.

To my surprise that tight feeling in my gut had soon given way to an equally ill-defined nostalgia as I gazed about the room in which Fitz and I had shared so many cheerful conversations over drinks. Being in that familiar setting had afforded me an ineffable feeling of somehow being closer to my lost friend. I believed my sharing those feelings with Annie had gone a long way toward dispelling any similar uneasiness on her part.

Annie rested her head on my shoulder for a moment in a way that suggested a combination of personal affection and mental fatigue, then she straightened up and said, "I think we made a wise decision in getting Kenny involved in helping us peddle *Watcher*. He seemed to be onboard, even enthusiastic with the plan."

"Why wouldn't he be?" I replied. "He may wind up getting more out of it than he would've with Fitz. He'll get a fat fee and his name in the credits as a producer even if the studio will want their own man to handle the actual nuts and bolts of the production. Not a bad deal."

"Good for Kenny," Annie said. "A success like that could carry him for the rest of his career."

"As far as I'm concerned, he's welcome to anything he gets . . . as long as he helps us get the best deal for Pilar and Danny," I said. "Speaking of whom, how do you think they are holding up?"

In the four nights I'd been living in the guest cottage, I hadn't seen much of Pilar. I was busy at my regular job during the day, and Pilar was out of the house on every one of the evenings I'd spent there, doing whatever it was that Pilar did with whomever it was that she did it. She was never up before I left for work, and this Saturday I'd only seen her and passed a brief greeting as she was on her way out the door "for a luncheon." There was never an explanation offered as to whom and about what she was meeting, and I never asked; I had my own business to mind.

To anyone not familiar with his normal behavior, Danny might've seemed almost unaffected by events, but there were subtle signs that things were not yet back to normal, even for a resilient five-year-old such as Danny. Most evenings after dinner he preferred being held close and read to by me rather than playing games or roughhousing as we normally would've done. Annie had mentioned to me that on a couple of nights Danny had woken and cried out. As the guest room was next to his, it was Annie rather than Pilar who'd heard him and gone in to comfort him until he'd fallen back asleep.

Annie passed over my open-ended question as it related to Danny, probably because she had nothing to report that I hadn't seen for myself, and focused her comments on Pilar. "I think Pilar's doing okay. It looks as if she's channeling her mourning and anger into action, looking for work to occupy her, to take her mind off of things. When she's home she spends most of her time with Danny. She's handling the situation a lot better than I would've expected. She's a lot tougher than I realized."

"Do you think she's staying off the stuff?"

"I'm pretty sure she is," Annie replied. "I can't be certain what she does when she's out, but there are no signs of anything when she gets home. And Dr. Appel hasn't been around."

"You let me know right away if he shows up," I said in a tone that left little doubt as to what my plan of attack would be if he did.

My comment got a knowing look out of Annie. "It looks as if your little talk with him after the funeral got through."

"Maybe, but I rate Appel is a weasel. If he sees any crack in the wall, he'll try to slip back in as Pilar's supplier. I'm not going to let it happen." If Pilar was resolved to break her bad habit of turning to drugs when things didn't go her way, I intended to do anything I could to help her—if it meant breaking a fat nose here or there, that was just fine with me.

"It's too early to tell for sure, but if Pilar can pick up some work soon to keep her occupied, she'll probably be okay," Annie added. "She hasn't mentioned anything about Fitz's death since our talk after the funeral. I don't know if that's a good thing or not."

"Yeah, she hasn't asked me anything about the investigation either," I said. "That's good, as I don't have anything new to tell her."

"What do you make of Kenny's saying that Stephen had something on Appel?" Annie asked, sitting up a little straighter and adopting a more no-nonsense expression.

"I don't know. Fitz didn't mention anything like that to me on the night of the party when we discussed his frustration with Appel's supplying Pilar. My impression was that his plan was to have Willis come down hard on him. Maybe that's what Fitz was hinting at with Menske. I'll give Archer a call on Monday and tell him about it. If there's anything there, I'm sure he'll figure it out quicker than I could . . . Come to think of it, a not-so-friendly visit from the police may be just the right touch to keep Appel out of our hair."

Apparently satisfied with what I was proposing regarding Dr. Appel, Annie moved on. "What did Jack have to say when you met with him?"

"Not much." I'd mention it to Annie earlier in the day, but with everything that we'd been up to, this was the first chance I'd had to fill her in on the details of my visit with Jack Willis. "He's sticking to the story that he told to the police about being out of town visiting his sister when the kidnapping and the murder went down. The last time I talked to him, Archer said Willis's alibi checked out. That doesn't surprise me; Willis is a hard case, but he was loyal to Fitz, and I doubt he'd have done anything to harm him. And I don't see him taking Danny; Willis is a strong-arm type, not a scammer. I could see someone like Willis laying a blackjack on me that night I drove to the canyon—that sounds like something he might enjoy—but the whole ransom payoff scheme just doesn't seem like Jack's style."

"Maybe he was working with someone else who planned the kidnapping," Annie suggested.

"Maybe, but it still doesn't seem likely from what I know of Willis and his relationship with Fitz. His attitude when I met with him made me think that he almost certainly knows more than he's telling, but there was no use in pressing him. Unless I can come up with something to use as leverage, he's not going to open up to me . . . and maybe not even then. From what he did say, it's a strong possibility that he might be planning to take his own revenge for Fitz's murder on whoever did it. And he's not looking for any help with that from me or anyone else." I don't know how my words assessing Willis's resolve affected Annie, but they sent a chill up my back.

"So, what is your plan?" Annie asked.

"Well, I've got to admit that I don't have much of one. I've talked with Archer several times, but from what he was willing to share with me, the police don't seem to be any too close to solving the crimes. They're pretty much working on a theory that whoever snuck in and stole the jewelry in Pilar's bedroom also confronted Fitz in his study in the hopes of grabbing more loot, then shot him when he didn't come up with anything or tried to resist."

"Do you buy that?"

"Not really. I'd sure like to, but from what I know of it, second-story guys don't usually tote guns. But who knows? I could see Fitz, in the mood he was in at the time, not being passive when confronted by a burglar, even one pointing a gun at him. But it still doesn't seem right. From the way Archer talked about it, I don't think he totally buys the idea either."

"At least they're not pushing the theory that you killed Fitz to get control of the insurance money," Annie pointed out.

"Not yet, but if they don't locate the burglar and tag him with the murder, I'm sure they'll be on my back soon enough."

"I still can't believe that they think you did it," Annie opined with what sounded like less conviction than I would've liked.

"I'm not sure that what the police *really think* has much to do with it. They often just seem to follow the line of least resistance. Like I said before, Archer knows that this isn't my sort of thing."

"That's something anyway," Annie murmured half-hopefully.

"Yeah, but Archer's good opinion of me will only stretch so far if the rest of the Department starts to like me as a suspect. My best bet is still to figure out who did kill Fitz, before the police run out of other ideas and try to pin it on me."

"So, what are you going to do now?" It was clear by the way she asked this that my pointing out my own exposure had heightened her concern.

"There's not much I can do. Archer suggested I try to meet with Paul Logan, Fitz's bookie, to see if I can find out why there was a meeting scheduled with him in Fitz's appointment book.

When the cops talked to him, Logan claimed he knew nothing about a meeting and that it never happened. Archer thought that, since I have a slight connection to Logan, he might open up to me. I doubt it, but I've scheduled a meeting with him during my lunch hour on Monday.

"Is it possible this Logan character had something to do with Stephen's murder?" Annie asked hopefully.

"I don't see how. You or I probably would've heard something if Fitz had ever gotten in over his head with the gambling," I said, then added, "but Fitz had a rule of never making bets that he couldn't cover.

"I figured that Logan's guys would blow me off when I called them to set up a meeting with him. I told them that I wanted to clear up anything Fitz might have outstanding. I was surprised to get a call back from the big man himself agreeing to see me. That got me wondering . . ."

"How so?"

"Well, if Fitz did or didn't have any debt outstanding with Logan's book, Logan would've had one of his underlings call me back with that information. Logan didn't need to call or arrange to meet with me in person. I doubt he wants to see me to reminisce about old times when my father used to place bets with him.

"Then I thought: The cops have already been by to see him about the entry in Fitz's date book, but my gut says that whatever he told them was probably a lie. So, Logan's antenna would be up regardless of whether he was involved with Fitz's death or not. He's probably as interested in finding out anything I know about any police investigation that might impact him as I am in finding out why Logan's name is in Fitz's date book. I've got to believe there's something to it; otherwise, Logan wouldn't be bothering with me."

"Sounds like it might be an interesting conversation."

"Yeah, hopefully not too interesting," I remarked. "Logan is not a guy with who' I would like to get in sideways."

At some point Annie and I moved into the living room to be nearer to the front stairway where we would hear Danny if he stirred. We passed the rest of the evening together in a manner reminiscent of late Saturday evenings spent on my high school girlfriend's parent's porch in the dark. Any thought of our 'running the bases' was cooled by our adult obligation as Danny's babysitters in Pilar's absence. Thinking back on it, I have to admit that I felt a certain unique titillation associated with limiting our encounter to those illicit, adolescent activities.

Pilar finally arrived home around ten o'clock. I wasn't particularly surprised, nor shocked, that she had Charlie Stoke in tow. At Pilar's suggestion we remained in the living room for drinks. While I mixed Manhattans for the ladies and poured whisky on the rocks for the gentlemen, Stoke pointedly took up a position on one couch next to Annie. Returning with the drinks, I occupied the spot left for me next to Pilar on the couch facing them.

As Pilar explained it, without being asked, they had been out to dinner "to discuss several prospects" that Stoke had lined up for Pilar to consider as starring roles.

'And why not?' I posited to myself. 'Stoke was still Pilar's attorney, as he had been Fitz's. Why shouldn't she turn to him for help in finding work.' Despite the revelations about Charlie's designs on Pilar that I had learned about during my lunch discussion with him, I couldn't help feeling somewhat pleased that he might be turning out to be a solution to the Pilar problem.

"Anything that looks good to you, Pilar?" Annie asked, apparently just as comfortable with the new situation as I.

"Yes. One or two seem very interesting," Pilar replied with

a serious, business-like expression rather than the relieved smile that might have been expected. "Charles is going to arrange meetings to discuss them next week."

"That's great." I echoed Annie's sentiment in my own less polished style.

"Well, let's wait and see," Stoke interjected. "As you no doubt know, nothing is certain in this business. What I will say is that there should be no problem in ultimately finding something worthy of Pilar's talents." He threw out a self-satisfied smile in our direction that landed somewhere between Pilar and me.

'. . . worthy of Pilar's talents,' that's laying it on mighty thick, I thought, even for a smooth talker like Charlie Stoke.

Annie and I added our own good news to Charlie and Pilar's by explaining that Ken Menske was on board with helping to unload the rights to *Watcher*.

"How much should we get you involved in the negotiations, Charlie?" I asked.

"Menske knows what he's doing, and knows, probably better than I, what he can and can't ask for," Stoke replied. "If you have any specific questions, you should give me a call. But until you're ready to get down to the actual drafting of a contract, Menske can probably handle most of it."

"What about you, Pilar? Are you okay with the plan? I know that you were interested in a part for yourself in *Watcher*."

Annie shot me an inquiring look, no doubt wondering why I was broaching a sore point that diplomatically would've been best left out of the discussion. But I had my own reasons for wanting to know why Pilar had suddenly lost interest in *Watcher*. Not too long after my lunch conversation with Stoke, and after I'd had a chance to at least partially recover from the shock that I'd become a viable suspect for Fitz's murder, it occurred to me that unlike a divorce, which would've been something of a crap shoot, Fitz's death had given Pilar absolute control over the rights to *Watcher*.

"That is true. . . .. I did want a part in the film. . . .. I wanted it badly," Pilar intoned, stretching her words out as if for dramatic effect. "But even before Stephen's death, I came to realize that it would have been wrong for me. I was not happy about it. But I knew in my heart that it was true."

Pilar offered the first truly warm, honest smile that I'd seen on her face since the one that she'd bestowed on me following Fitz's funeral. "At one point Kenneth suggested to me that if I would allow him to produce the film, he would create a part for me. But I knew that he was just being kind, that he knew better."

"You and Annie and Kenneth should do what you think is best with the script," Pilar added. "There is no need for you to involve me."

Unlike the rest of us, Pilar still had half of her drink in her glass when Annie and I announced our intention to head for our beds. Charlie Stoke, saying that he would sit with Pilar while she finished her Manhattan, permitted me to freshen his with a half-shot before he bid us a "goodnight."

At the foot of the main staircase, I planted a lingering, sweet dreams kiss on Annie's lovely lips. Then I turned and headed for the dining room door to the backyard, throwing a wave at Pilar and Charlie as I passed the living room.

I closed and secured the backdoor behind me. But instead of heading for my regular nighttime post in the chair by the window in the guest cottage, I crossed the patio, crept around the side of the house, and slipped through a side gate. I situated myself behind a low shrub, in the dark moon-shadow of a large tree, a position that afforded an unobstructed view of the front steps.

I felt a little guilty about spying on my hostess. But she was the one who had asked me to play the detective. And as I understood it a certain amount of selective snooping was part of the job description.

Well below the dewpoint, the night air, coming through the loose weave of my sports coat, was clammy and icy cold. Luckily, I didn't have long to wait; I'd only been in position a few minutes when Pilar and Charlie, having either slammed down or given up on their drinks, came through the door and paused on the top step.

If any unheard words passed between them, they would've been few given the mere seconds that elapsed before the couple indulged themselves in a body-molding clench and full-on kiss. It wasn't exactly a licentious scene, as if they were about to go at it right there on the stoop, but it was certainly well beyond what one would expect of a family solicitor bidding adieu to a client.

I had no idea what it all meant, if anything, toward resolving the mysteries in which I was embroiled. But it certainly clarified how the wind was blowing in one area.

## Chapter 17

Contrary to a popular belief perpetuated by the movies and detective pulp novels, bookies are not in the habit of killing their clients. Oh sure, they might break an arm or a leg now and then to get a tardy debtor's attention. But killing someone causes a lot of trouble, sprinkling coarse grit in the otherwise well-oiled machine-like symbiotic relationships that they've established with the local police and politicos. And it makes it that much more difficult to collect what is owed. Accordingly, I had little hope that foregoing my lunch hour so that I could meet with Paul Logan would provide anything of value in my search for the person responsible for killing my friend Fitz. But I was wrong.

Logan, something of a legend in my old Boyle Heights neighborhood—certainly for as long as I could remember—ran the seedier betting parlors and arranged all of the medium- and high-stakes floating poker and crap games in the neighborhood for Jack Draga, the mob's main man in all of Southern California. Not many of the enterprises Logan administered were legal, but neither did any of them attract much attention from the local law.

There was the occasional, pre-arranged raid now and then: a splashy show for the law-and-order councilmen. Someone in the know would shout "IT'S A RAID!" a few minutes before the vice squad would arrive, enough time for the patrons to make a rapid exit through the back door. A few low-level thugs would get hauled off and spend the night in the can, only to be bailed out the following morning, their fines eventually paid by Logan through his attorney. The raids usually came toward the end of business on days when there wasn't much action expected on the last couple of races at the East Coast tracks. It was a lark for both the arrestees and the arrestors, the cops and the press sometimes arriving a little ahead of schedule so they could grab a short beer at the bar before the festivities began.

The betting parlors themselves were usually located in a single large room, accessible through an unmarked door at the back of a busy saloon. Would-be patrons would knock—speakeasy-like—to be viewed through a peephole before being admitted by a tough-looking bouncer. There was no "Sid sent me" password, and I doubt that anyone, save the occasional lost drunk looking for the john, was ever denied admission.

Inside, the traditional layout featured a single cage where a lone, deadpan teller in his shirtsleeves took the bets and made the occasional payouts with an even deader pan. There'd be a two-part setup consisting of a small-sized bar and an over-sized bartender: the former intended no doubt to curtail the foot traffic through the door to the public bar out front and the latter to assist the bouncer to tamp down any untoward disturbance by a disappointed bettor. Wooden tables and unpadded chairs would be spread out around the room on an un-carpeted, un-finished, and often un-swept hardwood floor.

From time-to-time when I was between the ages of eight and twelve, my father would bring me along with him when he visited such rooms. While he made his bets, I'd be left sitting at one of the tables, my feet attached to skinny legs, dangling down barely touching the floor. I'd sit there alone nursing a root beer or an orange Nehi if I was in luck—or a grape one if I was unlucky.

On this occasion, I was saved a visit to the back room and an unscheduled, undesired trip down Memory Lane by Stan "Mace" Mason, a well-known and probably quite competent enforcer for Logan and a less well-known, less competent ex-boxer, who met me as I came through the entrance to the main saloon. I knew of Mace's reputation as a pugilist because of my longtime interest in boxing, both as a former participant in and a current less directly involved fan of the sport. I'd never gone toe to toe in the ring with Mason; he was ten years my senior and fought professionally as a slow-footed heavyweight, while I, an amateur, fought as a lanky, awkward middleweight. Mace was in mid-career when I was in my mid-teens and just beginning to learn the ropes. I'd seen him working out at Ernie Silverman's gym in the old neighborhood, but, due to Mace's greater weight and size and my tender years, Ernie never matched us up in the ring, even to spar.

I hadn't seen Mace in close to seven years, and I doubted he'd remember me, or, come to think of it, would've ever known I existed. I easily recognized him, as even though he hadn't had a professional bout of any note for some time, the passing years had not changed the looks of his puffy, broken-nosed face.

Mace's being on the lookout for me saved me the trouble of trying to elbow my way through the midday crowd at the bar to check in with the bartender. The numerous patrons lining the bar looked to be old-timers, seeming to have been occupying their same self-assigned positions at the varnished counter since the beginning of time. They stood there frequently raising a shot glass of liquor or a mug of beer to their lips; less frequently imparting information to their neighbor by shouting it as if their companion was known to be deaf; and on occasion—no doubt to get some much needed exercise— shifting from their right foot to their left or from their left to their right, resting each in turn with little weight on the brass railing that ran along the length of the floor at the base of the bar. The almost still-life quality of the scene made one half-heartedly wonder whether it was the bar that was holding them up or vice versa.

"You Marshall?" Mason asked in a less-than-friendly tone as soon as I'd walked through the western-style swinging half-doors to the saloon. It was a delivery no doubt intended to provide his idea of a fair warning to anyone whom he met and might have occasion to deal with physically.

"Yes, that's me," I answered in a contrastingly friendly and non-threatening manner, which seemed to cut no ice with Mace as his expression remained unchanged.

"The boss will talk to you upstairs." Mace turned and headed with a mariner-like rolling gate toward the back of the room. I followed in a more land-lubberly fashion.

Mace led me up a flight of stairs marked at their foot by a brass sign that read "Private," through a door at the top with its own "private" sign—this one faux-gold-plated–and into a large office. Logan was seated on a cracked and worn leather swivel-chair behind a gargantuan desk with nothing on it except an oversized ashtray with an oversized cigar smoldering in it. The rich-smelling, expensive-looking, probably Cuban cigar was a stark divergence in elegance to Logan, who, despite his elevation over the years in the ranks of Jack Draga's criminal organization, had managed to retain the look and aroma of a cheap hoodlum.

I hadn't seen Logan in more years than I had Mason, and I realized my childhood memories of him were vague at best, and distorted. Seated, he looked to be a little better than medium height, maybe five-foot-ten or -eleven inches tall. His stocky build tending to fat, and a scar over his left eye—no doubt a trophy from some long past, dubious battle—made for a discordant contrast with his tailored dark blue suit and wide silk tie, the likes of which I hadn't seen since a not-too-distant series of brief tete-á-tetes with Sid Rice, the well-known, well-heeled criminal attorney. Logan's looks were consistent with those of the average enforcer for loan sharks and bookies, which was how Logan had gotten his start.

Being smart rather than sophisticated or stylish was what had set Logan apart from the crowd in the illegal gambling business and protection rackets and why he was now seated behind a clean desk about two times the size of mine at the Examiner. What really defined Logan, however, was a constant, sinister, evil grin, which never altered as he looked at you, so unchanging that you had a feeling as if it had been chiseled into his face by some demonic sculptor.

He didn't get up from his seat or offer a friendly hand. "Sit down," he ordered and pointed at one of two uncomfortable, non-padded chairs across from him. I didn't see any purpose in defying him, although some irrational and foolhardy urge in me longed to do so. Instead, I sat as ordered.

Logan stared at me, probably to give his unsettling countenance a chance to have its full effect—he needn't have waited so long.

"You probably don't remember me, Mr. Logan," I said, trying lamely to take the initiative. "But you did some business with my father several years ago."

"I remember your old man. Square shooter, always cash, never credit. Smart. You don't want to let us get our hooks into you." Logan picked up his cigar in short, thick, well-manicured fingers, shoved it between his lips and puffed on it two or three times without breaking his disconcerting, wolfish expression. He lowered and positioned the side of the cigar along the edge of the ashtray, tapped off a quarter inch length of white ash, exhaled an even stream of smoke, and said, "You're right, I don't remember you, but I know who you are. You're the guy who shot Maurizio."

'Damn it,' I thought. I was beginning to think my having shot and killed Mark Maurizio, another one of Draga's crew, was going to become the defining moment of my life, my *magnum opus* as it were. Maurizio had been wandering way off the reservation at the time, so Draga had given me a pass for dropping one of his guys in self-defense, but I couldn't be certain that everyone in the organization had the same businesslike outlook about it. "Not a problem for us I hope."

"Nah, I hated the guy. Stupid wop, had it coming. You probably saved us the trouble," Logan said as if I'd done him a small favor, such as running by Chinatown to pick up his laundry. "So, what is it you want from me?"

Mason had taken up a position standing behind me, slightly to my left. I turned my chair just enough so I could see him if I craned my head in his direction. Looking toward Mason but talking to Logan, I said, "I don't mind Mace staying here while we talk, but could you not have him stand behind me; it spoils my concentration."

Mason looked past me in Logan's direction. Logan must've given him a high sign, as Mason moved to the side of the desk. I turned my chair back, now facing them both.

I didn't really think that I was in much danger, but I didn't know where the discussion might lead. Mason was a brawler, not a boxer. In the ring he used to stand toe-to-toe with another of his ilk, exchanging mostly unblocked punches until one or the other hit the canvas with a collapsing-brick-wall-like impact. I had no chance of winning that sort of a contest with Mason. But in a big, open room such as Logan's office, I'd have a better than even chance of holding my own if I could avoid his connecting with a solid blow before I could get to the office door and make good my escape. Contrarywise, if on a wink from Logan, Mason sucker-punched me from behind, it would be lights out.

I knew the police had already talked to Logan about Fitz's death, so I saw no reason to rehash it with him. "As I explained on the telephone, Stephen Fitzgerald and I were good friends. I'm the executor of his estate. I know Fitz ran bets through you from time to time, but as far as I can tell from his records, he doesn't owe you anything currently. Is that right?"

"As far as I know. I'll check with the book and get back to you," Logan had shifted smoothly from sinister looking to bored. I found it hard to believe that Logan would've gone to the trouble of calling to set up the meeting with me without bothering to check on the status of Fitz's account. His comment confirmed my suspicion that he was interested in getting information from me rather than doling any out. "But if it was anything big, I'd already know about it."

"Okay, good. But here's the thing, because Fitz was murdered, the insurance company is making a big stink," I lied. "They're not going to pay off until they know what happened."

I'd had no contact with the insurance company to that point, except for having Stoke send them a letter notifying them of Fitz's death and requesting that they begin the process of paying off on the policy. My comment to Logan was just to smooth over my reason for talking to him.

I continued with the soft soap, making a statement I had no basis in fact to assert. "I know that you don't go around shooting your customers. But your name in Fitz's datebook kinda stands out like the proverbial broken nose. I picked up on it and so did the police. The insurance guys are bound to want to talk to you about it." I was walking on thin ice with Logan, and I knew it, but if I had any hope of getting anything out of him, I was going to have to take some chances.

My effort to downplay the issue was apparently a flop. If there had been any hint of friendliness that I might have missed in Logan's looks before, I wasn't going to find it now. "If the insurance dicks want to talk to me, let 'em come. They got nothing on me. I'll tell them the same thing I told the cops and that I'm telling you before I have Mace here throw you out: There was no meeting on the twentieth with your guy, Fitzgerald. Hell, I've never even met the guy. His man Willis was the contact; he made all the payments for Fitzgerald and collected when anything was due him."

"Yeah, I remember now, it was Jack that came in that day," Mason, no doubt normally a man of few—but in this instance ill-chosen and ill-timed—words, blurted out. "You remember don't ya boss?"

Logan shot Mason a malevolent look, which under normal circumstances he may have reserved for use just before he let loose on someone with a 'forty-five.' Mason's reaction was almost the same as if he had been plugged. He didn't fall down dead, but he did stop talking and looked as if he might melt into a puddle on the floor.

"Get out!" Logan yelled at him. Mason turned quickly and was out the door before my mind had had time to fully process the significance of what I'd just learned.

Logan turned back to me with the look of someone who realized he'd just given himself away by an overreaction to having missed filling-in his hand with his last down card. "Okay, maybe Willis was here that day, but I didn't see him. You can give that to your insurance dicks. If they buy it fine, if not, tell them from me they should save their nickel if their thinking about calling to talk with me . . . and, oh yeah, they can go to hell. And you can get out of my office and go to hell too. I don't want to see you around here, and if you know what's good for you I won't."

I've never been accused of being overly aware of what was good for me, but I was more than convinced that Logan's suggestion was a sound one. I slipped out of Logan's office as smoothly as I could manage it given my elevated nervous state, making barely audible, innocuous parting comments, and descended the stairs at a measured but steady pace, trying to appear unaffected, but, once again, no doubt failing. As I passed through the saloon, I saw Mason sandwiched in between the regulars, leaning against the bar, downing a double shot of what looked like, but no doubt wasn't, strong tea.

I'd reasoned that there would've been no point—and a lot of risk— in pressing Logan for more information in his frustrated, angry state of mind. Mason's slip of the tongue had revealed more than I'd expected I would glean from the meeting with Logan. I hoped that his verbal faux pas wouldn't earn Mace—or me for that matter—a fitting for a Chicago overcoat.

Safely out of Logan's saloon and, hopefully, his not-sometaphorical line of fire, I walked along a crumbling sidewalk toward my next rendezvous. It gave me plenty of time to consider the significance of the little that I have learned from my brief, heated meeting with Logan.

The fact that it was Willis who had made it to the meeting rather than Fitz didn't explain why the meeting had been penciled in on Fitz's diary. And Mason's comment, ". . . you remember, don't ya boss?" had put the lie to Logan's claim that he hadn't been at the meeting with Willis. If it was just a payoff on a gambling debt, why would Logan meet with Willis, and why lie about it? Logan's anger at Mason, which he quickly redirected at me, convinced me more than ever that finding out the reason for the meeting would be a key to solving at least one of the mysteries. There were a lot of open questions but damned few answers. And to my thinking my best bet on getting some of those answers would be through another, less cordial, less passive visit with Jack Willis.

But that was for another time. Right then I had other fish to fry in the form of a scheduled two o'clock meeting at another neighborhood bar, a few blocks over from Logan's place, with one Lee Buntz, a childhood friend and a well-known second-story man. If anyone could give me a handle on who had broken into Fitz's house and taken Pilar's second-tier jewelry on the night of Fitz's murder, it would be Lee.

## CHAPTER 18

Lee Buntz was sitting alone at a table situated at the back of the bar in the darkest corner available when I arrived ten minutes late. My tardiness didn't seem to bother him as he flashed a worldly-wise, yet sincere, friendly expression when he saw me approaching.

As always, Lee was dressed fit to kill: A well-tailored, well-pressed dark suit, with an appropriately color-coordinated contrasting silk tie, hung well without padding on his slender, lithe torso. A highly polished Florsheim or Johnston & Murphy shoe, just visible under the table at the end of a crossed leg, bounced jauntily below a one-inch pant cuff. Gold cufflinks with rose colored semiprecious stones peeked out below his coat sleeves on lightly-starched white French cuffs, a tastefully sized diamond stud stick pin pierced his tie, and a solid-gold wristwatch with an alligator band graced his left wrist—all of which I assumed were on permanent, involuntary loan from one or more of Lee's numerous victims. Lee's sartorial display added credence to his reputation of being something of a lady's man despite his having a face that, while it might not actually stop a clock, would certainly slow one down.

Lee and I had been best friends in grammar school but had lost contact after I'd moved away from the old neighborhood. We'd run into each other recently at the courthouse in downtown L.A. soon after I'd started my job as a crime reporter. Lee had given me a number where I could leave a message for him, saying we should get together to talk about old times. That had sounded good to me at the time, but being busy learning my new trade, and then with Fitz's death and everything that flowed rapidly from it, this was the first I'd seen of Lee since the initial, chance meeting.

"Marshall, pull up a chair," Lee said in a bright, good-natured voice, which conjured memories of our not-too-distant childhood. "What can I get you to drink?"

"Nothing for me, Lee," I replied as I sat across from him. "I had to skip lunch, so I'm afraid anything too strong now would knock me on my can."

"Something to eat then? How about a burger? They make a great one at the joint next door. You can eat while we talk, and I drink."

"That would be great, Lee." I sat back in my chair, feeling as if the ensuing years since our shared youth had suddenly disappeared. The lingering tension from my visit with Paul Logan had begun to ease, not totally cooled but moved to a low flame on a back burner.

"Hey, Jimmie, have someone run next door and get my friend here a burger," Lee called over to the bartender. "Put it on my tab."

"I should pay you for it," I protested.

"Nah, this way I can hit you up for a steak sometime—on you." Lee chuckled at his own little joke.

I smiled back at him, knowing it was no joke—but a cheap enough payback if anything meaningful came out of our get together. We reminisced for a while until my lunch arrived, delivered by what looked to be a nine- or ten-year-old kid wearing a dirty shirt, ripped flannel pants, and a woolen flat cap. I gave the kid a nickel for his efforts. The burger looked substantial enough to provide the needed cushion for it, so I relented and ordered a short beer.

While I ate, Lee began the conversation. "You said you had something important you wanted to talk to me about."

I was glad Lee had broken the ice by getting right down to the reason for my having called him. As much as I'd have enjoyed under normal circumstances to have continued to talk with him about old times, my heart wouldn't have been in it while Fitz's murder was front and center on my mind.

"Yeah, it is . . . to me anyway," I started in. "I don't know how much you've heard about the break-in and killing on the Westside a couple of weeks ago."

"Some. . . What's that got to do with you?" Lee's tone was wary.

"The man who was killed, Stephen Fitzgerald, was a good friend of mine."

"I'm sorry to hear that," Lee said with sincerity.

"Thanks."

"And, naturally, you're looking to find out who did it," Lee added sympathetically, but still with a note of caution.

"Yes, but there's more to it. For reasons I'd just as soon not get into, I'm something of a suspect. Right now the police are working on a theory that whoever broke in also killed Fitz. But if that doesn't pan out anytime soon, I'm sure they're going to start taking another hard look at me. So I'm searching for ideas to throw in their path. I don't want to get you involved, Lee, but anything you could come up with that might help me out would be appreciated."

Lee waved his hand dismissively, the crystal on his watch catching and refracting a stray ray of light. "I'm already involved," he said, any guardedness on his part now gone. "There's a burglary involved, so the word is out that the police are looking to talk to me, along with everyone else in the trade. That's why I'm laying low, sitting here in this dark corner. That's why I was a little slow in returning your call. I don't know why the police always want to talk with me every time there is some penny-ante break-in. It's a little insulting."

It was common knowledge that Lee was one of the best in the business. He'd been arrested several times and charged once or twice, but never convicted. If the police hauled him in for something small, it wouldn't be because they had any thought that he'd pulled the job, rather that he might tell them something that would point them in the right direction. Knowing Lee, if they did manage to corral him, I doubted that he would give anything up. Given our personal connection, I was hoping that I would have better luck than the cops in getting something useful out of him.

"Tell me what you know about how it went down," Lee directed.

I ran through in detail what I knew of the burglary. I stuck to the basics in describing the murder scene and the robbery and said nothing about the kidnapping.

Lee listened carefully to what I was telling him, asked no questions, and thought about it for several seconds before commenting. "Well, first off, this was no one in the trade. Professionals never break in while anyone is at home; they wait until they know that the owner is away for the evening or out of town. If a quick search didn't produce what they came for, they'd slip back out the same way and just as quietly as they'd come in. And someone who knew what they were about would never go for the junk. They'd leave it—not worth the risk of trying to fence it.

"Whoever did this was an amateur—pure and simple—but someone who knew the layout of the place, knew where to go to find what they were looking for. The fact they took the cheap crap and left the good stuff means they didn't know the difference and didn't know where the valuable stuff was kept or how to get to it.

It sure sounds like an inside job. If I were you, I'd look at the hired help.

"You know, the cops may not be off base with their idea that the guy who broke in also killed your friend. Real pros never carry guns for fear that someone—more often than not themselves—will get hurt. If they're caught in the act, they've blown it. Why turn a simple burglary into a murder rap? Sure, they'd try to get away if they could, but they'd never want to get into a shootout. A rookie, on the other hand, would be more likely to carry a gun and might confront the owner with it if he was frustrated by not finding what he was looking for."

I'd been nodding my head in agreement, slowly and repeatedly as Lee spoke, like a patient Chinese waiter taking down a frequently changing food order from an unruly, drunken group of Caucasians. What Lee had been telling me tracked with Lt. Archer's assessments. Lee hadn't broached the idea that the burglary might be a phony to cover the true reason for Fitz's murder. But why would he? That was the stuff of three-reelers, not real life.

"I'll ask around some to see if I can find out anything," Lee offered. "But don't get your hopes up. If the killer has any brains at all, he's already dumped the loot and the gun in the harbor."

After finishing my late lunch and reminiscing some more with my old friend, I returned to the Examiner to finish out the workday. My long lunch hour was no issue with my boss Carl Greenberg, as I'd sold him on the idea that my involvement as Fitz's executor and my relationship with Lt. Archer would give me something of an inside track on the story of Fitz's murder as it developed, but that it might require my being missing in action from my regular duties from time-to-time. Greenberg didn't care how or when I got my work done as long as I met my deadlines.

The afternoon passed slowly, and my work was less than

effective, my mind constantly milling over what I had learned during my protracted lunch hour. Lee Buntz, while more definitive in his comments, hadn't really told me anything the police and I hadn't already considered: The break-in looked to be the efforts of an amateur, and the way that both the kidnapping and burglary came off suggested the involvement of someone knowledgeable of the layout and the routine of the Fitzgerald household.

But try as I might, I just couldn't see any of the hired help being intentionally involved; they were all too devoted to Danny, Fitz, and Pilar. Willis had been in Bakersfield visiting with his sister—if she and his other friends could be believed—on the nights when Danny was kidnapped and when Fitz was shot. Dotty, as per her usual routine, had been at home with her three kids. Viola was unmarried and lived alone, so she had no alibi—but that didn't mean much of anything as it would've been the case for just about every other spinster in L.A. And the mental picture of Mag being a shadowy sneak thief or gunning someone down in hot or cold blood offered an almost cartoon-like image.

The possible significance of the Willis-Logan meeting on the twentieth of July, the meeting that Mason had let slip and that Logan had obviously intended to keep on the q.t., had captured and preoccupied most of my thoughts all afternoon. But no meaningful answers had come to me at my desk in the newsroom despite my best mental efforts. The only plan I could come up with was to pay my old, not-so-forthcoming pal Jack Willis another visit to see if he would be willing—or not-too-gently persuaded—to shed any light on the reason for his clandestine meeting with Paul Logan. Willis's place in Culver City wasn't too far out of my way home, so my plan for the evening was to swing by and pay him a short, hopefully more productive visit than the first one.

It was the last gasp of dusk when I walked into the always packed parking lot next to the Examiner's offices. In the post-sunset glow and the only just a little stronger, round-the-clock light of electric bulbs fanning out into the gathering shadows through the newsroom windows, I saw a man leaning against the driver's side of my worn-down Ford. I could make out just enough of him to recognize that he was big and tall, towering as it seemed above the car. The glow of a burning cigarette accented his right hand hanging casually at his side. From the little I could make out of his face, he looked vaguely familiar, although the shadow from his felt broad-brimmed fedora pulled well-down on his forehead made it unlikely that I would place him. His eyes were obscured, but not his mouth with its full, soft, almost innocent looking lips closed into the hint of a humorless smirk.

I knew he was trouble as soon as I saw him; no one hangs around parking lots in downtown L.A. after hours to share pleasantries or the latest joke. My first thought was that he might be one of Logan's goons sent to reinforce the idea it would be good for me to keep to myself what I knew about Logan's meeting with Willis, or to take me out of the picture altogether. But I quickly dismissed those thoughts, as Logan, having met me and knowing my father's character, would've rightly guessed that the former wouldn't have worked in my case, and the latter wouldn't have been worth the effort and risk as I hadn't really found out anything that would come within an extended country mile of linking Logan to Fitz's murder.

I was tired and cranky after putting in a long, yet less than productive afternoon at the paper following my seeming equally unbeneficial meetings with Logan and Buntz. I wasn't in the mood for more trouble—or for that matter any pleasantries or jokes. I gave the idea of turning and walking away from this guy brief consideration but guessed he would've just come after me— trouble has a way of hanging on once it's found you.

He took a step away from the car as I approached. His movement was smooth and agile, like someone who knew how to handle himself. He dropped the cigarette from his fingers and ground the butt into the pavement with the sole of his shoe. "Are you Marshall?"

"That's me." I didn't owe anyone money, so I saw no reason to deny the fact. "Who's asking?"

Apparently, this guy must've had some outstanding debts of his own coming due, as he didn't respond to my question. "Dr. Appel has asked me to speak with you, to advise you to keep your nose out of his business," he said in a low, threatening voice. I was close enough now to see his eyes: deep set, cold, dark, colorless, just visible beneath the brim of his hat.

Most thugs aren't as soft or well-spoken as this one, which is probably what put me off guard; that, and the fact I was tired and wanted to go home to get some much-needed shut-eye. The way his lips quickly switched from a passive expression as he spoke back to a cruel smirk should've alerted me, but I was preoccupied with composing witty suggestions as to where Dr. Appel could stuff his advice.

His fist flashed forward and smacked me on the side of the jaw faster than a striking cobra that's become bored with the sound of a charmer's flute. A boxer's instinct to roll away from the punch kept me from kissing the asphalt. I was able to stay on my feet and stagger away from the blow to regain my balance and some semblance of a clear head before turning back to face him. I was saved the bother of finding out if I could hold my own against my unknown attacker in a no rules, bare-knuckles street fight by the fact he was now holding a small, but lethal- looking revolver pointed in my general direction.

My immediate assessment was that he didn't intend to shoot me in the middle of an open public parking lot where at that hour there was a better than even chance that someone would see him do it. He probably just didn't want to take the chance of getting his nice suit dirty in a tussle he couldn't have been any surer of winning than I was. I stood still, knees bent, hands forming fists at my side, poised to do I don't know what. His telling sneer was unchanged. I calculated my chances of getting out of this situation alive at a lot better than fifty-fifty if I kept my head and controlled my rising temper. I could see no way of shaving those odds further in my favor, so I didn't try.

He backed away slowly for a couple of steps, his gun now directly pointed at my chest, his eyes linked with mine. Then he turned as smoothly as if executing a practiced dance move and stepped off into the gathering night, the pistol, hammer still thumbed back, hanging down at his side. He needn't have taken the risk of shooting himself in the leg as he walked away, as I had no intention of following him, armed or, as I was, unarmed, into the pool of deep blue that engulfed his retreating figure.

Though I'd hinted at a little physical intimidation of my own when I'd chatted with Appel at Fitz's wake, I'd had no real intention of roughing up the doctor; I just wanted to scare him—a little bully-like bluffing for a good cause. Apparently, my ploy had been taken seriously by Appel but hadn't been as affective as Annie and I had thought.

I dropped any idea of looking for revenge on my recently departed assailant almost as soon as he was out of sight and the sharp pain in my jaw had turned to a dull ache. I half blamed myself for letting my guard down. And picking fights that could be avoided with big guys who were quick to pull guns didn't much appeal to me.

I lightly rubbed the side of my face as I slipped in behind the wheel of my car. There would be some swelling and bruising, which a clumsy guy such as myself could easily explain away. I saw no reason to share with Annie the details of my little adventure in the parking lot. Why rile her up? I could envision a scenario in which she'd lay into Dr. Appel about it on her own if he showed his face. She tends not to be as philosophical or even-tempered as I am about such things.

However, my recent painful and embarrassing encounter gave me even more incentive to mention Ken Menske's comment about Fitz's "having something on Appel" to the police. Better to let Archer's boys handle the Appel problem; Annie and I had more important things to worry about.

## CHAPTER 19

Nursing a sore jaw and wounded pride but congratulating myself on my cool-headed, mature approach to defusing what otherwise could've turned into a lethal confrontation, I drove the ten miles from downtown to Willis's Culver City apartment. My less-than-friendly talk with Dr. Appel's strong-arm type in the Examiner's parking lot had delayed me long enough to allow the evening traffic heading west out of L.A. to clear out, making my second drive to visit with Fitz's ex-chauffeur, missing-when-needed bodyguard, and go-between with a mob-connected bookie a lot quicker than the first trip.

Willis opened the door on my second loud knock, partially dressed in wrinkled suit pants and his undershirt—quite a comedown from his appearance on my previous visit. He was uncombed and unshaven, shoeless in stocking feet, the smell of whiskey strong on his breath—at least three shots worth by my calculation. His remarkably hairy, ape-like arms hung by his side. In his right hand and tending in my general direction, he held a .45 automatic, the inevitable weapon of choice of ex-military types. I was beginning to wonder if I had some mystical attraction that made the barrels of handguns want to point at me like the needle of a compass toward the North Star. However, this time the weapon's business end was more aimed down at the floor rather than directly at me, which I took as a positive indication that Jack had no immediate plans to shoot me.

As soon as he saw who it was standing at his door, he

turned away without any change in expression or comment, walked back into the living area, de-cocked the gun as he went, and laid it down on a low table in front of a ratty, threadbare couch of indiscernible color. Neither invited in, nor told to get lost, I followed him into the room.

"What do you want now?" he growled in an authentic tough-guy voice, not bothering to look back at me.

"I want some straight answers," I replied at his back in my own tough—if not so authentic—tone. I doubt that the tenor of my voice scared him, but it was enough to get him to turn back to face me.

"Go to hell." Not exactly a King Vidor comeback line, but his delivery made his point clear. He looked down and shot a glance at the gun on the coffee table but apparently decided that shooting was too good for me. Instead, he threw an unwarranted and, luckily, well-advertised swing in my direction, which, due to a combination of his semi-drunken state and my anticipating his action, I was able to avoid. His follow through spun him off balance, his back partially toward me again. A solid push sent him sprawling across the coffee table toward the couch. I stepped up behind him quickly and snatched the Colt automatic off the table, set the safety, and put it in my coat pocket before Jack could regain his balance and reconsider the option of using the gun on me.

I backed away to give myself room to react if he decided to renew his attack. Willis would be a formidable opponent sober, but in his current state no match for me. "Come on, Jack. We both want the same thing here," I said, hoping to avoid any further fisticuffs.

My words seemed to calm him down. At least he didn't throw any more punches, although he still looked as if he'd like to.

"I don't think you had anything to do with Fitz's death," I continued. "But I know now that it was you, not Fitz, who met with Logan on that Tuesday a couple of months ago. A meeting everyone involved wants to pretend never happened. I want to know what it was about and why it's such a big secret."

He didn't answer right away, as if he was giving my request some consideration. But any optimism I had that he was about to be forthcoming was soon crushed. "I was just paying off some bets for Fitz," Willis offered grudgingly.

"Bull!" I replied succinctly. His remark was an obvious lie, a poor effort considering that he'd taken his time to come up with it. I knew he was lying, and he knew that I knew it, but he didn't seem to care. Willis eye-balled me with an expression that seemed to say, 'Yeah, I know it's bull, but that's all you're going to get from me.'

"If you were just paying off debts for Fitz, why would the meeting with Logan be in Fitz's diary, why would you meet with Logan to make a routine payment, and why was Logan so keen to keep it a secret?" I continued to press for information, although I sensed it was next to useless. "If there's something else you've got going with Logan on the side, I don't give a damn. But if it has something to do with Fitz's death, I need to know about it."

"You don't want to know . . . Better that you don't know." Willis, looking down at his feet, muttered this as if he were talking to himself. Then he looked up directly at me, clear eyed, apparently somewhat sobered by his thoughts. "Fitz wouldn't want you involved. I said I'll handle it, and I will."

"'Fitz wouldn't want me involved,' what the hell is that supposed to mean?" I responded angrily. "We were friends. Of course he'd want me involved."

Willis's comment had cut into the discussion like a heavy ax splitting kindling—with me playing the role of the log. Fitz had unwittingly involved me when he'd made me the trustee on Danny's account. The insurance payout into the trust gave the police a hundred thousand reasons to look at me for Fitz's murder. I was tangled up to my neck in this mess whether Fitz intended me to be or not—up to my neck with a possible noose around it.

I saw no benefit, and possibly some downside, to sharing with Willis my personal reasons for wanting to solve the mystery of Fitz's murder. He wouldn't be moved by any concern for my wellbeing and might be even less forthcoming with information if he thought the police were actively looking in my direction, and not in his.

It was clear Willis wasn't going to tell me anything more, and I saw no peaceful way to make him spill anything he didn't want to. Frustrated almost beyond reason I briefly considered but rejected a less diplomatic alternative. In his weakened state, I probably could have beaten him to a pulp, but it wouldn't have gotten me anything but a bunch of sore knuckles and a guilty conscience; Jack wasn't the type to talk if he didn't want to, no matter what the pressure. Besides, I still had a feeling that we were both on the same side and should be working together, not at odds.

"Okay, Jack," I said in a firm, no nonsense voice, "this is how we're going to play it: You think about what I've told you. If you get back to me with an answer in the next twenty-four hours, fine. We'll decide together what needs to be done. If you don't get back to me, I'm going to the cops with what I know. Logan has already lied to them about the meeting. Now you're in the picture. Lt. Archer is going to put the screws to Logan, you, and your sister. If your alibi doesn't hold up—which I doubt it will—you're going to be in deep bo pucky with the cops. It's up to you, but all things considered my guess is that you'd be better off working with me."

I left Willis without waiting for an answer. I wanted him to think long, hard, and sober about what I'd said

Following my visit with Willis, I drove to the house, arriving too late for dinner. That was okay as my disappointing encounters with Dr. Appel's gunsel and an uncooperative Willis had crushed any appetite—but not my desire for a stiff drink. Annie had waited up for me, and everyone else was asleep or gone for the evening. We sat together in Fitz's study in our regular spots on the couch, while I briefed her on what I had and hadn't learned during my visit with the taciturn Paul Logan and his careless minion, Mace Mason. I briefly mentioned my late lunch with my childhood friend Lee Buntz, commenting that I didn't expect much to come of it. And I finished up with my follow-up visit with Jack Willis. As intended, I left out any mention of my run in with Appel's heavy; I saw no reason to upset Annie or to embarrass myself.

"Are you really going to go to the police if Jack doesn't get back to you?"

"Probably, but maybe not right away. I'd prefer that he come around on his own. Jack was pretty loyal and committed to Fitz. If he somehow knows or suspects who did it, he may still be looking to take his own revenge on whoever killed him. He knows that I wouldn't help him commit murder if that's what he has in mind."

"That sounds like Jack," Annie commented. "I could see him wanting to deal with it personally."

Annie as Fitz's fulltime employee had been around Willis and had seen a lot more of him in action than I had, so her opinion carried weight with me. "Yeah, I can see how he might feel that way in the heat of anger. But some time has passed, and from the way he reacted when I confronted him, my impression is that if he knows anything he hasn't done anything about it yet. That could mean he either doesn't really know for certain who the killer is, or he can't get to the killer for some reason."

Annie picked up on my line of reasoning quickly. "Jack's not the type to cool off once he gets his back up. But if he hasn't been able to find the killer himself by now, why wouldn't he have told the police whatever it is he knows so they could find and arrest whoever did it?"

"I don't know, but there's got to be something about the deal that Willis would rather not let the police in on."

"Something to do with this Logan character?" Annie asked suggestively.

"Stands to reason," I replied. "It's gotta have something to do with the meeting on July 20ᵗʰ that was penciled in on Fitz's calendar. A meeting with a lowlife like Logan, a meeting everybody wants to pretend never happened, is bound to involve something they don't want the cops to know about. And Jack's meeting me at the door with a gun in his hand and his taking a swing at me for no good reason makes me wonder if he isn't a little worried about it himself."

"What could it mean?" Annie stood, took my empty glass from my hand, went over to a cabinet-bar, and with practiced ease poured us another couple of neat scotches.

"Damned if I know," I answered when she returned, handed me my drink, and again eased down beside me. "But it's got to mean something. You handled all of Fitz's appointments. So why did he arrange this particular one, write it in his book himself, not tell you anything about it, and then send Willis in his place?"

We sat quietly, thoughtfully sipping our drinks until Annie broke the silence. "It's not the only time."

"What's not the only time?" I asked, stirred by her comment.

"There was one other entry in his diary that I didn't arrange and didn't know anything about before it happened: It was that appointment at the beginning of August with Dr. Peterson," Annie replied and sat up as straight as a schoolgirl answering a question in class that no one else could field. "I noticed it when we were going through his calendar, but it was so long ago I didn't give it a thought until just now. Stephen booked the appointment himself."

"Who is Dr. Petersen?" I asked.

"He's the doctor for the life insurance company," Annie answered. "The first I heard of him was when I received a bill for the physical examination. When I asked Stephen about it, that was when he told me about the insurance policy he'd taken out. He handled the whole thing himself. It was odd, as Stephen never wanted to be bothered with those sorts of things; he always had me handle them for him. Do you think that it means anything?"

"I don't know. . . Maybe." I answered, not totally truthfully. "But at least it's something to think about. God knows, unless Willis decides to open up, I've got little else to do with my time. I'll check it out, but it's probably nothing."

Annie gave me a look that expressed her dissatisfaction with my response but didn't press me. Knowing Annie, I suspected that her speculations about this new consideration had progressed a lot further than my increasingly troubled thoughts.

After Annie retired for the night, I went back through Fitz's calendar to look for the two doctors' appointments I'd noticed before. The first, a date at the end of June, long before Fitz's death, was with Dr. Joseph Herschkowitz, Fitz's regular doctor. The other, with a Dr. Paul Peterson, had been scheduled for the fifth of August. I looked up Peterson's office number in the telephone book. "Prospect 4-6005," I mumbled, circled the number with a pen, and jotted it down on a scrap of paper that I jammed into the pocket of my shirt.

The next morning I left for work an hour earlier than my usual 6:30 am. The quick drive in light traffic to the Examiner's offices in L.A. didn't provide much time to analyze further the new information that Annie had laid on me the night before, or to dispel the vague feeling that it might lead to something, something that perhaps—to paraphrase Jack Willis's remark— 'I didn't want to know.' After putting in a few hours at my desk, which had helped to divert my attention, around nine o'clock I retrieved the piece of paper with Dr. Peterson's information from my pocket, unfolded it and spread it out flat on my desk, and dialed the number.

A cheerful woman's voice answered after the first ring. "Dr. Peterson's office. How may I help you?" A mite overly friendly I thought, considering she had no idea who it was she was greeting on the other side of the line and offering to provide assistance, but maybe she was just in a better mood than I.

"Hello. My name is Shane Corrigan," I lied in a disguised voice, slightly high pitched with just a hint of Irish tenor about it.

"How can I help you, Mr. Corrigan?" she asked again. My newly found friend was intent on being helpful, as well as cheerful, and despite my earlier misgivings, I was starting to like her, sight unseen.

"I was told by the United States Western Life Insurance Company that Dr. Peterson performs physical examinations for individuals applying for life insurance. Would that be correct?"

"Yes, we do that. Would you like to make an appointment?"

"Well, therein lies the problem, don't you know? I'm a bit squeamish about such things," I continued, trying to sound squeamish, which wasn't all that hard considering I'd always found visits to a doctor's office daunting. "Could you tell me exactly what such an examination would involve?"

"Certainly. It's quite simple really. There would be blood and urine samples, of course, and a brief examination by the doctor. He would discuss your medical history—past illnesses, allergies, that sort of thing—listen to your lungs, and generally look you over."

"Well, that doesn't sound too bad, does it, Darlin'?" I commented, now well into a Victor McLaglen mode and cadence.

Overhearing my faux brogue, the reporter at the desk across from me shot me a questioning expression. I responded with a toothy, McLaglen-like grin.

"No . . . no it isn't. Shall I book an appointment for you, perhaps next week?" From the eagerness in her voice and the fact that she didn't miss a beat at my over-familiarity in referring to her as "Darlin'," I surmised that business must've been slow at Dr. Peterson's office.

I was beginning to feel a little guilty about shining her on and decided to cut the conversation short, as I'd already succeeded in confirming what I wanted to know. "No, not yet thank you. I haven't actually applied for the policy just yet. I'll get back to you. Thank you."

My next call was to Dr. Herschkowitz's office at a telephone number that I'd found in Fitz's book and written down before leaving for work. When the doctor's receptionist came on the line, I explained that I was Stephen Fitzgerald's executor, and said I had some legal matters that I needed to discuss with the doctor "to clear up some minor questions concerning the estate," which was only partially untrue. The receptionist had me hold while she checked the doctor's schedule. It took her a while to come back on the line, so I expected she had to check directly with the doctor.

"Dr. Herschkowitz can meet with you for a few minutes at three o'clock this afternoon. Will that be satisfactory?"

"That would be great," I replied.

# CHAPTER 20

Fitz must've thought having an office on Wilshire Blvd. was a sign of a true professional, since Dr. Herschkowitz's surgery was on that street, just like Stoke's chambers, although Herschkowitz's digs were a much smaller, less opulent layout on the west side of town, just across the border from Beverly Hills on the edge of Westwood Village. I was right on time for our three o'clock meeting. The receptionist, a cuddly-looking, short curly-haired blonde in what looked like a Hollywood workup of a nurse's creamy-white uniform, minus the little cap and the sensible, rubber-soled white shoes, showed me directly into the doctor's office.

Dr. Herschkowitz, a small man, looked even smaller sitting in a high-backed chair behind a desk that may have been even larger than Paul Logan's, certainly cleaner absent Logan's manhole sized ashtray and smoldering cigar. The doctor wore a stiffly starched white lab coat and wire-rimmed glasses that magnified his dark brown eyes. He sat upright, clear-eyed, and attentive. A fringe of white hair circling a bald pate reminded me a of the bust of a Greek philosopher that I'd once seen but whose name I couldn't recall at that moment. The whole package made him a vision of calm and confidence: the sort of man into whose hands one might feel a good deal more assured when putting one's life into them. He didn't get up to greet me, instead motioned me to take a chair across from him.

"How can I help you, Mr. . . . . Marshall?" he said, with a

smile and a slight pause between the mister and Marshall, while he read it off a scrap of paper in front of him. His smile looked genuine, so I took him at his word that he would be helpful. He was already aware of Fitz's death, so I got right down to it.

"I have one question for certain and, depending on the answer, maybe a couple more," I said. "Just how sick was he, Doc?"

It was a guess—a long shot, I admit it—but it paid off. Herschkowitz didn't say anything, but his smile had made an exit—it probably didn't have far to go.

"Look, Doc, he's dead," I continued, breaking a silence that I sensed might otherwise extend into the dinner hour. "Murdered, okay? You're not betraying any confidences here, and maybe your answers can help find his killer."

It didn't take long for him to reach a decision. The missing smile, now replaced by a deep frown, was at least still well short of an outright scowl. "Alright. Your friend was very sick, dying in fact—cancer. He would have died in the next five . . . six months at the most. Whoever killed him did him something of a favor."

'Maybe more than you suspect,' I thought. I don't know whether the doctor expected me to be surprised or shocked. When I was neither, he looked a little disappointed.

"The coroner's report didn't say anything about cancer," I said, pressing for more information.

"Coroners are very busy men, Mr. Marshall." The doctor must've been a quick study, as he didn't need to look down at his little piece of paper to get my name right the second time around. "As I understand it, it was obvious that he died from a gunshot. Once the medical examiner established the cause of death, he would stop looking. Mr. Fitzgerald's condition wasn't obvious. In fact, I wouldn't have caught it if he hadn't complained of tiredness and sore muscles during a routine examination. That caused me to run additional tests."

"What about an insurance physical?" I asked. "Would that have caught it."

"Almost certainly," Dr. Herschkowitz replied. "It's the sort of thing that they would be looking for. They would run blood tests and . . ."

With my having bulldozed a gap through his barrier of professional silence, the doctor seemed as if he was about to gush forth with additional technical information, information I probably wouldn't understand and might've just as soon not known if by chance I were to be questioned about it in the future by the police.

"That's all I needed to know," I impolitely interrupted his ramping up presentation, rose from my seat, and headed for the exit. "Thanks, Doc," I said over my shoulder just before I passed through the door.


I suppose that I needn't have been so rude to Fitz's doctor, but I wanted to catch Dr. Peterson at his office before the end of the workday. I stopped at the first payphone I found and looked up the address that I'd neglected to write down earlier. As it worked out there'd been no need to rush as Peterson's office was also on the Westside not too far from Dr. Herschkowitz's location.

When I arrived at the address on a side street just off of Overland Blvd. I found that Dr. Peterson's office and examination room were attached to the side of what presumably was his home. It was a common arrangement for general practitioners in those days; the separate entrance allowed for patients to come and go without disturbing the occupants of the house.

As I pulled up to the curb on the far side of the tree lined street, I saw a young woman in a white nurse's uniform, whom I assumed was my recently acquired telephone friend, locking the office door. I couldn't see her face clearly from where I was parked, but her short strawberry blond hair, tight little figure, and well-curved, stockingless calves provided ample compensation.

I waited while she walked to a car that rivaled mine for wear and tear; got in, displaying even more of her fine legs as she did so; and drove away—oblivious to what might have been. I was more than half sorry that my mission with her boss would not require our augmenting our newly established relationship in person. Ah well, Annie would've probably objected anyway.

When her car reached the end of the block, rounded the corner, and disappeared, I got out of mine, ambled across the quiet tree lined street and up the walkway, and used the knocker on the front door to announce my arrival.

After a brief pause the door was answered by a short, heavyset, middle-aged man. He wore thick-lensed, wire-rimmed glasses on a button nose positioned near the middle of a round face. His head was topped by a mass of closely cropped, well-coiffed brown hair. He was still clad in his lab coat, a match to the one worn by Dr. Herschkowitz, though perhaps a little less neatly starched, a little less white, and somewhat threadbare. He didn't say anything, instead, he stared at me with a questioning expression.

"You Peterson?" It was probably a stupid question to ask, but it would've been even stupider if I'd started to direct my questions at the wrong guy.

"What do you want?" Not a direct answer to my inquiry but close enough.

"We need to talk," I said abruptly and sandwiched my way through the doorway and into the room, brushing past him.

"What the hell? You get . . ."

"'What the hell?' My question exactly," I growled as I turn

to face him down. "As in 'What the hell are you doing signing off on the insurance physical for a man that is dying of cancer?' Stephen Fitzgerald. You remember him don't you, Doc?"

"I don't know what you're talking about," he shot back, the standard reply of those with much to hide and little hope of doing so.

"Look, Peterson, I don't give a rat's ass what kind of scam you've got going here, but unless you tell me everything I want to know I'm heading to the police. If they get involved, the best that you can hope for is that you'll lose your license and probably do some time for insurance fraud. On the other hand, if you tell me what I want to hear, maybe nothing happens, and you can go on running your little scam 'til the cows come home."

He looked as if he was about to break, but I decided to give him another little push just to make sure and get something else out on the table to see his reaction. "And if you think that you can get to your buddy Logan to have him take care of me before I can get to the cops, your timing is way off."

My mentioning Logan took the trick; the skin on Peterson's face seemed to tighten over his cheek bones and his eyes got as big as H.C. Andersen's dogs'. He had the look of a man who has suddenly realized that he has misjudged the timing of his stepping from a rowboat to the dock.

"Okay, okay," he stammered when he finely regained a modicum of composure. "I do a lot of off the books work for Logan, but this was the first time he asked me to sign-off on an insurance exam. I figured that Logan was just setting it up to get paid money that was owed him when the Fitzgerald guy died. I didn't think that it would work though because the insurance company was bound to baulk at paying off on a guy that dies of cancer within a year of taking out a big policy. But Logan thought otherwise and was paying me a grand to do it. He supplied me with faked blood and urine samples that would cover me if the insurance company came back at me. I could claim that the lab had screwed up or that Fitzgerald had somehow slipped me the fakes."

"Would the insurance company buy that? It sounds kind of hokey to me."

"Probably not, but they couldn't prove otherwise. Whether they bought it or not I be cut off from other work for the insurance company going forward anyway."

"If that's so, I'm surprised that you agreed to do it," I said, not really surprised at all, but thinking that if I sounded sympathetic he might be more forthcoming. Which, as it turned out, he was.

"Paul Logan is not a guy who' it's easy to say no to," Peterson offered. "Anyway, the other work that I do for Logan pays a lot better than the piss-ant fees I get from insurance companies for doing physicals."

I nodded knowingly. Clearly Peterson had carefully worked out the economics and risks involved in his various, less-than-professionally sanctioned enterprises. That was good to know, because Peterson's having a logical mind would go a long way toward getting him to buy off on what I was about to lay on him.

"Okay, here's the way we're going to play this, Doc: I'm not going to take any of this to the police unless I have to. If it does get back to you and Logan, Logan's not going to know that it came from you or me. That way Logan won't get the idea that you ratted him out, and you can play your 'I have no idea how the samples got switched' routine with the cops and the insurance dicks."

I paused to let Peterson absorb what I'd proposed, then I added, "The best way for you to handle this is to pretend that this meeting between us never happened. Nothing good can come of it if you get nervous and spill your guts to Logan. He won't thank you for it, and probably would arrange to have both of us killed. And even if he only took me out, I'm going to leave a poison pen note for the police that will lay everything out and name names—yours included. You better hope that I don't wind up dead, because that would tie you in as an accessory to my murder on top of all of your other troubles."

I left Dr. Peterson with a lot to ponder and no good choices. But that was his problem, not mine. I too had much to consider and some tough decisions of my own that would need to be made soon.

Annie and Pilar were out with Danny when I got back to the house, so there was time to sit alone and think things through over a couple of cold ones. Even with what I had learned from confronting Dr. Peterson, it was hard for me to accept that my pal Fitz had been running a scam on the life insurance company to fund Danny's trust account. Annie's having pointed out the anomaly that Fitz had arranged his own appointment for the insurance physical, the sort of thing that he never did himself, had got me to speculating that there might be something dodgy about the whole setup.

It was all starting to fit together: Fitz, when he learned that he was dying of cancer, cooked up a scheme to take out a large insurance policy to fund a trust for Danny. Fitz was smart enough to realize that the insurance company was going to cry 'foul ball' at paying off on a thirty-five-year-old guy who dies of cancer five or six months after taking out a big policy, so his plan was to arrange for his own death in a way that would allow for the cancer to remain unknown.

Dr. Herschkowitz had answered the sixty-four-dollar question when he confirmed that a routine examination by the doctor for the insurance company should've caught the fact that Fitz had cancer. That convinced me that Peterson in all probability was in on the gag, as there was no way that Fitz would've passed the physical without his help.

My throwing out Logan's name when I confronted Peterson

was something of a shot in the dark but not totally. Fitz wouldn't have known how to find a doctor willing to play along with his scheme, and I doubted that Jack Willis would either, but Logan would probably have several from which to choose. Arranging for it all was undoubtedly what the guarded meeting between Logan and Willis had been about.

It took a little longer to work out how Danny's kidnapping fit into the plan. Peterson had said that he'd been paid a grand for his services. And from what I'd learned of such things from the short time that I'd been working the crime beat, I doubted that the payment to a professional shooter would run any more than that. But arranging the whole thing through a mob connection, such as Logan, would come with a much higher fee. I doubted that there was a price list for such things, but $15,000 sounded like it would be in the ballpark: a thousand for the doctor, another grand for the shooter, and a cool $13,000 payday for Logan and his boys.

However, an unexplained withdrawal in cash of that amount from his bank account just before Fitz's murder would raise a red flag, so the fake kidnapping and ransom payment was dreamed up to cover it.

There were still some niggling loose ends that I needed to work out, but I was now fairly certain that my general conclusions were close to accurate. As Dr. Herschkowitz had pointed out, the coroner wasn't going to look beyond a bullet hole in the chest for a cause of death. And presented with an unsolved murder committed during an apparent burglary gone bad, the insurance investigators weren't going to waste their time to see if the victim was already dying from something else. A double indemnity payout to boot, with me controlling the cash, Danny would be set for life—even if a potentially unstable, unreliable, pill-addicted Pilar's career tanked at some point in the future.

The bottom line was that Fitz had arranged his own death— it wasn't murder; it was sort of a suicide. Having worked through it, my first thought was to let the whole thing drop, pretend to myself that it was none of my concern—which, as I saw it, was true to a point. The police or insurance company investigators might figure it out as I had, or they might not. But if they didn't tumble to it, Danny would wind up with a hundred thousand bucks in the bank, which would be jake with me.

My number one task of identifying the murderer and my number two, more personal one, of locating the crew who had kidnapped Danny had resolved themselves. I still had a bone to pick with the idiot who'd knocked me out while I was handcuffed to the door of my car, but I'd get over that eventually.

All of that was fine as far as it went, but if the police didn't figure out the scheme for themselves, they'd keep looking for the killer and the kidnappers. And when they didn't come up with anyone else, they'd probably start looking at me again. I would still be the number one suspect under Buller's wrong, yet admittedly more plausible, scenario.

I could blow the whistle on Fitz's insurance and kidnap scam to try to take the heat off me. I'd hate to screw up the big payoff for Danny, but I'd hate it even more to go down for Fitz's murder. But dropping a nickel on Fitz's scheme still wouldn't prove that I wasn't involved. The theory that some unidentified, hired killer had jumped the gun by killing Fitz while the kidnapping was underway and before he'd collected his fee, didn't make a lot of sense; the timing of it stunk.

Buller—and maybe even Archer if I waited too long to come clean—would find a way to twist my unproven theory to say that the whole thing was my idea from the start, and that I'd killed Fitz to pocket the $15,000 in addition to getting control of the insurance money. He would reason that I'd lost my nerve and was letting the police know about the insurance scam because I'd calculated that they were bound to discover it on their own, and if I was the one who pointed them in the right direction, they'd stop looking at me for Fitz's murder. In his scenario I wouldn't get my hands on the $100,000 in insurance money, but I wouldn't hang for killing Fitz, and I'd have the ransom money to stuff away in my mattress to ease me through my old age.

Buller wouldn't be able to prove it, but I had to admit his was a better theory than the one I would be offering—a theory without any actual proof to support it. I was going to need more than the fact Paul Logan had neglected to mention his meeting with Jack Willis to the police. The problem was that I had no idea of where to begin to find the evidence I needed. The back of my head was starting to ache again—this time from more than the still swollen knot on my skull.

Pilar, Annie, and Danny arrived home a little after seven o'clock. Pilar headed straight to bed with hardly a word to me, and Annie put an already half-asleep Danny down for the night before joining me for our usual nightcap.

I explained to Annie what I'd learned and my thoughts on what it all meant, none of which seemed to come as much of a surprise to her. But my explanation of the risks they presented for me got her attention.

"You've got to go to the police," she said, demonstrating a grasp of the soundest and most logical approach to the problem.

"Yeah . . . yeah, I hear you. You're right, I know I should, and I probably will. But I'd sure like to have something more to give to them when I do. My pointing a finger at Logan and Peterson is just that; I have nothing solid to prove their involvement. If the police go to Peterson, he's not going to make the same mistakes he made with me. He's going to deny everything and fall back on his 'I was duped' alibi. And if he knows what's good for him, he's sure as hell not going to drop Logan's name to the police.

"Without Peterson's support all I've got to offer is an off-the-wall theory with no real proof to support it. Archer would probably believe me, but even he could only stand by me so far. An unproven, alternative theory of the case offered by the number one suspect isn't going to carry much weight."

I slumped in my seat to graphically display my frustration and took another solid swallow of watered-down scotch. "A mysterious, unidentified—and probably never to be identified—mob hit man, who fakes a robbery and shoots Fitz in a very unprofessional manner before he has received his fee, isn't going to sound any more plausible to the police than it does to me."

"I can see your point," Annie commented "And there are other things about it that don't seem right to me either."

"Such as?"

"Such as, why would Stephen let it happen before he knew for certain that Danny was home safe? For that matter, why would he have let them take Danny in the first place. That's not like Stephen; he'd never put Danny in that kind of risk."

Annie was hitting on some of the things that were still bothering me. "Yeah, that is strange. And for that matter why have the faked kidnapping and murder happen so close together. If the kidnapping was just to provide cover for the big drawdown of cash, it would be better if the two events were as far removed from each other as possible. Now everyone is assuming that most likely there is some link between them."

"So, what can you do to get the proof that you need?" Annie asked. She sensed my frustration and showed it by the way she looked at me with her sympathetic, dark blue eyes.

"I want to take one more run at Jack Willis before I go to the police," I replied. "With what I've found out about the insurance deal and Willis's probable involvement, maybe I can pry some answers out of him. How he plays this could be important. His loyalty is to Fitz, not me. He's not going to admit to anything, and if his alibi holds up—which it probably will—there's nothing that the cops can pin on him. But if he realizes that the only hope of keeping Fitz's scheme alive and not screwing up the payout for Danny is to help me find a way to get off the hook, he may open up with some answers to some of our questions. Taking this to the cops can wait another day."

"I hope you're right," Annie said with a sigh.

"So do I," I answered in all sincerity but with much doubt.

## CHAPTER 21

Sammy Zissu's pawn shop was a small, nondescript storefront on Soto Street near the western edge of Boyle Heights, just up from Olympic Boulevard and a couple of blocks east of a dry arroyo mischaracterized, if not actually misnamed, as the Los Angeles River. The only indications of the shop's existence and purpose to a passing non-local were an undersized, hand-painted sign nailed over the door with Sammy's name and the word "PAWN" on it and the trade's traditional three gilded balls hanging above the sign. As far as I knew, the same sign and the same metal spheres had hung there since before I was born, certainly for all the years since I'd roamed those streets as a kid.

I opened the door and sauntered in with the style of a casual shopper on the lookout for a bargain. The interior was a narrow rectangular room, the walls on both sides covered with a sufficient number of worn musical instruments to outfit a small marching band, some artwork of dubious quality and attribution, and a number of unwound wall clocks, their hands displaying many erroneous opinions as to the time of day. This mishmash of forfeited family treasures hung above and behind long, narrow glass cases in need of a good cleaning, which, on one side displayed a trove of watches and jewelry of various values, and, on the other an arsenal of handguns of a variety of different conditions and calibers.

At the back of the room was a wood and wire teller's cage that looked like it had been pieced together from odds and ends picked up in a scrapyard. In this secure booth sat Sammy on a high stool. Behind him and resting upright in one corner, prominently visible, were a shotgun and a baseball bat. The two weapons intended no doubt to provide Sammy with an option depending upon the degree of intensity and distance of any presented threat . . . though I expected that the personal armaments on display were intended more to discourage problems than to deal with them. For actual confrontations, there was probably a fair-sized loaded handgun tucked in Sammy's cash drawer.

Sammy, a short, wiry man in his seventies, looked the part he found himself playing in life. A Romanian Jew, his naturally thick, curly, dark hair and his complexion had both turned shades of gray with advancing age. But his eyes were still as black as fresh coal dust and bright as polished onyx. He had a reputation for being as tough as a rhinoceros and as mean as a hungry watch dog, both as a haggler and in just about any other situation that might arise.

Like every other kid in the neighborhood, I'd known who Sammy was but never had any dealings with him. I wasn't a thief and didn't have anything of value of my own, so I wouldn't have had anything to hock or fence. In those days, kids never had any money anyway, so, like kids everywhere, we made do without it.

Sammy didn't move from his stool or, other than watching me with alert eyes, react in any way as I approached him and introduced myself.

"Okay," he muttered without emotion. He gave me a look as if to say, 'Go away. You bother me.'

That my showing up at his shop bothered him was no surprise given my purpose in being there. He had already been alerted to my probable visit by Lee Buntz. Earlier that morning Lee had telephoned me at my desk to inform me that Sammy had some information that might help me out and that he'd reluctantly agreed to talk to me. So Sammy knew I wasn't about to 'go away' until I heard what he had to say.

Even so, it didn't take long to realize that Sammy had no

intention of starting the conversation, so I kicked it off. "Lee Buntz says you may know something that might help me out."

"Maybe." Sammy Zissu, like Mace Mason, was obviously a man of few words. But unlike Mace, Sammy was apparently more careful about how he doled them out.

It looked as if I was going to have to draw on all of the limited interviewing skills I'd picked up during my brief tenure as a crime reporter if I was going to pry any information out of Sammy. "Mr. Zissu, you don't know me, I know. But Lee Buntz does and must have told you that I am someone you can trust not to betray a confidence. This is a personal matter. The man who was killed, Stephen Fitzgerald, was a close friend. I'm not a cop. I *am* a reporter, but I'm not here as a reporter. Whatever you tell me, I promise to keep your name out of it, unless you say otherwise."

Sammy gave me a long, hard look while he considered my plea. Finally, he again muttered, "Okay," followed by, "The Buntz kid told me who you are and about how you two go way back." A hint of a smile cracked on his stony face and his eyes seemed to shine a little brighter. "I did some business with your grandfather a long time ago. Did you know that?"

"You knew Saul?"

"Sure. He used to come in with stuff the studio was throwing away or selling cheap. We did quite a bit of business for a while. He never haggled over what I offered him. I liked that, so I always gave him a fair price. I never met your father, but your mother came in with your grandmother a couple of times. A pretty girl, your mother. I always remember the pretty ones." His smile got a little broader when he saw my reaction. "What? You think I was always this old? Anyway, it was before you were born."

"Okay," I laughed as I said it, a little disconcerted at the thought of someone lusting after my mother, even as a young girl. "She was a beauty, wasn't she?"

"What do you know? She was your mother; all mothers are beautiful to their sons. From me you're getting an objective opinion." His face suddenly shifted to sad concern; the faint smile gone. "But you said 'was' . . ."

My emotions suddenly matched Sammy's expression as I responded to his unasked question. "My mother died a few years ago, shortly after my father passed away."

"Too bad . . . too bad," Sammy whispered with what I took to be genuine sorrow. I realized then that I had suddenly become extremely fond of this grizzled old man.

Sammy, probably in an effort to break the mood, returned to the main issue. "About a week ago a young guy came in with some jewelry he wanted to unload. Sell, mind you, not hock. It was all paste but good stuff; it had some value. I probably would've bought it off him if I had known him, but he was a stranger to me, not from the neighborhood. I figured the goods were hot, so I sent him on his way. I didn't know anything about a murder at the time and didn't put it together until Buntz told me about the killing on the Westside."

"Can you describe him?"

"Mexican kid, early twenties, medium height, a little on the skinny side. Dressed in an open-necked cotton shirt and pleated slacks . . . standard fare for his type. Not a worker bee though, more of a hustler, if you ask me. Mean looking . . . got surly when I turned him down; acted as if he was going to get physical, but then thought better of it. Stormed out. That was the last I saw of him. You know him?"

"Yes, I'm pretty sure I do," I replied, 'Pretty sure' that was unless Javier Ruiz, Mag's ne'er-do-well brother, whom I'd seen arguing with her on the night of Danny's birthday party, had a twin that I didn't know about. An argument, come to think on it, that took place on the second floor of the house, a place where Javier had no business to be.

"Do you think he killed your friend?"

"Maybe," I answered, borrowing that noncommittal word from Sammy's repertoire.

From what I'd seen of him, I could picture Mag's brother as a sneak thief, if an easy opportunity with little or no risk presented itself. But I'd have been surprised to find that he had the guts to pull a robbery like the one that had gone down on the night that Fitz was murdered. And his confronting and shooting someone? That didn't fit my image of him either—which is probably why I'd never given any thought to his being a suspect.

Javier, using his knowledge of the layout and routine of the house, could easily have staged a break-in to snatch the usually doped up Pilar's jewelry from her bedroom. And he wouldn't know anything about the wall safe where she kept the good stuff and wouldn't know that what he did find was just costume junk. He wouldn't have thought it through enough to realize that the police would eventually tag him as an obvious suspect—maybe they already had but hadn't told me.

On the other hand, even Javier would've realized that trying to pull off a burglary while the family was alert and on edge dealing with Danny's kidnapping would be bad timing. And I couldn't imagine any scenario in which he would intentionally face down Fitz in his office; Fitz would've broken him like a burnt-out match. Javier would've thought he had what he wanted when he grabbed the paste and would've just snuck out the same way he'd come in. And even if Fitz had heard something and went to investigate, he would've met up with Javier somewhere else in the house, not in his study.

Javier probably wasn't the killer that I was looking for, but it sure as hell looked as if he was in the house that night, and that was something. My next step would definitely be a little chat with Mr. Ruiz.

# CHAPTER 22

Javier would've had to be slow off the mark not to realize that something was amiss when he came through the backdoor that evening to pick up his sister and saw Annie and I, with Mag bracketed between us, sitting at the kitchen table like a tribunal of angry judges. The troubled expression that appeared on his face was a natural reaction for someone with no doubt many guilts, which should've been, but probably weren't, all that troubling to his conscience.

"Sit," I ordered in a firm and unfriendly, but not particularly threatening voice.

Javier hesitated; his eyes angled more at his scowling sister than on me. Then apparently realizing that he'd better find out what this was all about before reacting, Javier decided to comply with my order. He didn't speak; he just sat with mingled angry, defiant, and sullen expressions instantiated by his thin, tightly closed lips.

"We know that you took Pilar's jewelry." I'd decided to hit him with it cold, figuring that any build-up on my part might alert him and give him time to consider denying it and making up some bull-roarer of a lie.

"What are you talking about?" he said indignantly through a barely open mouth. His question was more of a delaying tactic to give himself time to think than any confusion about what I was laying on him.

But I wasn't about to give him the break he was looking for. "Don't mess with us, Javier. We know you were here that night and took the stuff, we can prove it if we have to." It was only half a lie; Sammy Zissu hadn't committed to fingering Javier. Given Sammy's sideline as a sometimes buyer of stolen goods, he naturally would be reluctant to get involved. But I was fairly certain that he would come through for me in this case if need be.

Mag, who had agreed to keep silent when Annie had explained to her in Spanish what we knew and how we intended to confront Javier, suddenly broke her promise. She let loose with a barrage of angry invective at Javier like a small mother bird attacking a larger one that had ventured too close to her nest. I was mildly shocked that some of the impolite Spanish words, which I recognized from my early days in the Heights, were part of the diminutive and otherwise demure Mag's vocabulary.

Javier, probably used to such older-sisterly outbursts, seemed unmoved by her words. But her tirade bought him time to consider—and then act—while my attention was diverted, and Annie had turned in her chair to try to calm and quiet the irate, blaring woman.

Javier pushed back from the table and stood in one rapid and seamless motion. A knife appeared in his hand with the same suddenness and impact as an illusionist's producing a hissing snake and thrusting it at an astonished lady in the front row.

Having been alerted by his movement and the click of the blade opening, I stood quickly and faced him, knees slightly bent and arms straight down slightly away from my body, hands open, ready. Annie, a little slower to react, also stood and moved close in beside the still seated Mag, keeping the table between the women and Javier. She placed one hand on Mag's shoulder. Mag had stopped shouting. We all looked toward Javier: Annie and Mag at the knife in his hand, I at his sweating face and into his nervous eyes.

Anyone who says that he is not intimidated by someone threatening him with a knife is either a liar or a fool, or both. While a gun is generally more reliable if you're looking to kill someone, there's something particularly sinister about a knife, a more up-close and personal kind of weapon. I've been told—and my limited experience has supported the idea—that people who carry knives as their weapon of choice are not usually looking to kill anyone; the weapon is intended to intimidate or injure rather than to kill. I was alarmed by Javier's having pulled on us and prepared to react, if need be, but not scared beyond reason.

"Come on, Javier. Put the knife down. We don't think that you killed Fitz." I spoke in as cool and reassuring a voice as I could manage. "But we know you were here the night that it happened. If you saw or heard anything that can help us figure out who did kill him, you've got to tell us."

Javier didn't move toward me, which I took as a sign that he'd given up on any idea that stabbing me was a viable option. As I saw it, his remaining choices boiled down to giving in to my request or bolting.

"Javier, I doubt Pilar gives a damn about the jewelry, nor will anyone else . . . if you can help us find the killer." Given Pilar's temperament, I had no real idea how she would react when told that Javier had taken her stuff. I would try to talk her down, if I could, but it didn't really matter, as Javier had no options. He could either tell us and later the police what he knew, or he could wait for a couple of less-openminded cops to come looking for him and tell them then. Javier wisely opted for the former.

"Okay, okay, but I don't know much," he began, his voice and apparent attitude still hostile. "It was about two. I came in through the back gate and across the yard. The idea was to go in through the back door—I had Mag's key with me—go up the back stairs, make a quick snatch, and get out the same way. I was going to break one of the windows in the backdoor on my way out to make it look like a break-in, but the window was already broken when I got there."

"You didn't think that was strange?" I interjected.

"Yeah, I did, but I didn't know what to make of it. I just let myself in that way. Never used Mag's key." He paused.

So far what Javier was telling us jived with what Annie and I already knew or suspected. Before Javier had arrived to fetch her, Mag had told us that she'd followed the instructions she'd been given by Fitz and hadn't told anyone, including her brother, about Danny's kidnapping. With the all-too-often bad luck of an amateur thief, Javier had stumbled upon the worst possible night to pull off his little caper.

"Go on. What else happened?" I prodded to keep him going.

"I'd just grabbed the stuff when I heard a shot. Senora Fuertes stirred, like she was about to wake up, so I beat it down the hall and the back stairs. I ran across the yard to the back gate."

'Javier's reaction must've been damned quick to get past the door to the guest room and down the back stairs before Annie awoke and came out to investigate,' I thought. The image of a groggy Annie bumping into a desperately fleeing, panicky, and no doubt armed with a blade Javier in the upstairs hallway was unnerving. I saw no benefit in dwelling or expanding on that unpleasant thought, so I moved on. Instead, I asked, "Is that all?"

Javier was quick to respond. "No. I'd seen the lights were on in Sẽnor Fitzgerald's office when I came across the yard the first time. Sẽnor Fitzgerald was sitting at his desk, and there was some guy standing on the other side. The guy was gesturing; it looked like he was doing most of the talking."

"Did you see who it was? Could you describe him?" I tried to not let my excitement show.

"No, I was too far away. I didn't want to get too close. I was on the far side of the pool when I saw them. I thought about splitting but then figured with them talking like that there'd be no chance that they'd hear me upstairs. I went the long way around, past the diving board, so I wouldn't get too close to the light."

Javier still held the knife but no longer as a threat. I doubt he even realized it was in his hand hanging limply at his side.

"You're sure it was a man, not a woman? . . . tall, short? . . . skinny, fat? . . . dark, blond?" I barraged him with questions that in the end achieved nothing.

"Pretty sure it was a guy . . . a big guy. That's it."

I kept pressing Javier, more to ease my frustration than in hope of getting any additional meaningful information. But it was futile; he'd told us what little he knew. All the cajoling and threatening I could bring to bear wouldn't help him remember something he hadn't seen. And more pressure might just cause him to start making things up—consciously or otherwise—to get me off his back.

When asked, he indicated that he still had Pilar's jewelry. "I tried to sell it, but the guy I talked to wouldn't touch it. That scared me. When I heard later that day that someone'd killed Señor Fitzgerald, that scared me more. I thought if someone found out I had the stuff, they'd think I killed him. So I just kept everything."

"So you didn't know about Fitz's being shot until after you tried to unload the jewelry?" I asked, searching for a crack in his story.

"No, no. I heard the shot, sure. But I didn't know it was Señor Fitzgerald that got it. I didn't know until I read about it in the paper that night after I tried to sell the stuff. Mag hadn't told me nothing about what happened here until later after it was all over." He glanced at Mag with a slight frown, as if looking for a way to somehow make this her fault. "If I'd known someone had snatched the kid, I wouldn't have broke' in that night."

What Javier was saying agreed with what Sammy Zissu had told me earlier in the day and worked to confirm my feeling that Javier was being straight with what he was telling us now.

I didn't speak for a long beat, as I considered the options. Finally I said, "Okay, this is what we are going to do, Javier: When you get home tonight, you give all of the things you took to Mag. She can give Annie the stuff when you bring her here tomorrow—early. After you drop her off, you head downtown to the central police station, ask for Lt. John Archer, and tell him what you told us—all of it. Annie and I will talk to Pilar, tell her you came clean and are helping with the investigation, but it'll be up to her whether or not she presses charges. She won't want to lose Mag—Danny loves Mag. So she may be willing to overlook this, particularly if your information helps the cops. But I can't guarantee which way Pilar will go with it. Either way, your only real chance is to come clean."

Javier nodded pensively, which I took as an indication that he understood my instructions and would comply with them. Mag, after having quieted down from her initial outburst, uncharacteristically, but understandably, had not spoken during my exchange with Javier. I'm not certain how much of our conversation she was able to follow with her limited English. I imagined she spent most of the time mentally composing the tongue lashing she would lay on her brother in colorful Spanish phrases during their drive home.

"Do you believe him?" Annie asked after Mag and Javier had left.

"Pretty much, don't you? If Javier had killed Fitz, he would've beat it when we confronted him, not stayed around to hear what we had to say about what he already knew. You saw how quickly he backed down. I can't see him facing down Fitz in the middle of the night, somehow getting the drop on him and then gunning him down. It's no big surprise that Javier is a thief, but I don't see him as a killer."

"I guess," Annie responded without enthusiasm, as if half glad that Mag's brother hadn't killed Fitz, but more than half disappointed that we hadn't come up with a solution that didn't point to Fitz as having arranged for his own death.

"I don't see how I could've missed seeing him in the hallway when I came out after hearing the shot," Annie added.

"You were asleep. The shot woke you. It probably took you longer to react than you realize," I pointed out. "And you headed for the front stairs, not the back. So Javier could've been at the far end of the upstairs hallway, and you wouldn't have seen him."

"What he said fits with how we think it probably went down," I continued. "Still, there are some things that don't add up. Why would the killer act before he was paid and while the kidnap scheme was going down? Like you said, Fitz wouldn't have wanted those two things to happen so close together; the police were bound to think that the two were somehow connected. It just doesn't make sense.

"And, if Javier is telling the truth about seeing someone in Fitz's office when he was sneaking into the house, that doesn't sound right either. What kind of hired killer is going to take the time to have a chat with his target before killing him. If he was going to shoot him here in the house, he'd get it over with and get out as fast as possible." I was thinking out loud, more trying to get it all straight in my mind rather than explaining things to Annie, things she already knew as well as I. I felt that we were on the right track but wasn't sure we were headed in the right direction.

"So, what now?" Annie asked.

"So, I don't know 'what now.' As I see it, all we've accomplished is to throw a spanner into the police's theory that Fitz was killed during a burglary gone bad. With that theory knocked down, the cops are going to have to look elsewhere for the murderer. I'm afraid that moves me back to square one in the frame.

"I may have to tell the police about Fitz's insurance scam right away rather than wait for them to figure it out for themselves," I allowed. "But before I do that, I think I'll go over and have another little, maybe not-so-friendly chat with Jack Willis tonight. If nothing else maybe I can get him to fill in some of the holes in our theory. If Jack's still on a bender, he'll be a lot easier to handle than if he's sober. And maybe more likely to tell me what he knows."

# CHAPTER 23

It was after nine o'clock by the time I'd finished mulling over things with Annie, fixed myself a cold roast beef sandwich, popped and drank a beer, and once again drove the few miles to Willis's place in Culver City. As I walked along the outside, unlit, second-floor walkway to Jack's front door for the third time, I reached inside my coat and eased off the safety on the short-nosed Colt tucked into its holster under my armpit. I doubted Willis would try to get violent again, even when I confronted him outright with my conclusions about his involvement in Fitz's little scheme. But you never know how someone might react if he felt cornered, so I'd taken the precaution of arming myself before paying him this visit.

This time there was no answer to my initial knock. I banged on the door again, a little louder. Still no answer. Trying the handle, I was surprised to find the door unlocked. That got my attention, as Willis had never impressed me as an easy-going, trusting type inclined to a neighborly open-door policy toward visitors.

I eased the door open a few inches at a time, slowly, cautiously for some reason—maybe because that's the way I'd seen them do it in the movies. The stench of not-too-recent death that assailed me was not as bad as I'd experienced once before, but it was unmistakable and enough that I stepped back with a jerk, pulled a handkerchief from my back pocket, and covered my nose before drawing my revolver.

Now better prepared for what I anticipated I was going to find inside and for anything else that might be lurking about, I pushed the door open further with my foot and began again to edge forward slowly, hesitantly, a slender finger-like gun barrel pointing the way.

The interior was too dark for me to see anything clearly from where I paused in the doorway. I reached out and fumbled with my left hand for the wall switch, reasoning that, if there happened to be someone with deadly intent waiting in the apartment, my chances would be better with the room suddenly illuminated than they would be with me trying to peer into the almost black living room and with my whole body silhouetted in the doorway against the steel blue night sky.

Flipping the switch, however, lit only a low-wattage, shaded lamp on a small table against the wall to my left. The weak light filling the immediate area didn't offer much, but it was enough to see that the room was unoccupied—unoccupied that was if you didn't count the corpse of Jack Willis. That there was no one else waiting for me inside was no big surprise, as no one with any sense of smell would hang around that stench if he didn't have to.

Willis's body and a straight-backed kitchen chair were lying together on their right side in the middle of the living room floor. His mangled face, covered with cuts and dried blood, was barely recognizable.

Willis must've been sitting in the chair when it had gone over. His body was positioned against it as though he were still seated, leaning slightly forward as if to hear what was being said to him. He was held in place by a set of handcuffs, one loop secured to his left wrist and the other attached to the arm of the chair. While I couldn't see it beneath his body, I expected that a similar arrangement held his right side in place. A knotted, gore-soaked rag that looked as if it had been used off-and-on as a gag lay on the floor near the body like a small island in a miniature sea of nearly dry blood.

I breathed slowly to calm my nerves while I made my cursory scan of the room from the doorway before inching forward, careful not to step in the still tacky blood surrounding the corpse. Someone had beaten the hell out of him and cut him up with what looked like an intent to inflict maximum pain before finishing him off with a single slash across his throat.

I fought back and won a close bout against the recent cold beer and undigested roast-beef-on-rye raising a riot in my gut. Once I'd calmed down and was reasonably satisfied that no one was about to jump out at me, I scanned the room. I didn't make a study of it, concentrating as I was at the time on Jack, but my later recalled impression was that the room looked much the same as it had on my last visit: not exactly neat, maybe a little less so, but not as if there had been a knock-down, drag-out struggle. Jack's .45 automatic that I'd previously left on the coffee table had been removed and wasn't visible anywhere else in the room. From his condition it certainly didn't look as if Jack had had a chance to put it to any effective use.

I gave some thought to examining the body more closely and to having a look around the apartment for clues that might help my cause. But I decided against it; I had already visited Jack's apartment twice before, and the police were bound to find a few of my fingerprints scattered around. I certainly didn't want the cops to find some of Jack's blood on me or more of my prints in places that couldn't be easily explained. So instead of nosing around as I was tempted to do, I backed carefully out of the apartment—again like they do it in the talkies—flipping the safety and holstering my revolver as I went.

Clear of the room, I closed the door as I'd found it. Then I banged on those of other apartments until I located a woman who'd let me use her telephone to call the police. That accomplished, I sat down on the second from the bottom tier of the exterior stairway and waited quietly for Lt. Archer and Sgt. Buller and the rest of their crew to arrive.

I assumed that my 'packing' might make the police a little nervous until they were clear on what they were about to find upstairs and exactly how I fit into the picture, so the first thing I did when they got there was to surrender my Colt, which I did by announcing its presence and holding open my jacket with two fingers while Lt. Archer pulled it from my shoulder holster. He gave me one of his little smiles as he did this, acknowledging in his own way the wisdom of my decision.

As soon as I'd given them a somewhat less than forthright explanation of why I was visiting Jack Willis late on a Wednesday evening and a much-understated description of what they were about to find in his second-floor apartment, they left me again sitting at the bottom of the stairs, this time under the not-so-relaxed eye of a uniformed patrolman.

After twenty minutes or so, Sgt. Buller returned alone. To my surprise he didn't follow his usual pattern of presenting to me in harsh style a convoluted explanation of how and why I had pulled off this mutilation and most recent murder. Instead, his attitude was surprisingly sympathetic. "That's a bad one. As much as I've seen, things like this still hit me hard. It must've scared the hell out of you."

I nodded but didn't say anything, thinking Buller might be setting me up, trying to get me off guard before slamming me with one of his cockamamy theories. He must've sensed this as he followed with, "Even I don't see you as having anything to do with this. Archer has told me enough about you, and I've seen enough myself to know this is not your style."

It was as lefthanded a compliment as I'd ever received. I was tempted to ask him what he envisioned my "style" of torture and murder to be but thought better of it. It was probably just as well that I kept my smart mouth shut, as after a slight pause and what could've been mistaken for a vaguely insightful smile, Buller added, "But I'm still not convinced you're totally clean on the Fitzgerald kidnapping and murder." Then he turned away, leaving me alone with that thought, and went back upstairs to Willis's apartment.

'Sergeant Buller—not unlike the Lord—giveth and taketh away,' I mused philosophically as he climbed the stairs. But though down deep he may have wanted to, Buller was right that he couldn't tag me for this one. Willis had been dead for at least two days before I'd found him, and even a novice murderer isn't likely to return to the scene of the crime just so he can pretend to discover the body and call the police.

Still, it was hard for me to take too much umbrage with Buller's comment as, if I hadn't already crossed a line by withholding evidence, I was getting damned close. And while I had no hard proof, I knew Fitz had been trying to run a scam on the insurance company and had almost certainly arranged for his own death. But I wasn't even close to figuring out all the pros and cons of the if-when-and-what I should tell the police or the insurance company about any of that. What was now clear was that I was close to running out the clock on the time I had to think about it.

The detectives ran me downtown and kept me there for over three hours. Sgt. Buller, having regained his less-than-friendly demeanor, questioned me briefly a few times, asking the same questions over and over, with me giving the same answers again and again—Lt. Archer notable by his absence. In between sessions they left me sitting in one of their dreary interrogation rooms, empty except for a beat-up wooden table; a couple of equally distressed, utilitarian chairs; a large, smudged, probably two-way mirror; and me. As usual in such situations, they kept me supplied with lousy coffee, which I drank sparingly. My chair seemed to get harder and harder as I sat there. And even my frequent bouts of pacing about the room didn't do much to relieve the problem; when I sat back down, the chair seemed, if anything, even more unyielding. From time to time I would close my eyes and pretend to sleep, trying to appear unconcerned about having been hauled in and left to stew for long periods of time, but I don't think I fooled anyone who might've been looking at me from the other side of the wall mirror.

Little if anything was accomplished in the way of my providing more information during my sessions with Buller. On the other hand, Buller—whether intentionally or unwittingly I couldn't say—told me that Willis had been methodically tortured, and his apartment ransacked. That wasn't much of a revelation as those things—at least the part about Jack being worked over—had been obvious to me from the start. He also told me that I had been right in surmising that the killer had handcuffed both of Willis's wrists to the chair before he worked him over.

'Handcuffs again,' I thought. 'Someone is doing a big business in handcuffs.' Maybe I should consider myself lucky that my attacker only used a sap on me that night in Topanga Canyon rather than a knife or a gun. But then I didn't have any information that he might want—perhaps ignorance really is bliss, at least it appeared to be in my case.

Finally, Archer, accompanied by Buller, came in to talk with me for what I hoped would be the final round of probing. Archer lost no time in tunneling into the mother lode of what he wanted to know from me. "So, explain again what you were doing at Willis's; and why were you carrying a gun?"

"I talked with Paul Logan, like you suggested," I replied, anxious to get on the table that piece of information I had not previously passed on to the police. "He wasn't about to tell me anything, but his guy, Mace Mason, the ex-fighter, let slip that it was Willis, not Fitz, who made the meeting with Logan on the twentieth."

"Why didn't you come to us with that information right away?" an obviously annoyed Archer pressed.

"I was going to, but I wanted to give Willis a little time first, to see if he would come around and open up to me; I doubted he would for you. I met with him on Monday night, the same day that I had the sit-down with Logan, but Willis was drunk and surly and wouldn't say anything."

"From the condition of Willis's body, that must've been just before he was killed," Buller pointed out.

I tried to ignore Buller's disconcerting—and suggestive, if not outright accusatory—comment and kept talking before Archer might pick up on it or Buller could further twist it into a theory against me. "I was going to take another run at Willis when he sobered up, but I was pretty busy on Tuesday. Then the situation with Javier came down the pike . . ."

"Javier? What are you talking about?" Archer broke in.

I explained—without naming names that didn't need to be named particularly Lou Buntz's or Sammy Zissu's—how I'd learned through my *sources* that Javier had been the one who had snuck into the house and taken Pilar's low-end jewelry the night Fitz had been shot, and about Javier's seeing Fitz talking with someone in his study. I didn't mention the fact that Javier had pulled a knife on me when I'd confronted him, figuring that that had already been settled between the two of us, and that the police knowing about his misstep wouldn't do Javier's hopes of their going easy on him much good when he turned himself in.

"And again, why didn't you call us with that information as soon as you found it out?" Archer wasn't smiling, and I realized that my belated revelations were putting a strain on the personal relationship we'd developed over the last two years.

Buller was displaying a smug little smile, no doubt happy about my discomfort in trying to navigate the trouble waters I had sailed into, or at the storm clouds he could see appearing on the horizon of what had before been my sunny relationship with his boss.

"I wanted to give Javier a chance to come clean on his own," I stammered, sincerely contrite.

"You're too damn' nice, Marshall," Archer said with a frown, but apparently somewhat appeased. "It's going to get you into trouble one of these days—maybe it already has. You'd better hope this Ruiz kid shows up at the station pronto."

The significance of Archer's pointed remark wasn't lost on me, but I saw no positive purpose in commenting on it. Instead, I continued to unload, wanting to get all of my reasoning out as quickly as I could manage to do it. "I wasn't sure what the meeting between Logan and Willis was all about, but I guessed that it must've been significant. Logan wasn't going to give anything up. And like I said, I figured I'd have a better chance of getting a straight story out of Willis once he'd sobered up and thought about it than you guys would, so I decided to take a shot at him."

It was a poor choice of words, which I regretted as soon as they were out of my mouth—mentioning 'taking a shot' at a man who you have just discovered murdered is not a great approach when making an explanation of your actions to the police. Not wanting to get into it any further, or to give anyone else time to think on it, I moved on quickly. "I didn't think Willis had anything to do with Fitz's death, but I couldn't be certain. He'd answered the door with a gun in his hand and had been combative before when I broached the question of his meeting with a disreputable character like Logan. I couldn't be certain how he might react when I confronted him again about it—a meeting that Logan obviously wanted kept a secret. I thought it might be a good idea to be armed for this meeting, just in case Willis decided to overreact."

What I was telling Archer was mostly true, if not the whole truth.

"You realize that your confronting Willis on your own gave him a heads up and would've allowed him time to work up a cover story with Logan before he talked with us," Archer pointed out.

"I hadn't thought about that," I admitted and tried not to look as foolish as I felt for not having considered it. At that point, I came damned near to opening up with everything I knew about Fitz's insurance scam and his arranging for his own death. But for reasons I still can't explain—or perhaps for less-than-ethical reasons I'm still reluctant to face—I held back on that information.

"Willis's turning up dead of course makes it look like he was involved, but Jack was loyal to Fitz to a fault; I don't see him killing him. Maybe it has something to do with the kidnapping," I suggested.

I thought about recommending that Archer and Buller take another look at Willis's alibi for the time of the kidnapping and Fitz's murder, but I realized Archer would already be way ahead of me on that. Under the circumstances in which I had been tardy in supplying him with important information, I doubted Archer would've taken kindly to me telling him how to do his job.

For the same reason, I didn't bother to state the obvious: that whoever had killed Willis was probably the same guy who had shot Fitz, or at least it had been arranged by one guy—my money was on Logan.

Archer interrupted my thoughts with an abrupt, sobering question. "Are you telling me everything you know, Marshall?"

I paused and looked the lieutenant in the eye before answering, "I've told you everything that I can prove." I paused again and swallowed hard before I added, "I have some ideas, but I'm not ready to share speculations until I've given them a lot more thought."

"Well, don't wait too long. Whoever killed Willis did you a favor by cutting him up. Otherwise, you'd be number one on the hit parade of suspects for this one too," Archer said. "And you'd better hope this Ruiz kid is waiting for me when I get back into the office in the morning. If he isn't, you and I are going to have a big problem."

"I think he'll be here," I responded weakly to Archer, expressing the least certain comment that I had made to him that night—or more accurately that morning, seeing as how my visit with the police had extended into the early hours of the next day.

Finally, no doubt sick of looking at me and wanting to be rid of me before our personal relationship took another hit, Archer cut me loose. He'd gotten next to nothing out of me because, as usual, I knew nothing they couldn't figure out for themselves if they cared enough to think on it. I'd given additional serious consideration to sharing my idea about how Fitz's shooting went down, but with Willis—the only witness who might back up my ideas—now in the morgue, I thought it would be counterproductive for me to start offering a theory that in the absence of any actual proof would look to be self-serving.

This time Archer didn't walk me out of the building or express any words of reassurance, but he did arrange a ride for me back to Culver City to pick up my car parked near Willis's apartment house. In the battle to maintain our personal relationship, I rated those offsetting actions by Archer as a tossup.

The return trip from downtown L.A. to Culver City in the back of a squad car at 2:30 on a Thursday morning gave me plenty of time to think things over: If Willis had arranged with Logan for a pro to kill Fitz, then killing Willis was probably Logan's way of covering his tracks, of breaking the connection between Willis and him. That thought made me feel some remorse for uncovering the Logan-Willis connection, which may have gotten Jack killed. But I assuaged my conscience by reasoning that if Willis had opened up to me in the first place, as I'd asked him to do, I probably wouldn't have talked to Logan at all.

As I was the one other person who knew of the meeting between Willis and Logan, I briefly considered that I also might be a target of Logan's clean-up efforts. But having now passed what I knew, if not all that I suspected, about the meeting to the police, they would quickly follow up with Logan. When that happened, Logan could tell them any fairy tale he wanted to about the meeting; a dead Willis wasn't going to contradict him. There would be no reason—other than sheer bad temper—for Logan to send a hired-gun after me once the cat was out of the bag about the meeting. And there would be a lot of police eyes giving Logan a hard look if I suddenly showed up dead. Having me killed would be an unnecessary risk for Logan with no real benefit. My reasoning was cold comfort, I admit; I had little confidence that Logan was as inclined to consider the situation as rationally and objectively as I might hope he would.

It looked as if my only clear chance of confirming that the kidnapping was a fake and that Fitz had been shot by a professional killer arranged through Logan had died with Willis. I could give up Dr. Peterson, but he'd be crazy to admit anything to the police that he didn't have to, and Logan sure as hell wasn't going to back me up.

Logan probably had arranged for a different hitman to kill Willis than the one he'd supplied to shoot Fitz. Knowing something of how Logan-types operate, I surmised that both of the killers were long since out of town and would never be seen or heard from again.

## CHAPTER 24

As soon as I got to the guest house, I telephoned into the newsroom and dictated the facts on Jack Willis's murder to a re-writer. I wasn't breaking my deal with Lt. Archer as I limited my story to my firsthand knowledge of the facts without disclosing that I had been the one who'd discovered the body or with any mention of Willis's connection to Paul Logan. I did include in the report the fact that the murdered Willis had worked as chauffeur for the recently murdered movie producer, Stephen Fitzgerald, but offered no comment on the possibility of a connection between the two deaths. It was long before first light when I finished dictating over the line. That would leave plenty of time for the night editor to get the story into the morning edition and out on the newsstands well ahead of the other local newspapers, as the reporters for those rags wouldn't hear of the killing until the police released a statement later that morning. That would make my boss happy and more than make up for the fact I had no intention of showing up in the newsroom until much later in the day.

My plan had been to treat myself to a nice long, uninterrupted, and for the first time in a while, untroubled sleep. I was still sacked-out at 7:30 a.m. when Javier had come by the house—hopefully on his way to police headquarters—and Mag had dropped off the stolen loot to Annie.

Annie had opted to let me sleep through Javier's visit, but when she opened the morning paper and read about Jack Willis's killing, she decided I'd slept long enough. She woke me and alternated supplying and withholding much needed black coffee as an inducement to wheedle the entire story of my discovery of Willis's body out of me. I spared her a description of the condition of Jack's corpse, just telling her that he'd been beaten and murdered at least two days before I'd found him.

It took Annie, normally quick on the uptake, a few moments longer than I would've expected to process what I was telling her. I put that down to a normal person having a hard time coming to grips with the idea of people—people they knew—turning up murdered from time to time. It all must have seemed unreal to her—fictional like a book or a movie—not something that happened to regular people.

At least this time it was I, not she, who'd found the victim. While I'd had a visceral reaction when first encountering Willis's mangled body, I realized now, watching Annie, that I'd otherwise taken it in fairly unemotionally, in an almost matter-of-fact fashion. It made me wonder if my experiences over the last couple of years weren't causing me to become inured to violent death . . . Not exactly a talent that I would like to add to my repertoire.

"Who killed him?" The fact Annie asked the obvious question, a question she would've known I would've already answered if I'd known it, was a further indication of her bewildered state.

"Who knows?" I replied with a rhetorical question of my own. "But my thinking is that it's the same guy who shot Fitz or someone just like him sent by Paul Logan."

My non-specific answer and speculation seemed to bring Annie out of her semi-stupor. "How did Lt. Archer react when you told him about the insurance thing?"

'The insurance thing,' Annie's euphemism was an indication that she was as uncomfortable with thinking about Fitz orchestrating his own death as I was.

"I haven't told him yet," I said and steeled myself for what I knew was coming next.

"You haven't told him?" Annie made no effort to hide her frustration with me. "You have to tell the police everything. Why are you waiting? The longer you put it off, the less they are going to be willing to believe what you tell them."

"I know, I know," I responded weakly. "But a lot of things still don't make sense. Jack was my only hope of having someone who could swear that I had nothing to do with either the kidnapping or Stephen's murder. With Jack now dead, all they have is my word that I wasn't involved; that, and whatever goodwill I have left with Lt. Archer, which may not be much.

"What I don't get is if Fitz's killing was a setup and Jack knew about it, why bother to kill him? He wasn't going to rat on Logan; Jack was in the whole thing just as deep as anyone, maybe deeper. That's probably why he wouldn't tell me anything the two times that I talked with him.

"It just doesn't make sense," I repeated. "I want to take some more time to think it over, but if I don't come up with the answers today, I'll talk with Archer. I promise."

"Oh, John called this morning while you were still asleep." Annie said as if she were commenting casually on an unexpected call from an old boyfriend.

"John?"

"Lt. Archer," she clarified. Then with an amused smile she added, "He said I should call him 'John.' I think he likes me better than he does you."

"I'm sure he does," I replied without any sort of good humor of my own. "What did he have to say? How did he sound?"

"He sounded like he always sounds . . . but then, he's not

angry with me, is he?"

"True enough."

"Anyway, he said that Javier had turned up at the station, so 'you're off the hook,' whatever that's supposed to mean."

"It means your boyfriend isn't going to jail for aiding and abetting a fugitive." I said, relieved that my bet on Javier had paid off.

Annie shrugged. "I guess that's good news." She made a credible job of pretended indifference toward my fate. "John didn't say anything about Jack's being murdered or your being involved. I only found out about that when I got the paper. Maybe John assumed that I already knew about it, as he also said to tell you that they'd called Jack's sister, and she admitted that his alibi was a setup. He was there alright, but he'd arranged it with her himself. John said that when they pressed her about it, she admitted that she suspected that his visit had been so Jack would have someone to swear that he was out of town for those specific nights, but she said she doesn't know why."

"That fits," I commented quietly, more to myself in a whisper than out loud to Annie.

"What fits?" she asked. "What do you mean?"

"It pretty much confirms that Jack knew that the kidnapping was going down that night. It also lines up with what I've already concluded: that it wasn't Jack who slugged me with a blackjack that could've killed me the next night when I dropped off the ransom. There wasn't much love lost between us, but Jack had no reason to risk knocking me off."

"Wouldn't Stephen have made it clear to whomever he sent to meet you not to hurt you? Maybe we're wrong about Stephen's arranging for Danny's kidnapping," Annie suggested.

"Maybe, but I doubt it," I responded. "It's more likely that whoever was sent to make the swap got nervous and slugged me even though he'd been told not to rough me up. That sort of fits with the whole amateurish, staged way it went down. It sure as hell wasn't the same guy who shot Fitz; there's no way he could've gotten back here that fast."

"Who could it have been?"

"I don't know. But maybe figuring that out is now my best hope of getting myself off the hook. If Fitz was killed by a hired gun as we suspect, the shooter isn't about to hang around L.A. And now with Willis dead there's no one left standing who can finger the real killer except Logan, and he's not going to give anything up.

"But if I can find out who was with me in Topanga Canyon, that could prove my alibi and that I couldn't have killed Fitz. It'll probably blow Fitz's insurance deal sky-high, but that may be how it has to be. Much as I love that kid, I'm not going to take a fall on a murder rap just so Danny can wind up rich."

"Why not go to the police now? Why wait?" Annie asked with an exasperated expression, which seemed to say, 'That's what I told you to do in the first place.'

"Unless I can at least point them in the right direction toward who was with me in the canyon, it's just my word that I was slugged. I'd still be the person with the strongest motive for killing Fitz." I drank the last mouthful of now room temperature coffee Annie had given me and got out of bed, announcing, "Right now I'm going to take a shower, shave, and get dressed. But first things first—What's for breakfast?"

"Whatever you want to make for yourself," was Annie's standard reply. "Dottie doesn't come in 'til noon."

I was still in the kitchen in my pjs, robe and slippers, breaking the yokes on two fried eggs as I attempted to flip them over-easy in the pan, when Pilar entered. Her serene, rested looks made me envious; she'd probably clocked at least three more hours of restful sleep during the night than I had. To no one's surprise, she verbally exploded in a display of innovative Latina fireworks when Annie and I returned her jewelry and explained Javier's involvement. But she calmed down quickly enough when we made it clear that he'd turned himself into the police and would be providing information that might be helpful in finding out who killed Stephen. I didn't bother to explain to her that his information wouldn't add much other than establishing that Stephen had not been murdered by a thief, or that it had put me back in the picture as a suspect. I certainly didn't want Pilar to lose confidence in me or to have even a shadow of suspicion that I might have had a hand in her child's kidnapping or her husband's death.

I also didn't mention that Javier's telling us he'd seen Pilar asleep in her room when he was taking her jewelry had established that she couldn't have been the one who shot Fitz. While that should've been good news from her perspective, I'd never seriously considered the idea she might have been the shooter. And I doubted that anyone else had either, so there was no need to comment on it. And knowing Pilar's disposition, even mentioning the fact she might have been under suspicion would've probably set her off again.

By the time I excused myself to take a shower and get ready for work, I was fairly certain that Pilar, while she hadn't said it outright, would not press charges against Javier.


A hot shower, the water beating down on me, seemed like the perfect place to mull things over; I took my time with it. With Willis now a literal dead-end, I needed to come up with another approach to the problem. Annie and I had reasonably resolved the how and why answers to a lot of old questions, such as why Danny had been kidnapped and why Fitz had been shot. But we'd come up with no answers to the "who" questions, the key one being, 'Who was it that had been sent to meet me in Topanga Canyon?'

The more that I thought on it the more convinced I became that the kidnapping drama had been a Stephen Fitzgerald solo production. The whole hand-off of the ransom in the middle of the night and in the middle of nowhere was melodramatic, a scene that would work well on the big screen, but not so much in real life. How Fitz would come up with the $15,000 to fund the insurance gag, a substantial amount in 1937 in the middle of a depression, was his problem, not Logan's. Logan and his mob wouldn't have touched the kidnapping; why take the risk? And as Annie had pointed out, there was no way that Fitz would've let Logan's guys anywhere near Danny. But handing a sleeping Danny off to someone that Fitz trusted for what should've amounted to no more than an overnight babysitting gig probably wouldn't have seemed at all risky to Fitz.

Admittedly, there were now new questions to answer: Who had killed Willis, and what were they searching for in his apartment? But those were questions for the police, not me. And Lt. Archer and his loyal companion Sgt. Buller were much more qualified to find the answers to those questions. My best bet was to concentrate on who had helped Fitz pull off Danny's fake kidnapping.

I reluctantly finished my shower as the guest house's supply of hot water started to abate. I shaved, got dressed, and went back into the kitchen to fix myself an early lunch, two mangled fried eggs having not done the trick. My head still ached every time I thought back to the night in the canyon. Hoping that a cold bottle of beer would ease my pain and help me think, I alternated drinking from the bottle, eating a sandwich, and occasionally holding the cold glass flask against what remained of the lump on the back of my head. I knew a lot—or thought I did. The pieces were starting to fit together, but there were still big holes in the puzzle.

It took a while, but then something Archer had told me at Fitz's funeral triggered a new idea, an idea I was almost certain was right. When I'd gently needled Archer about staking out Fitz's funeral, he'd said they were "as interested in who wasn't at the funeral, as who was." I hadn't thought of it at the time, but I realized now that a longtime protégé, the frequent recipient of Fitz's largesse, had been missing from the crowd of mourners.

I ran down the hall to Fitz's office and flipped through his address book until I found what I was looking for, then jumped in my car, and sped toward an address in Van Nuys.

## CHAPTER 25

I punched Dick Melvin square in the nose when he opened the door, knocking him back and down on his keister, but not out. Maybe I was losing my touch, or maybe I'd had time to cool down during my hour-long drive, an hour in which I became more and more certain of my conclusions about Melvin, certain enough anyway to take the risk that I might be breaking an innocent man's nose.

It all seemed to fit so perfectly with what I knew of Fitz and Melvin's relationship and with the comic opera feel of the kidnapping. 'It was like a scene from a movie script,' I'd commented to Archer when he'd questioned me that morning when I arrived at the house with Danny. Well, it *was* a scripted scene, a scene written by Fitz in his best dramatic style. And who better to play a key part than an actor who owed much of his career to Fitz and who on the night of Danny's party had been promised a major part in *Watcher*.

My knuckles ached from the punch, but I have to admit that, at that moment, any pain I felt was overshadowed by a certain self-serving satisfaction on my part—maybe I'm not always the "nice guy" that some people seem to think I am. And to be fair, the temporary pain in my hand was nothing compared to the relentless throb in the back of my head where he'd slugged me more than two weeks earlier on a chilly, black night at the end of a dirt road in front of an old oak tree and an even more antiquated boulder.

"You son-of-a-bitch!" I bellowed at him, rubbing my throbbing knuckles. "You could have killed me! You stupid bastard! Why did you hit me with that damned blackjack?"

I could see from the look on the part of his face that wasn't already smeared with blood that Melvin was considering denying it, but wisely decided otherwise.

"I . . . I didn't know. I . . .," he stammered, his voice trailing off.

"'You didn't know,' Well, alright then," I responded, choosing scathing sarcasm over further physical violence—at least for the moment. Picking him up by his shirt front, I pushed him down on a nearby couch. "I should stomp on what's left of your face."

His hand quickly shot up to touch his bleeding nose. 'Actors', I thought. Even in the face of a death threat, albeit hollow, Melvin was more worried about a broken nose that might mar his money maker mug than the fact I had justifiably threatened to kill him.

"Did Fitz tell you to do it?" I asked, more to see if Melvin would lie about it than because I thought it might be the case.

"No . . . No!"

"So, it was your idea?"

He nodded but didn't speak. Maybe he thought that if he didn't admit to it out loud, I'd overlook it or go easier on him— maybe it worked since I didn't hit him again, although I was tempted.

"Alright, tell me about it." At that point, my tone of voice was scaring him more than the pain in his nose or the thought I might add to his injury. "Tell me everything."

Melvin, at a rapid pace broken only by occasional pauses to

catch his breath and wipe the still flowing blood from beneath his nose, confirmed what I'd already figured out: Fitz had handed over a sleeping Danny to Melvin on the night of the fake kidnapping. Melvin drove him to his sister's house not far from his apartment in Van Nuys, where they kept Danny in a warm bed, mildly doped-up on occasional teaspoons of cough medicine until Melvin handed him off to me.

He tried to gloss over it, but it took only mild, verbal prodding to get him to admit that the handcuffs and knocking me out were his ideas. Fitz had planned a straightforward handoff, but Melvin got cold feet, fearing I might recognize him or try to be a hero. He claimed he didn't know why Fitz arranged for the fake kidnapping and had no idea who shot Fitz or why. That made sense, as the fewer people who knew about Fitz's underlying insurance payoff, the better from Fitz's point of view. The only unexpected comment Melvin provided was that, as far as he knew, Willis wasn't in on the kidnapping scheme. That still seemed unlikely to me, particularly since Jack had gone out of his way to establish an alibi for the night Danny was taken and in light of his recent demise. But who knows?

Melvin was supposed to keep two hundred bucks and give the rest back to Fitz as soon as the heat died down. And Fitz had also promised him a speaking part in the *Watcher* film. Either one of those payoffs would've been enough of an incentive for a character like Melvin to go along with Fitz's scheme with no questions asked.

"So when you heard the next day that Fitz had been shot, you decided to keep the money for yourself, is that it?" I asked, more as a statement of fact than as a question.

"I . . . I didn't know what to do. I was afraid the police would think I had something to do with Fitz's death. I was scared."

I believed him, not about why he'd kept the money, but the parts about his not knowing why Fitz had staged the fake kidnapping or anything about Fitz's murder—and particularly the part about his being scared.

Satisfied that there was nothing more that Melvin could tell me, I asked, "Where's the money now?"

"It's here. I'll get it." He walked into the bedroom with me following close behind. I didn't figure him to have a gun, but then I wouldn't have figured him for a blackjack either, so I was being extra careful and staying close. The money, still in the brown leather briefcase, was hidden on the back of a shelf in his closet— not the cleverest of hiding places, but then he hadn't been expecting my visit.

"You're not going to tell the police, are you?"

"I don't know," I lied. With hindsight, I should've called the police right then and waited for them to arrive.

Instead, after hanging around long enough to determine that Melvin's nose wasn't broken and to assuage my only slightly guilty conscience for having come close to doing so by helping him clean off and patch up his battered face, I drove to my house in nearby Glendale. I went there rather than making the longer trip to West L.A., as I wanted to put the call in to Lt. Archer to drop a nickel on Melvin as soon as I could and to arrange to unload my burden of a briefcase full of cash.

Lieutenant Archer wasn't at his desk, but he called back within twenty minutes of my leaving a message. Archer should've been impressed with my detective work, but if he was, he hid it well. I explained to him my theory that the kidnapping had been a ruse set up by Fitz working with Melvin and probably Willis.

"Why would Fitzgerald do that, steal his own money?" Archer cut to the core of the issue.

"I don't know for sure," I responded vaguely. "He must've wanted the money to pay for something off the books. My best guess is it has something to do with the meeting between Willis and Logan. Melvin says he doesn't know why Fitz set the deal up; he just went along with it for the $200 and the promise of a part in Fitz's movie."

I didn't share my theories about Fitz's insurance con and using part of the money to pay off a hired gun. I reasoned that it still would be better for me if Archer worked it out for himself, which I was almost certain he would after talking with Melvin and revisiting Fitz's appointment calendar. I'd feel a lot better about it if it was Archer rather than I who cratered the insurance pay out to Danny. And Melvin's confirming to the police that it was he who slugged me when I went out to pay the ransom would be enough to get me off the hook as a suspect in Fitz's murder and go a long way toward establishing that I wasn't a party to the fake kidnapping of Danny.

Archer didn't press me any further over the phone, for which I was grateful even though I doubted he was omitting questions for my benefit. "I guess if this guy Melvin confirms what you're telling me it gets you somewhat off the hook for Fitzgerald's killing, but not totally," he remarked when I finished my explanation. "You still have the only strong motive that we've identified, and I suppose you could have arranged for someone else to pull the trigger."

I was pretty certain that Archer didn't believe I had anything to do with Fitz's shooting. I surmised that he was just pulling my chain with his speculative comment. He reinforced my assumption by adding, "At least, it moves you back down the list—good for you."

"What about Melvin?" I asked. "Are you going to arrest him?"

"Well we're certainly going to talk to him to confirm your

story," Archer replied. "Mr. Melvin has something of a problem; the only two people who might've confirmed his story about the kidnapping being a hoax are dead. On the other hand, if you and Miss Fuertes are satisfied, I think we can close the book on the kidnapping. I guess he's guilty of assaulting you, but it seems to me you deserved it for being stupid enough to handcuff yourself to a car door in the middle the night in the middle of nowhere.

"I think that Dave and I will pay Melvin a call this evening, shake his tree a little bit, and see if anyone falls out. Maybe while we're confirming your alibi, we can get a lead on who killed Fitzgerald or Willis."

"Hang onto the money for now; don't give it back to Miss Fuertes yet," Archer directed. "We may need it as evidence if we do decide to push the kidnapping rap against Melvin."

"Okay." I hung up the telephone feeling less relieved than I thought I should be. I didn't think it would take Archer long to follow up on the lead I'd given him and to reach the same conclusions I had: Fitz, working through Jack Willis and Paul Logan, had arranged for his own murder as part of an attempted insurance scam. And Logan had covered his involvement by having Willis killed. There would be no way for Archer to get anything out of Logan, and the shooter if he was smart would've left town right after punching Willis's ticket. My guess was that Archer would realize he'd reached a dead end. He'd probably pass on what he knew to the insurance company, write his theories into the case file, and move it to the inactive pile to gather dust.

If after chatting with Dick Melvin, Archer would be satisfied that I was no longer a viable suspect, then I supposed that I should be contented as well. But I wasn't. Too many things still didn't add up. Among those was Melvin's comment that he was supposed to return the ransom money to Fitz in a few days. If that was true, Fitz certainly didn't expect to be killed that night. Too many questions. I couldn't kick the feeling that it wasn't over for me just yet.

## CHAPTER 26

There was no food in the house, but there was beer. From my perspective it was the best of all possible worlds, as I wasn't hungry but had worked up a mighty thirst. Despite being elated at having found a way to get myself out from under suspicion for Fitz's murder, I was still troubled. A cold brew or two might be the perfect catalyst to help resolve the open questions that still niggled at me: Why was Fitz killed while the fake kidnapping was still in progress? Why had the shooter acted before being paid? And why did he shoot Fitz in the middle of the night at the house when he knew other people would be around? There would've had to be better times and places to pull it off. Fitz wouldn't have wanted any of it to go down that way.

And why had Willis been killed? Killing Willis to shut him up didn't make any sense, as Jack would've had just as much reason to keep quiet about the plan as Logan. As far as I knew Willis had nothing that would tie Logan to Fitz's death, and, having some idea of how Logan types operated, I doubted that there was anything. Even if Jack had come clean about the whole deal, it would be only his word.

And why had his killer worked Willis over before killing him? Torturing someone like that didn't sound like a normal activity for a professional killer. I was no expert, but from what I'd heard they generally got in, got it over with, and got out as quickly as possible. There must've been something that this guy wanted big time for him to take the time and trouble to work Jack over.

My father used to say, "Things have a way of working themselves out." I never quite understood how he arrived at that stoic perspective, but I knew he was right this time when I answered a knock at my door and the killer was standing there with what I guessed was Jack's .45 automatic pointed at my chest—I just hate it when my old man is right.

He was somewhat larger than the average-sized guy. He wore a rumpled grey suit, no hat, and no tie. His sandy brown hair was uncombed and looked like it had been that way for some time. Steely blue-grey eyes, which ironically matched the patina on his gun, seemed to say, 'I can hardly wait to blow you away.'

He backed me into the room and kicked the door closed behind him with his heel as he entered. His face looked mean enough, but otherwise it was non-descript except for a scraggy two-day-old beard that looked like it might be starting to go grey and a white scar on the right side of his upper lip that provided a gap where the hint of his budding moustache seemed to be making no progress.

It's strange how I can clearly remember those details now, when, at the time, I was staring at his gun and thinking of nothing but what might be poised to emerge from the barrel pointing at my thumping heart. Walking backwards isn't a skill most people bother to master; it's even harder when you're focused on something else—such as not getting shot—but I was too scared to stumble.

With his free hand he pulled a pair of handcuffs out of his side coat pocket. That revved up my heart rate to a high hurdle pace. "Sit down," he said in a hard voice, matching the expression on his face that now included as unfriendly a sneer as I've ever encountered.

"No," I said. I know that it sounds crazy, I knew it then, but I also knew for sure that if I let him handcuff me to a chair, I was a dead man. It certainly wasn't quick, cool-headed thinking on my part. Instead it was based on a scenario that I'd played out in my mind several times as a result of my own unfortunate experience of handcuffing myself to my car door before being knocked unconscious, and of having seen a manacled, maimed, and murdered Jack Willis on the floor of his apartment. Jack might've still wound up dead if he'd resisted, but there was no doubt that his last few moments on earth would've been a whole lot less painful.

"I saw what you did to Willis. You can shoot me, but I'll be damned if I'm going to let you work me over first," I said as resolutely as I could manage.

He looked puzzled. I didn't suppose he was used to people arguing with him when he had a gun pointed at them. It was a desperate longshot bluff on my part, but as I saw it the only chance I had. At least it got him to hesitate, which bought me some precious seconds. He looked as if he was trying to think it through, perhaps with the deep analytics of a chess grandmaster, or perhaps with the hectic thought processes of a cheap hood. Either way I rated the odds against me at no better than eight to one that he'd just put a bullet in my kneecap and questioned me at his leisure between my screams of pain.

Still, a forty-five makes a sound that could blow out the average person's eardrum when fired in close quarters, so maybe he was afraid of cutting our encounter shorter than he intended by disturbing the neighbors. If he tried to pistol whip me, he'd have to get close, maybe close enough for me to work inside the reach of his gun. I was bigger than him and, as I've said, a trained fighter of sorts, although a rusty one. My chances in a close fight were not great, but a lot better than trying to dodge a bullet. If I saw a chance to act, I was going to take it.

"Where's the dough?" he asked, apparently giving up on trying to mentally cope with my initial lack of cooperation and deciding to move on to the primary reason for his visit.

I knew better than to say I didn't know, it would've just

made him mad, maybe mad enough to actually shoot me instead of only considering it. The fact that he knew that I had the ransom money had to mean that he'd seen me at Melvin's apartment and knew that I'd left with the briefcase.

"I don't have it here. I put it in the bank, my safety deposit box. You followed me here. You must've seen me go into the bank."

It had been over two hours since I'd left Melvin's apartment, and I doubted this guy had sat outside my place for all that time thinking about it before knocking on my door, so I knew he hadn't followed me home. That also meant he couldn't know for certain that I hadn't stopped at a bank on my way back from Melvin's apartment. Why he hadn't trailed me home when he saw me leaving Melvin's with the briefcase, I'll never know for sure, but he hadn't. Maybe he'd been hiding too far away to see the briefcase clearly, or maybe he'd just wanted to check if some of the money was still with Melvin before he paid me a visit. For whatever reason, it was good for me that he'd waited; bad I feared—more than likely fatal—for Dick Melvin.

The briefcase with the money still in it was on a shelf in my bedroom closet. Okay, not the most original of hiding places, but then I wasn't expecting a visitor either. It would've been hard but not impossible for him to search my place while holding a gun on me. If he did try, it might give me the chance to get in close enough to try to jump him.

I kept talking to keep him from noticing the Swiss cheese bubbles in my story. "Look, you want the money. I like money too, but I'd rather stay alive. You can shoot me, but then there's no way you'll ever see the cash." I let that sink in, then said, "I suggest we wait here until morning, you over there in the chair by the window and me here on the couch. Tomorrow when the bank opens, we go there together. You get the money and leave, happy. I stay in the bank, alive. That will make you the winner and me the place horse. That way we both finish 'in the money,' you literally and me figuratively."

I'm not certain he knew what the definitions of "literally" and "figuratively" were, but he seemed to grasp the basic concept. "How do I know you're not lying?"

"I don't lie," I lied. My indignant tone must've been just right; he didn't question me further, slipped the cuffs back into his side pocket, and sat in the chair I had indicated, but kept the gun leveled at my gut. I eased myself with no sudden movements onto the couch. With my change in position, the gun was now pointing in the general vicinity of my nose, which didn't make the situation any more appealing, but at least I didn't have to worry any longer about my increasingly rubbery knees giving out on me.

Having a gun pointed at me would work to keep me awake for twelve plus hours. I had no honest expectation I could keep a running discourse going until morning, but I hoped I wouldn't have to wait that long. He didn't show much interest in small talk, so I started off by trying to clear up a few open questions of my own.

"What I don't understand is why you shot Fitzgerald before getting paid?" I asked.

At first, I didn't think he was going to respond, but after a moment he said, "I didn't shoot him. I was supposed to, yeah, but somebody beat me to it. I hadn't even decided how I was going to pull it off yet.

"That Willis guy set up everything. The dummy even told me about the kidnapping they'd set up to get the money to pay me. I never met Fitzgerald, but I was watching the house the night he was killed."

"Why?"

The nasty smile returned. "I knew the kidnapping was a scam. I figured when you came back with the kid, you'd still have the money, and I could score the whole bundle."

'And kill Fitz and me,' I thought, but didn't say it out loud—I didn't want to put any more ideas along that line into this guy's head. And I certainly didn't want to interrupt his flow of words. Once he got started my visitor seemed to enjoy dominating a conversation, an occupational hazard for someone in his line of work I would've thought.

"So, they send me out here to do this job on the Fitzgerald guy, but then they tell me I have to cool my heels for a couple of weeks or so, while he finishes up some deal he's got going and pulls off the kidnapping caper, and then a few more days for the heat from that to die down. They say they'll cover my expenses while I wait it out; I should consider it a paid vacation."

"They being Paul Logan?" I asked, trying to slip the question in unnoticed.

The killer flashed me a sly, knowing smile. "Yeah, Logan." His quick response to my question and willingness to mention Logan by name reinforced my suspicion that he still harbored an idea of taking me out after I retrieved the cash for him in the morning.

"So I say okay, but I'm thinkin' why not grab it all if I can? I start staking the house out, driving by now and then, clocking the local police patrols to get their schedule, and waiting for something to happen. Those stupid bulls run around on a better schedule than a streetcar. I can park on the street after dark for almost an hour before I have to move to avoid being there when they swing by. Then I come back and park in the same spot five minutes later.

"So that night I pull up to my usual place where I can see up the driveway through the open front gate. There's a big black sedan parked by the front door with a driver sitting in it. After a few minutes you show up in a hurry, park next to the sedan and rush up the steps, past some little guy just coming out. The little guy gets in the car, and it drives away. From all the comings and goings I figure the deal must be coming off, so I wait. Just before I was going to have to move to miss the patrol, you come out holding a little suitcase, kiss some babe, jump in your car, and take off. I turn my heap around to try to follow you, figuring I can grab the money when you get where you're headed, but I lost you at the cross street."

I didn't like the sound of that, as I reckoned the chances of Dick Melvin and me surviving his 'grabbing the money' when we made the exchange would've been nonexistent. Despite that troubling mental image, I strived with some success to remain passive.

"Sunset?" I asked.

"I guess. I don't know the street name. This is your town, not mine."

That night coming out of Fitz's neighborhood, I'd turned right on Sunset and then taken Sepulveda north over the Santa Monica range into the San Fernando Valley. It was the shortest route to my destination if not the easiest at night on a winding mountain road. In the dark one set of taillights looks much like another; it was easy to believe that this guy, unfamiliar with the area would've lost sight of me quickly.

"So I figure my best bet is to go back to stake out the house and wait for you to come back with the dough," he continued. "About one-thirty, after the patrol has made its regular sweep, I settle in for another look-see. The porch light is on, and I can see there are still lights on in the house, so I figure everyone is still up waiting for you to come back with the kid. The little guy that I'd seen before was at the top of the steps just going back into the house."

My muscles tightened and I came close to jumping up involuntarily from my seat—a sudden movement that probably wouldn't have turned out well for me. "Dr. Appel? You saw Appel again?"

"I don't know who he was. But it was the same guy I'd seen before."

"Was there anyone else with him? His driver?"

"Not that I saw, but it was dark, just the light on the porch."

This new information almost made me forget my own immediate peril. I was tempted to press my captor for more information but thought better of it. If I pumped him too hard, he'd be likely to shut down and start rethinking our current situation, which also probably wouldn't improve my status. I opted to let him resume his dialog as he saw fit.

"So, I'm just sitting there, waiting on the street in my car in the dark for another twenty minutes, when I hear a shot. It's a quiet neighborhood, the shot was plenty loud, sounded like it was popping off right next to the car, could'a heard it a mile away. That cooled it for me. I beat it outta there before the cops showed up."

"Did you see anyone come out of the house after the shot?" I asked hopefully.

"Nah. I wasn't curious. I just got outta there."

My mind was running wind sprints, piecing together the meaning of Appel's returning to the house. I'd seen him that night when I'd arrived there. He'd been called in to tend to Pilar while the kidnapping was going down. After injecting her with something to calm her down, he would've known that Pilar would be out of commission and that Fitz and Annie would be alone in the house after I left to hand off the ransom.

The doctor had been quick to send his muscle around to try to scare me off after I'd cornered him at Fitz's wake and told him to stay away from Pilar. He probably thought that scaring me would be all it would take to shut me up, and that I wasn't enough of a threat to bother having his guy take the risk of killing me. But Fitz was a different matter. Given Fitz's mood, I can only imagine what words might have passed between him and Appel before I'd arrived on the scene. Taking advantage of the circumstances to permanently ease Fitz out of the picture so he would have a free reign over Pilar and her habit might have been too good a chance for the doctor to pass up. After I'd left to make the drop, Appel and his guy could easily have returned to the house to shoot Fitz, and Annie if necessary.

Appel didn't impress me as the type to pull the trigger himself. And why should he when he had a guy like his chauffeur on the payroll, a guy who pulled a gun on me in the Examiner parking lot with less concern than as if he were unwrapping a stick of gum and popping it in his mouth. The hired gun who was laying all of this on me hadn't seen Appel's man, but that didn't mean that he wasn't there.

Those thoughts steamed me up to a point that I once again almost forgot about my own immediate danger. I was focused on ideas for various ways in which I could deal with Dr. Appel and his hatchet man. But my uninvited guest, apparently now enjoying our one-sided conversation, wasn't finished filling me in on his exploits.

This gunman must've had some Mediterranean blood in him, as his free hand waved around erratically as he spoke, his gestures becoming broader as he became more enthralled with his tale. His other hand, weighed down by the heft of his forty-five-caliber piece moved around some but with less emphasis. The business end of the gun was still pointed in my general direction, but not always directly at me. I estimated my chances of being hit if the gun went off accidentally, as he jerked it around, finger on the trigger, at about fifty-fifty.

I didn't particularly like those odds, but I needed to keep him talking. "Why didn't you come after me right away, if you thought I had the money?"

"I had to lay low for a while to wait for the cops to back

off. People I know told me you weren't in on the deal, so I paid the Willis guy a visit instead of you."

Again, the 'people' he knew must have been a reference to Logan. I made a mental note to scratch Logan from my Christmas card list if I was lucky enough to survive to send out any in the coming season.

"When I talked to him, Willis said he'd pay me my fee when he got the money back even though I hadn't been the one who'd pulled the trigger on Fitzgerald," the assassin explained. "But when I told him I wanted the whole wad, he stopped talking. That Willis was a tough nut, I'll give him that; he wouldn't spill anything. After a while, he kept passing out on me, so I gave up on him.

"I didn't have no other ideas, so I staked out Willis's place. When you showed up, I thought maybe my guy might've been wrong about you being in on the deal. But when you called in the police right away, I figured maybe not.

"Anyway, that's when I started following you. You were all I had. You led me to the guy in Van Nuys."

"Melvin?" I don't know why I bothered to clarify the obvious.

"Was that his name?  He wasn't as tough as Willis, by a long shot; he gave you up right away. Too quick."

My heart went out to Melvin. I'm not sure how long I would've held out if I'd been in his shoes, certainly not as long as Willis. Still, it took this guy over two hours to show up at my door; I suspected he'd worked Melvin over some, just for the drill. Luckily, I never found out how I'd stack up compared to Willis and Melvin. I was saved by a heavy, insistent knocking at the front door and Lt. Archer's voice shouting, "Open up, Marshall."

Archer was the conscientious type. I'd been counting on his going over to Melvin's right after we talked—had hoped he would anyway. After finding what I expected he had at Melvin's, he would've made a beeline to my place. Now that he had and was loudly announcing his presence, I was going to have to talk fast and get it just right if I had any hope of surviving the next few minutes.

The gunman jumped up, raised his automatic and steadied his aim at what I expected was a reasonable approximation of where my heart was again pounding away.

"Who's that?"

"That would be the police," I said as nonchalantly as I could manage, not moving from my seat on the couch. I kept talking, fast enough to get everything out, but not so fast as to scare or confuse him. "You can try to shoot it out with them, or you can slip out the back. I promise to take my time getting to the door. I'll give you another five minutes before I tell them you were here."

I could see he was conflicted. A man of action, shooting me and then blasting away at the police was no doubt what he would've decided on his own if I hadn't suggested an alternative.

"How do I know I can trust you?" he asked.

He couldn't, of course, but I hoped he'd overlook it. Ironically, it was the first honest advice I'd given him.

"I'm a man of my word," I said, trying to sound like he'd be a fool not to take me at it. I held my breath and waited for his decision.

"Okay," was all he said as he ran toward the back of the house. When I heard the backdoor slam shut, I got up and walked at a leisurely pace to the front door, which isn't easy when your heart thinks you're in the process of running a hundred-yard dash.

The banging and shouting were reaching a crescendo. As I opened the door, I narrowly missed being knocked over by a uniformed cop who was about to break it down. Without the door to provide the expected resistance, his momentum carried him halfway into the room.

"Come in," I said as he stumbled past me.

"What took you so long?" Archer grumbled in a not too friendly tone as he and Buller and the rest of the posse filed in, accepting my invitation.

"I was indisposed," I replied, not exactly a lie on my part but admittedly a misleading response. I was overdoing the wisecracks, probably a nervous, almost giddy reaction to the sudden relief I felt at no longer having to find ways to entertain someone who'd just as soon be amusing themselves by cutting me into small pieces.

It was easy to keep my word to my visitor, as Lt. Archer did all the talking for at least the first five minutes. Archer and Buller had driven over to Melvin's, but not right away, which explained why it had taken so long for them to get to my place. Archer told me in matter-of-fact police jargon that Melvin had been worked over and killed in much the same manner as Willis.

Had they gone right after I'd called, they might have caught up with my new acquaintance in the act of beating Dick Melvin to a pulp and carving him up before killing him, I thought. But they probably wouldn't have arrived there in time to save Melvin, so their delay may have been just as well, as things could've gotten dicey if they'd cornered Mr. X in the act of searching the apartment.

I felt sorry for Dick and a pang of regret for having led the killer to him. I supposed that if he'd turned the money over to the cops as he should've he'd probably still be alive. He got greedy, I know, but if the statutory penalty for being greedy was death, the world would be a lonely place for the few of us who survived.

"So, what do you know about this, Marshall?" Archer punctuated his dissertation with the key question, then added another, "Who did it?"

"I don't know his name, but he was here a few minutes ago. You just missed him."

Funny how a few, carefully selected words, can kill a conversation. It was a moment of high drama frozen in time like a painting of a barroom scene by a 17th century Dutch painter. I wish I had a picture of the expressions on Archer's and Buller's faces; I'd hang it on my wall as one of my treasured possessions.

"He was here? You let him get away?" Buller asked, the first to break the stunned silence.

"I'm not sure that 'let' is the right word, Sergeant," I shot back in an angry tone of voice that I didn't really feel but thought might help to make my point. "When someone is pointing a forty-five at me, I pretty much let them have their way. The best plan I could think of to resolve the situation without anyone getting killed was to suggest that he leave before you broke down my door. I didn't much like any of our chances if you barged in here and found some thug with a gun in his hand waiting for you.

"Besides, he looked to me like the type you're bound to have a picture of somewhere in your collection. I can ID him. I'm sure you'll be able to find him and pick him up without undue risk. Certainly, without any risk to me."

They didn't argue with my logic, but I could see they still weren't pleased—it was just frustration on their part.

While Archer sent a couple of uniforms out to scour the neighborhood in what we both knew would be a wasted effort, I filled them in on what I'd learned.

"So, he said he didn't kill Fitzgerald?" Buller touched on the key point. "Do you believe him?"

"Why not? He was damned open with me about everything else. I think he still had hopes of somehow killing me after he got the money. He copped to killing Willis and referred to Melvin in the past tense, so, yes, I believed him. After acknowledging killing the others, why would he lie about shooting Fitz?"

I told them what the hired killer had said about Dr. Appel being back at the scene when the killing had taken place. "Like I told you a couple of days ago, Appel reacted to my warning to stay away from Pilar with his drugs by sending his heavy to try to intimidate me.

"They'd called Appel in that night to calm down Pilar while the kidnapping was going down," I explained. "I saw him leaving as I arrived. The situation was a perfect setup for him to come back and take out Fitz. My visitor didn't see Appel's man, but I'd bet my money that he was there and that he did the actual shooting. Appel isn't the type to handle something like that himself. Appel's goon is probably the 'big guy" that Ruiz saw standing in front of Fitz desk when he was sneaking in that night.

"The kidnapping was bound to send you guys off looking in the wrong direction for the killer. Of course, Appel wouldn't have known about Javier picking that night to grab Pilar's jewelry, probably still doesn't. The fact there happened to be a robbery being pulled off at the same time would've just been frosting on the cake from Appel's point of view, since it also got everyone off on the wrong track."

Archer and Buller were nodding their heads as if in seeming agreement as I finished stating my theory. "Sounds about right," Archer mused, "particularly if Appel's chauffeur is as hard a case as you describe. There was no one home at Appel's place in Santa Monica when we went out there to talk with him after you mentioned his strong-arm tactics earlier. The neighbors hadn't seen him or his driver for a few days. We have the Santa Monica guys keeping an eye on the place, but there's been no activity. We'll check it out again."

Lieutenant Archer and Sergeant Buller took me into "custody" as a "material witness," which meant that once again I was going to spend the better part of an evening at police headquarters, this time looking to no avail at several binders of mug shots of remarkably unattractive individuals.

Before I asked, Archer informed me that he'd arranged for a patrol car to spend the night in front of the Fitzgerald house as a precaution. We both doubted that Danny, Pilar, and Annie were in any danger, but Archer had also realized I wasn't about to hang around the station looking at pictures rather than being with them as long as Dr. Appel and his sidekick were on the loose. In spite of Archer's precaution, I still insisted that they let me call Annie to let her know where I was before I would agree to start on what I knew would be a protracted trek through the police's rogues-galleries.

There was no way I would be able to cover in an agreed-to short telephone call all of the details of what had happened in the past couple of hours. Any attempt to do so would've just raised more questions than could be answered at that point. So I just told Annie that we'd located a witness who had seen someone at the house about the time Fitz was shot, that I was helping the police run down the lead, and that she wouldn't see me until sometime the next day. I don't know whether it was my tone or the words I chose, but Annie seemed to understand that there was no point in pressing me for more information. Archer had been adamant that I should not mention anything about Dr. Appel or his driver until they had followed up on it. The lieutenant's approving nod as I hung up the telephone was an indication that the call had stayed within the agreed parameters.

Archer also let me call in a report on Dick Melvin's murder. He was giving me another jump on my competition as long as my article stayed within the facts that he would be releasing to the rest of the press later that night, which of course would disclose nothing of the identity of the killer or the connection to the murders of Fitz and Willis.

It was past ten o'clock by the time I'd finished my unsuccessful perusal of the police's black sheep family albums and dictated and signed another typed statement for their collection. Once again, Archer arranged for a black and white to drive me back to my house in Glendale. They kept the little brown briefcase with the ransom money, which I would've insisted on their doing even if they hadn't demanded it.

Archer honored me with one of his friendlier smiles when they let me go, which I assumed was an acknowledgment that I was once again in his good graces.  His parting, quite unnecessary advice to me was, "Be more careful, Marshall, and try to stay out of trouble."

I intended to do just that. Although I wasn't too worried about another visit from my new *friend*, who, now that the money was beyond his reach, was no doubt somewhere well east of San Bernardino and still opening the distance between us. If I could just break the unfortunate habit of carelessly answering my door without knowing who was on the other side, I'd probably be okay. In my case, the logic was sound, if a bit overly optimistic.

## CHAPTER 27

The next morning I awoke at first light, refreshed and ready to face with a clear conscience what I anticipated to be the first day of a bright future for yours truly. It was too early to call Annie, so I showered, shaved, and slipped into the last clean shirt in my closet and a pair of slacks that still had a couple of days' wear left in them. Then I made a quick call to the city desk, told them that I wasn't coming into work, and headed out to grab a hearty early breakfast at Barney's on Sunset on my way to West L.A. If I timed it right, I should be pulling into the driveway of the Fitzgerald estate just about the time Danny, under Mag's watchful eye, would be eating the last of his morning Cream of Wheat, and Annie would be finishing her shower. Pilar wouldn't make an appearance for at least another hour and a half at the earliest.

For once my prognostications proved accurate. Danny and I had just enough time to make something of a mockery of his breakfast routine, much to Mag's good-humored chagrin, before Annie made an appearance in the kitchen.

Mag took Danny upstairs for him to brush his teeth and to dress him for the day's planned activities—many of which I'd mentally devised on my drive over to the house. I sat with Annie and drank black coffee while she, never much of a breakfast eater, picked at a croissant and drank a cup of her own.

"We were right about Dick Melvin," I said, giving Annie co-credit for my idea in a tacit recognition that ours was a team effort. "He admitted that the kidnapping had been a set up by Fitz. But he didn't know why it was being pulled off or who else, if anyone, was involved."

"Do you believe him?"

"Yes, I do." I said sadly. "He was doing it for Fitz for a couple of hundred bucks and the promise of a part in Fitz's film. Slugging me was his own idea. He still had the ransom money. The police have it now."

"You turned him in to the police?"

"Yeah . . . but, unfortunately, not right away." I paused. I was coming to one of the parts in the recounting of my previous evening's adventures that I'd been dreading. "Annie, I don't know how best to tell you this . . .. Dick Melvin's dead."

"Dead? . . . How? . . . Why? . . ." The unexpectedness and gravity of what I'd just told her caused Annie's normally high-speed thought process to slip into neutral. Her face had turned white, and her three one-word questions were followed by a stunned silence.

I decided that her current somewhat off-balance state of mind might be the best time to get all of the bad news out on the table. "The same guy who killed Willis got to him."

Annie stared at me dumbfounded, then asked, "But you said that you talked to Dick?"

"It happened after I left him. The killer tracked me to his place, then paid me a visit at my house. He was after the ransom money."

"He followed you!" Annie's eyes were wide in amazement, but not in a good way like someone who has just found an extra gift beneath the Christmas tree; more like someone who has just realized that they are in love with an idiot. "He could've killed you!"

It was clear Annie's confusion had been short-lived and never all that deep. Any hope that I could ease gently into the rest of the story was a forlorn one, so I finished up the part about my encounter with the deadly stranger in summary form. "The police scared him off before that could happen."

"Scared him off? You mean he got away?"

"Yeah, but now that he knows the police have the money and it's out of reach, he has no reason to bother us, and isn't going to take the risk of hanging around."

That comment seemed to sooth Annie; her questioning continued but in a more analytical style. "So the man who came after you is the one who shot Stephen?"

"No, it wasn't him. He was going to do it just as we figured, but not that night. I suspect that the plan was to delay until Fitz had finished the script and made his own arrangements to cash out on *Watcher*. My uninvited and unidentified guest was, however, the one who gave us the clue as to who *did* shoot Fitz. According to him, he was staking out the house that night and caught a glimpse of Dr. Appel going back in just before Fitz was killed. He hightailed it as soon as he heard the shot."

Annie's reaction to this information, a stunned silence, matched my own when my visitor had laid the same revelation on me.

"As I told Archer, it's more likely that it was Appel's driver who did the actual shooting," I continued. "Appel isn't the type to do his own dirty work. Archer and Buller are going to pick up Appel and his man, probably already have. I don't think they'll have much trouble getting one of them to give up the other to save his own neck."

"So they returned to the house, went in, and shot Stephen."

Annie was clearly back on an even keel, her normal rational self. "That's pretty brazen."

"Yeah, it was," I said, not pointing out to Annie, who was the only other person who would've likely been up and about in the house at the time, that the killer was undoubtedly prepared to leave no witnesses. Instead I commented as a bit of a diversion, "Fitz must've had more dirt on Appel than he indicated to me for Appel to take the risk of killing him."

Satisfied with my explanations, Annie moved on. "So you've now disclosed Stephen's little insurance scenario to Lt. Archer?" I noticed and was pleased she was doing me the courtesy of not referring to the lieutenant as 'John,' although I expected that they now had every intention of sticking with first names when addressing each other one on one.

"Well . . . not totally," I dissembled. "He knows that the kidnapping was staged by Fitz, but I left it to him to figure out why. I thought it would be better that way."

Annie didn't look as if she was totally onboard with my assumptions about not sharing everything that we thought we knew with the police, but she let it pass.

When Pilar came downstairs, I told her that the police had developed a sound lead in Fitz's case and were expected to make an arrest soon. I explained that as a condition of the police's sharing information with me, I couldn't say anything more for the time being. Pilar, apparently satisfied, accepted that position more readily than I would have expected of her.

Annie, Pilar, and I spent the rest of Friday playing with Danny. He seemed more his normal self, perhaps sensing and reacting to the improved mood of the rest of us. Pilar was as radiant and exquisitely beautiful as I had seen her since Fitz's death. I supposed that Charlie Stoke could take some deserved credit for that change.

Annie didn't ask for more details of my adventure and seemed satisfied and outwardly relaxed. With the family out of danger and no longer requiring our undivided attention, Annie and I were free to spend a different sort of emotionally cathartic and physically intense night together in the guest cottage.

Saturday and Sunday slipped by peacefully at the Fitzgerald house, a carbon copy of the previous Friday afternoon. Relaxed and happier than I'd been for some time, I was back at my desk at the Examiner on Monday morning, blocking out the story I would finalize and release as soon as I got the word from Archer that Appel and his thug had been arrested and charged.

When I didn't hear from Archer that morning, my positive attitude and feelings of serenity began to abate, and I was starting to get antsy. It was around three in the afternoon when a response to my latest telephone call of an hour earlier came through from Archer.

"Hello, Marshall. I understand you've been trying to get ahold of me."

"Well, yeah . . . John. I was sort of hoping you would fill me in on what's happening." I'd put extra emphasis on calling him 'John.' In the past—and as I planned to in the future—I'd always called him 'Lieutenant' or 'Lt. Archer' to his face. He would almost certainly catch my gentle dig at his having establish a first name relationship with my girlfriend; Archer's sharp enough to field that sort of lazy flyball. If he had in this instance, I could mentally picture the grin on his face at the other end of the line.

"I'll bet you were. Sorry I didn't get back to you sooner, but we've been pretty busy. And I don't have much of anything to tell you yet."

"What about Appel? What did you find out from him?"

"We haven't been able to locate him. We sent a couple of uniforms around to pick him up the night you were here, but the house was dark. I've kept the boys in Santa Monica checking the place, but as far as we can tell, Appel hasn't been to the house for days. Buller and I spent the better part of Saturday talking to the neighbors. No one has seen him or his car for days; they assumed he was away on business or a vacation."

"What about his driver?"

"No one's seen him lately either. Some of the neighbors confirmed your description of him but didn't know his name or anything else about him. We've checked with all the agencies in town that hire out chauffeurs, but none of them have supplied a driver for Dr. Appel. Without a name for Appel's guy, and only a half-assed description from you, he's going to be hard to trace." I caught a hint of uncharacteristic frustration in Archer's voice.

"Did you search the house? Maybe there's something there that will tell you where Appel has gotten to or give you a name to put with his strong-arm helper," I suggested.

"The D.A. isn't going to get us a search warrant for Appel's house on just the second-hand word of an unidentified, unlocatable hired killer who says he saw Appel on Fitzgerald's front porch on the night of the murder," Archer explained.

"I guess not." I breathed the words in a frustrated whisper.

"The timing of Appel's disappearing does look suspicious; no one's seen hide-nor-hair of him or his driver since the night Fitzgerald was shot," Archer offered. "But maybe he *is* just away on business and took his guy with him or gave him the time off. There's no reason to suspect that they somehow got wise to the fact we're on to them and took off. We have a bulletin out to look for the car registered to Appel, and the locals are still keeping an eye on Appel's house.

"The professional license records indicate Dr. Appel moved

out here from Newark about five years ago. Maybe his guy came with him. I sent a wire to the Newark police asking them to check and send us any info they can find on Appel. We'll probably have you back in soon to look at some more mug shots of thugs with mob connections from other cities to see if you can identify your visitor from the other night. But until something or someone shows up, there isn't much more we can do."


Working for a major newspaper has its advantages; I had easy access to the same—perhaps even greater—reference materials as the police. So following my conversation with Lt. Archer and almost before the earpiece on my telephone, now back in its cradle, had time to cool from the warmth of my hand, I had a copyboy pull the California medical license directory for me and was thumbing through its pages. Not surprisingly, there was only one Dr. Johann Georg Appel listed, his address 854 4th Street in Santa Monica. I wrote the address down on a scrap of paper, folded it, and stuck it in my jacket pocket.

I fought an irrational but nonetheless strong urge to leave my current project half-finished in the typewriter, sprint out the door, and drive at top speed to Santa Monica. But I knew it would be a waste of time; the cops were already watching the place, and the odds of my stumbling onto anything or anyone that they had missed were poor. Instead I turned my attention back to completing the work that I was being paid to do for Mr. Hearst's newspaper.

That clear reasoning and cool resolve lasted for all of thirty minutes and resulted in my completing less than ten lines' worth of decipherable copy. In one well-coordinated string of motions, I pull the sheet of paper from my machine; handed it to another reporter, with only slightly less seniority, to decode; grabbed my hat; and was headed for the exit. It probably would prove to be a futile effort on my part, but then so would be trying to do anything else.

## CHAPTER 28

The house on Fourth Street was a modest, single-story, two- or three-bedroom, typical East-coast-cottage structure on a small lot. Not surprisingly, the numbered street was four blocks inland from Ocean Blvd and its adjacent, palm-tree-lined palisades that overlooked the Pacific. The front of the house was dimly lit by a nearby streetlamp. A narrow driveway, consisting of two concrete strips standard wheelbase distance apart, ran up the left side of the house. A cement walkway from the street to a narrow, covered porch and the front door was bracketed by two patches of grass fighting for their lives in the salt air that drifted in constantly from the nearby ocean.

I parked on the far side of the street directly across from the house. Reaching over to my Ford's passenger side, I opened the glove compartment, took out a flashlight—the same one I'd used to read the fateful note in the parking lot of Ray's Bar & Grill three weeks earlier—and my Colt revolver from where it had been since the morning after my unfortunate confrontations with Dr. Appel's goon in the Examiner parking lot and a gun wielding Jack Willis in his apartment.

I slipped the gun into the side pocket of my sport coat, got out of the car, jaywalked across the quiet street, and marched directly up to the door. There were no lights on inside that I could see. And, as I'd anticipated, there was no answer to my knock. I tried the door. It was locked.

I walked around to the back of the house to a fence-enclosed area almost too small to qualify as a backyard. There was a closed and locked detached garage at the end of the driveway. I checked and found that all of the windows at the back of the house were closed and seemingly locked, as was the backdoor. Through an unshaded window next to the door, I was able to shine my light into what looked to be a small bedroom that had been converted into an office of sorts. The room was unoccupied.

Having completed all of the tasks that I'd contemplated during the trip out to the beach town, I returned to my car to consider the other options available to me, the ones I'd been reluctant to think through thoroughly during my drive from downtown L.A. There were no other cars parked on the street, so if the police were watching the house, they must've been doing it only when they had nothing better to do. Since no one had been around the place for days, the idea of my doing a one-man stakeout in my car didn't hold out much promise of paying off.

My thoughts were 20-80 divided on a plan of coming back after midnight to break in and search the place, though I expected only a slim chance of finding something in a flashlight search that might point to where Appel had disappeared, or to the identity of his heretofore unnamed associate. If I found any information of value, I thought I could slip it to Archer anonymously to get Buller and him off the dime. On the other hand, there was that risk that any such action on my part might coincide with a drive-by from the local buttons and land me up to my neck in hot water—an image of a sweating missionary in a cannibal's stew pot came to mind.

I was spared further felonious considerations by the timely arrival of a taxi that pulled up directly in front of the house. The cab dropped off a shapely little blonde number with a short-cropped Betty Boop hairdo. She was wrapped in a tight fitting, floral patterned, mid-length sheath, and further over-dressed in what looked to be expensive silk stockings and shoes that had no hope of coordinating with the rest of her outfit. My guess was the shoes were at least a half an inch to an inch too high to provide for any margin of error if she unintentionally leaned too far in any direction.

I was out of my car and headed her way before she'd finished settling up with the cab driver. The angle of her feet to the pavement slowed her progress to the door and caused an entertaining view from my rapidly shortening perspective. Despite the urgency of my mission, I admit that I found the time to contemplate and appreciate the rhythmic motion of her hips, tightly encased as they were under the smooth cloth of her dress.

I wanted to catch up with her before she got to the door. I suspected that once she was inside, I would've had just as little response to a knock as I'd had the first time. She was just putting a key in the lock when I reached her.

"Excuse me, Miss."

She paused with the key poised motionless in the lock and turned her head, but not her body, just enough to look back at me. If she was startled by my suddenly appearing at her side, she did a good job of hiding it. With anything like a smile I thought that she would've been pretty, but with a suspicious frown coupled with colorless shadows on her face caused by the light from the streetlamp, she just looked hard. "What do you want?" she asked in an unfriendly, alto voice that seemed a perfect match for her looks.

"I'm looking for Dr. Appel. I've got an important message for the doctor. Do you know where I can find him?"

She turned the key in the lock and opened the door. "I'm Agnes Miller, his nurse. You can give me the message. I'll see he gets it."

In her goodtime party dress and skyscraper shoes, and with her long, bright red, lacquered fingernails, if she was a nurse, I was Porky Pig in pants.

"No can do, I'm afraid. Strict instructions: This goes to him in person, no one else." I smiled my friendliest, non-threatening, business-like smile and patted the breast of my jacket with my hand as an indication that the critical missive was safely tucked in the inside pocket. "When do you expect him back? I can wait."

"I don't expect him anytime soon," she said. There was something inexplicable about the way she said this that cooled my blood.

"Can you get in touch with him? I don't know for sure, but my feeling is that some people, including your boss, are going to be plenty upset if he doesn't get this message."

For a moment, her frown became a little deeper and her visage more than a little harder. Then, as if a cloud of doubt had passed, she almost smiled and was nearly pretty. "Okay, come on in. I'll give him a call.'

She led me through the house without turning on any lights until we reached the room I'd seen through the back window, which she referred to as "the doctor's examination room." Aside from some locked, glass-faced cabinets hanging from one wall, crammed with an assortment of small white boxes and vials containing a variety of colored liquids, and a low, chaise-like, dark brown leather couch pushed against another wall, there wasn't much to distinguish it as a doctor's office. There was a desk, empty except for what appeared to be a large, cloth-bound appointment calendar, and a run-of-the-mill, black, upright, two-piece telephone, a twin brother of the one on my own desk at the Examiner.

Agnes picked-up the phone and lifted the earpiece from its cradle. Holding both the neck of the phone and the earpiece in her left hand she dialed a number from memory with her right—no small feat considering the length of her fingernails.

"Hello, Dr. Appel? . . . This is Nurse Agnes . . . There's a young guy here who says he has a message for you. He says it's important . . . He wouldn't say who it's from . . ." She looked at me. "Young, big, kinda handsome . . . I guess." She actually managed to fling a smile at me. I was right; she could be damned attractive if she wanted to be. "What's your name?"

"No names." I shook my head slowly and resolutely, trying to look sinister and streetwise.

"He won't say . . . Okay." She hung up the phone and set it back down on the desk.

"He says he'll be right over. Shouldn't take more than fifteen or twenty minutes." She was smiling more and better looking than ever. I couldn't but think that her newly found goodwill was a major effort on her part. "How about a drink while we wait?"

"Sounds good," I played along. I was giving 'Nurse Agnes' credit for her effort, but her side of the dialog over the telephone had been as phony as any I'd ever heard. My bet was there was next to zero chance that the voice on the other end of the conversation was Dr. Appel's, or that he would be the person showing up at our little impromptu party in the next few minutes— if at all.

Agnes opened a side drawer to the desk, pulled out a pint of rye and two reasonably clean glasses, and poured a couple of healthy shots. She walked around the desk and handed one of the glasses to me. I took it and sat down on the leather couch, avoiding what looked to be a good-sized sticky stain a quarter of the way up from the foot. Agnes sat un-nursely-like on the edge of the desk. From the way she'd positioned herself, with her dress casually hiked up, I could see the top of the silk stocking on her right leg, the garter belt clips that held it in place, and a good bit of exposed thigh. It was quite a show, but then, I supposed that was the idea.

"Down the hatch," she toasted, raised her glass to her lips, and tossed back a solid, expert-sized slug.

"Chin-chin," I replied and followed suit, although with a smaller, more lady-like sip. Given the obvious quantity of drugs present in Dr. Appel's office, I'd been careful to watch for any slight-of-hand as Agnes had poured our undiluted, un-chilled libations. Once she'd thrown back a hefty slug of her own drink that had come from the same bottle as mine, I was less inhibited about modestly imbibing as we waited. I considered that a short shot of whisky might go a long way toward calming my nerves, which I admit were starting to react actively to the developing situation.

Agnes and I indulged in inane chit-chat while we waited. I could tell she was giving it her best, working against her nature to maintain an outwardly friendly and cheerful demeanor for more than a few minutes at a time. Still, she made a good show of it, going so far as to allude to the possibility of our continuing our conversation on a more personal basis once I'd completed the delivery of my oh-so-important message.

Less than ten slow minutes had passed when I heard the sound of a car pulling up the driveway alongside the house. Agnes heard it too and instinctively, involuntarily glanced over her shoulder at the door to the backyard. I took advantage of her distracted attention to stand, remove my revolver from my coat pocket and cock it.

When she turned back and saw the gun in my hand, her eyes lost their previous bedroom promise. She opened her mouth but didn't speak. Confusion, mixed with fear, spread across her face as quick and easy as soft butter on a warm biscuit.

I had no intention of shooting Agnes. I wasn't even pointing the gun directly at her, although I held it out in a way that she would be sure to see it and think otherwise. I pressed the forefinger of my free hand to my lips. A clearly frightened Agnes nodded, a sign she understood my mute signal for silence and would comply.

I could just make out the faint soft-shoe sound of footsteps as someone approached the back door.

"Cops, Lou! It's a trap!" Agnes shouted at the door. Apparently, she wasn't as scared of me as she'd let on.

There was a quarter note rest in the score before I caught the sound and rhythm of running feet receding from the door and I gained the presence of mind to react. I was barely halfway through the doorway when a bullet slammed into the frame just above me. A decent, but luckily unrewarded, effort for a fleeing man turning slightly as he ran and firing back over his shoulder.

A survival instinct caused me to pull back, only to be met by a smack to the side of my face with the base of the telephone wielded by an angry Agnes. I pushed her away. The blow hadn't done much to slow me down, but it sure soured what was left of any positive attitude I'd managed to retain toward that little blonde bombshell.

I heard the squealing of tires and felt the quake of the impact of a car scraping against the side of the wood frame house. Agnes's "Lou" would be halfway down the street before I could get to the driveway, but I went out the door anyway, crouching, gun poised but with nothing to aim it at.

Suddenly I heard tires squealing again and the black sedan shot back into view from behind the side of the house. It braked to a stop but not before slamming hard enough against the door of the garage to spring it. My first thought was that my adversary had changed his mind and decided to return to shoot it out. It was at that moment I realized that my poorly thought through plan was rife with several possible fatal flaws.

Before I had time to react, Sgt. Buller came into view from the side of the house, gun drawn, crouching low behind the car in what would be the driver's blind spot. A loud voice I recognized as Lt. Archer's bellowed from still out of my line of sight, "Throw the gun out, Cristiani. Show me your hands. Now!" I heard the clattering sound of what must've been a gun dropping onto the pavement on the far side of the car.

I was positioned too close to the house for Buller to have seen me peripherally, his focus at the time being on the car and its occupant. I decocked my gun and slipped it back into my pocket; it was clear that Archer and Buller had no need for my assistance. And I reasoned that if they turned and noticed an unexpected figure in the shadow of the house standing holding a gun, their reaction might prove more automatic than considered. In further hope of avoiding an unnecessary and potentially lethal confrontation, I slipped quietly back into the house.

Agnes, whatever else she might be, was no fool; the office was empty. I moved quickly through the house and out through the now wide-open front door onto the sidewalk. Agnes, running in her stocking feet, holding her shoes dangling from their straps with one hand, her dress hiked-up to above her waist with the other, was halfway down the block. I started after her at a cross-country pace. I estimated the length of my easy stride at about twice hers, so even running in leather soled street shoes on pavement I would catch up to her within a few seconds.

"Give it up, Agnes," I gasped as I closed to within two arm-lengths of her. "There's nowhere for you to go."

Apparently, that was all the gentle prodding Agnes was hoping for, as she stopped running almost immediately. She turned to face me, her expensive stockings ruined beyond hope, and the hem of her dress still firmly stretched against her hips, all semblance of modesty long since given up on as a lost cause. With bending knees she dropped to the ground with all the grace of someone looking to sit down in a chair that turns out not to be there.

I bent over her, hands on my knees, breathing hard to catch my breath before I reached my hand down to help her up. We took our time walking together back to the house, slowly, side by side without saying a word, like lovers who have just finished their first spat and are considering how long they should wait before making up.

## CHAPTER 29

It was back to the station house for me, this time in Santa Monica. After cooling my heels for an hour or so while Lt. Archer and Sgt. Buller questioned our two recent captives, I was treated to a shorter and much more cordial tandem interview with the two detectives. And, of course, there was another typed statement to be signed and added to the police's now extensive collection. I accused Archer of gathering data for my biography. Archer countered by pointing out they would provide good material to fill out my obituary, which no doubt would be forthcoming if I kept up my pace of unscheduled meetings and impromptu shootouts with gangsters and other assorted felons. As usual, my discussion with the detectives served more to fill me in with new information than providing anything worthwhile to them.

"Right after I spoke with you on the phone, we got a call and a follow-up wire from the Newark police," Archer explained. "It seems Dr. Appel was getting something of a reputation back there for writing generous prescriptions. The narcotics guys were starting to take a hard look at him. That's probably why he left there on short notice. The Newark police were happy to see the back of him; it would've been a long, tough case to make.

"Where they really came through for us was by alerting us to Appel's known association with a certain Lou Cristiani—a thoroughly bad actor—who fit your description of Appel's driver to a tee. Cristiani has a number of outstanding warrants, some for violent offenses. That, with your earlier statement, was enough for us to get a verbal okay from the D.A. to do a semi-official search of Appel's place. That's how we got there in time to save your butt."

"Yes, I've been meaning to thank you," I said with more sarcasm than gratitude.

"We arrived unnoticed just as you and the woman were headed into the house. Since she was unlocking the door, we figured Cristiani wasn't inside. You're at least a head taller than Miss Miller—her real name by the way—so we assumed you were safe enough for the time being. Dave and I decided to wait outside to see what developed. It turned out to be a pretty good plan."

"Except it almost got me killed," I pointed out with only a hint of rancor.

"Yeah, there was that. But you weren't killed, and we caught Cristiani. So, on balance, I'd call it a good night's work." Archer was beaming at his own joke; Buller seemed to find it amusing as well; I, not so much, although I had to admit that finding myself in the line of fire this time had been my own fault.

"Cristiani's not saying anything, and I don't think he will," Archer continued. "Once we pointed out that we weren't looking at her for anything right now, but that she was sailing close to getting herself jammed-up on an accessory to murder rap, Agnes has started to sing like Betsie Smith with her skirts on fire.

"She says she doesn't know anything about Fitzgerald. But she does know that Appel and Cristiani had a falling out over some payoff Cristiani thought he had coming to him. She claims to not know what it was about, but that Appel went missing right afterwards."

"We've found dried blood in the trunk of Appel's car," Buller interjected. "And the stain on the couch in Appel's office that you put us on to looks to be of the same vintage."

"So, you think this Cristiani guy may have done away with Appel," I summarized.

"Dollars to donuts," Archer quipped. "We figure it's just a matter of time until Appel's body turns up. The Newark warrants on this Cristiani character give us all the time we need to hold him until we locate Appel, alive or dead."

"What about his killing Fitz?" I asked.

"Well, therein lies a problem," Archer replied and shifted in his chair as if getting himself squared away to introduce his next revelation in a more formal manner. "And you're not going to like it."

"What?" Archer was right; I had no idea what was coming, and I already didn't like it.

It was Buller who delivered the bad news; I suppose to save his boss the unpleasant task. "Cristiani has a solid alibi for the night of Fitzgerald's murder. He was in the local lockup. Apparently, after dropping Appel off at the Santa Monica house, he drove over to a bar in Venice, got drunk, picked a fight, and got himself arrested."

"Damn," was all I could manage, but it summed up my emotions succinctly.

"He had a California driver's license under a fake name: Albert Jones," Buller added. "But even if he'd given his real name, the locals wouldn't have had the time to match it up with the Newark warrants before he was released the next day."

"What about Appel? Could he have gone back and done it?" I was desperately clinging to my fading theories, like a drowning man irrationally clutching to an anchor as he slipped deeper into an abyss.

Archer hauled me back to dry land reality. "Unlikely.

Cristiani had the sedan with him when he was picked-up, and Agnes confirmed that Appel didn't drive. So, unless Appel managed to scare up another car and drive it in first gear all the way to Fitzgerald's, I'd say that we can rule him out." With that observation by Archer, I could almost feel the bitter end of my line of reasoning slipping through my fingers.

With my Cracker Jack theory of the case producing no prize, I began to mentally revisit the other options. It didn't take long, as there were few left to consider. I was silent, but my mind was shouting, shouting things that I didn't want to hear.

"So, we're back right where we were before, with no idea who killed Fitzgerald," Archer pointed out, tactfully omitting, '. . . and with only one suspect with an established motive: you.' Instead, he added, "You've always been good at tossing out ideas, so if you have any, now would be a good time for you to pitch one."

I shook my head, an unspoken evasion. I'd been so certain of Appel and his guy Cristiani's guilt that I'd dismissed all other possibilities. Now, faced with this change in my grasp of the facts, the truth stood out to me as obvious and unappealing as a canker sore. It had been there all the time, right there in front of me, but I hadn't seen it; I guess I hadn't wanted to see it. I knew who killed Fitz—or thought I did—I just wasn't ready to say it out loud.

# CHAPTER 30

When I telephoned to the house before leaving the police station in Santa Monica, Pilar informed me that Annie was out for the evening on an informal job interview over an early dinner at Chasen's with some writer named Wilder and probably wouldn't be home for hours. I wanted to talk to Annie; I needed to talk to Annie, but it wasn't to be. I was on my own for this one. I knew what I needed to do; I just wasn't sure I could handle it emotionally.

I drove east on Pico Blvd., slowly, taking my time, hoping with each silent run through of my reasoning that I would come up with a different answer. But I didn't; no other answer made sense.

With Logan's greedy hired gun, Mag's would-be thief of a brother, and Dr. Appel and his hoodlum chauffeur out of the running, it didn't leave many suspects with a reason to want Fitz dead. Javier had seen Pilar in bed asleep when he'd heard the shot that killed Fitz, so despite having a viable motive due to her gaining control over the Watcher screen rights, she was in the clear. Charlie Stoke may have had his eye on a deeper, long-term relationship with Pilar, but it was hardly a sufficient incentive to drop by in the middle of the night to take down Fitz.

My *good buddy* Sgt. Buller had pointed out that Annie was in the house at the time of the shooting, so she had the opportunity. And the timing of Javier's making his escape along the upstairs hallway when he heard the shot that killed Fitz and before an awakened Annie would emerge from the nearby guest bedroom was almost too close to accept as feasible. But even Buller had been hard pressed to come up with a conceivable motive for Annie to have murdered Fitz. And, while the ransom and insurance money gave me a plausible motive, and Dick Melvin's murder had erased my last hope of a solid alibi, I had the privileged knowledge that, in fact, I had not killed anyone.

So that left Menske—short, fat, un-presupposing yet likeable Kenny Menske—the only one left with anything close to a motive for killing Fitz. Not much of a motive, I'll admit, but as Lt. Archer once told me, "It usually doesn't take much."

If Menske had known of Fitz's intentions to let him play a production role in the *Watcher* film, he would've had no reason to kill Fitz. But he'd lied to Annie and me when he told us that he knew Fitz planned to use him on the project. I didn't pick up on it at the time because I was focused on getting Menske's help in selling the script and the production rights to one of the studios. Now I realized that Menske hadn't known about Fitz's decision; if he had, he'd have argued that fact when pleading his case to take over the production—and now that realization on my part made all the difference.

My would be-murderous visitor of four nights earlier hadn't exactly lied to me; he'd just been too arrogant to admit any doubt about what he'd seen. We tend to see what we expect to see. And I realized, as I drove through the night and recalled Menske's behavior at Fitz's graveside, that it was equally true that we believe and accept as fact what we want to believe.

Anyone with the most casual of contact with Appel and Menske would not have had to see them side by side to realize the similarities in their size and build. In the dark of night, in the dim glow of a porch light one could easily have been mistaken for the other, particularly if the other had been recently observed in the same obscure setting.

Javier had said that he thought that he'd seen a tall man facing Fitz in his study on the night of the murder, as Javier was sneaking across the backyard. But from Javier's perspective, on the far side of the pool and through a window, even a small man like Menske would've looked tall standing in front of the seated Fitz.

I still didn't like facing up to my conclusion, which I admit lacked any direct proof. It was all conjecture on my part, no hard evidence, but I was almost certain that I was right. My only purpose in meeting with Ken now, rather than just passing my reasoning on to Archer and letting him deal with it, was personal; I needed to have a face-to-face, a reckoning with the man who had killed my friend.

My car rolled gently up next to the curb, directly in front of Menske's house in Beverly Hills, at around 11 o'clock. There were enough lights glowing through the front windows to confirm that Menske was still up and about. I sat quietly in my car with the lights off for a few minutes to run through my limited, poorly thought-out action plan and to assess whether I had calmed down enough to execute it.

When he answered my knock and saw me standing on his porch, Ken must have assumed I was dropping in unannounced to discuss the negotiations on *Watcher*. Despite the late hour, he seemed happy to see me and ushered me into his study, where we sat across from each other, much as I had sat with Fitz on the night of Danny's birthday party, the night when I unwittingly became a player in Fitz's convoluted drama.

I had my gun in my coat pocket, but I had no intention of shooting Ken—that is unless he panicked and tried to do something stupid, such as attempting to shoot *me*. I had no desire to harm Ken; I was emotionally way beyond any lingering thoughts of personal vengeance. My mood had become one of profound sadness rather than anger. I just wanted some time alone with Ken to understand in some way what had happened between Fitz and him.

As soon as I'd entered the house, Ken started to rattle off a string of comments about whom he'd approached and the status of his preliminary negotiations to unload the *Watcher* rights. I wasn't really listening, but I let him talk until we were well settled into seats across from each other, and I was in at least reasonable control of my emotions. Then, in as dispassionate a voice as I could manage, I said. "Kenny, I know you killed Fitz."

I'd never called him "Kenny" before, but somehow it seemed like the right approach to adopt when trying to casually accuse an acquaintance of murder. Maybe I wanted to seem sympathetic, which I wasn't, or maybe I wanted to put him off his guard—to this day I'm not certain what I intended.

He started to protest, but I kept talking to shut him up; I needed to get it all out before he said anything. "The way I see it, you were up that night, drinking and doing a slow burn about Fitz not giving you a piece of *Watcher*. You went for a drive to cool off. You drove by Fitz's and saw the lights. You knew he often worked late, so it was no surprise that he was still up. You decided to plead your case one more time."

Ken's face was empty, emotionless. He offered no sound through his half open mouth. Only his eyes were animated, seeming to shine wet with the intensity of afternoon sunlight off the surface of rippling water.

"You had no way of knowing it, but Fitz had much more important things on his mind," I continued. "He wasn't in any mood to talk, probably got mad and threatened to throw you out."

I couldn't be sure of the exact dialog but was comfortable that I was edging close to how it had gone down. Ken's lack of response and sustained stunned expression went a long way toward confirming my conjectures.

"His negative reaction got your blood up again. You, who'd always played second fiddle, always two or three steps down on the film credits, always the smaller paycheck. Now you thought he was cutting you out of the biggest deal yet." I could see that Ken was getting nervous, cornered, thinking more about an escape than what I was conveying to him, so I eased off a tad.

"Fitz's gun was out of the safe, lying there on his desk. I hadn't seen it when I was there earlier, but I wasn't looking for it, and it could have been buried under a pile of papers. But you must've seen it and grabbed it without thinking. That wouldn't have scared Fitz; he would've thought that he knew you too well to be afraid of you. But it would've made him mad, mad enough to come around the desk with the intention of tossing you out on your ear. You panicked and shot him. And when you realized what you'd done, you ran."

Ken's face was now pale, his gaping mouth looking like a fish that suddenly finds itself out of water, bleeding in the bottom of a boat. His eyes were frozen as if in a trance, looking straight past me at something that wasn't there or that only he could see.

"You have no proof," he mumbled, more of a weak, automatic challenge than a statement of fact. It had the sound of a line from a script that he'd run through several times until it was committed to memory. There was no conviction in his soft voice.

"No . . . No, I don't," I admitted, shaking my head slowly, sadly. "But that's not why I'm here. You've told me in so many words what I wanted to know; you've let me know that I'm right. You see, innocent people get indignant when they are accused of a crime that they didn't commit. They say, 'I didn't do it,' but guilty people say, 'You have no proof.' I'm not looking for proof; I just want to be sure about it, to understand it. I'll let the police find the proof; they're good at it."

If Ken had retained any resolve to counter my reasoning, it had dissolved like the battlements of a sandcastle assaulted by the first wave of an incoming tide. The expression on his face, now close to tears, mirrored the one he'd shown at Fitz's graveside. "I don't understand it. I don't understand . . . Fitz wouldn't listen to me. He got mad, started yelling at me . . . I was desperate . . . I needed this picture. But he wouldn't listen . . . He came at me . . . I don't remember, I honestly don't remember . . . He was dead. I was holding the gun . . . I knew what I'd done, but not how or why . . . I ran." Ken made no attempt to hold back the tears. "I killed my best friend."

I was fighting to counter tears of my own, but that problem dissolved quickly when Ken rose from the couch with a revolver in his hand. The gun must've been tucked away in the cushions of the couch.

Startled, my reactions were wholly instinctive. I didn't even think of reaching for the gun in my pocket; there would've been no time to do that anyway. Instead, I threw both hands up, palms out, not all the way over my head in full surrender, but halfway there, shoulder height.

"Here take this." His words and the tone of his voice brought me back to reality. Ken's right hand was fully wrapped around the handle, but he held the gun limp-wristed, barrel pointed downward, the hammer un-cocked, his finger off the trigger. Ken didn't intend to shoot me; he was trying to surrender the weapon.

My hands began to oscillate back and forth like the wig-wag warning signal at a railroad crossing. Having once again found a way to establish my innocence, I had no intention of being found at some future moment in possession of the murder weapon with my fingerprints scattered over it.

"No, no you keep it," I stammered. "It'll be better that way."

I dropped my hands, rose up from the chair, and reluctantly fought a renewed urge to sympathize with Ken. In a sudden, mindless act he'd destroyed his own life as surely as he had that of his "best friend." I looked at him sternly and spoke in as unemotional a voice as I could muster. "I'll give you some time to think it over, Ken, but don't wait too long. I expect the police will figure it out for themselves soon enough without any help from me. My advice to you is to get a good lawyer like Sid Rice, the guy who handles this sort of thing for the studios. He may be able to get you off with manslaughter, minimum time, if you confess. If you wait for the police to come for you, you might wind up getting yourself hanged."

I left Ken standing alone in his office, the gun in his hand hanging by his side. I hoped that he wouldn't use it on himself, but that would be up to him. In my book, whatever punishment a court might throw at Ken, it would be nothing, almost a relief, compared to what he was putting himself through.

## CHAPTER 31

Two days later, I got a mid-morning call from Lt. Archer to tell me that Kenneth Menske, accompanied by Sid Rice—the "extremely high-priced and effective Attorney to the Stars," as Archer put it—had just paid him a visit at police headquarters. Menske had freely admitted to shooting Fitz, and "just in case we had any doubts about it," had turned over the gun that he'd used to do the deed. Archer was giving me a heads-up because he was going to release the story to the press later that morning and, per our arrangement, didn't want me to get the news later than the rest of my colleagues.

As Archer told it, Menske had gotten in "just under the wire," as he and Buller, having worked through a similar theoretical scenario as I had, were about to pull him in to give him the third degree. Ken undoubtedly would've cracked; he wouldn't have been the type to hold up well under that kind of pressure, probably wouldn't have wanted to.

Archer's news took a load off my conscience, which had been struggling with a question of how long I should wait before sharing my knowledge of Ken's guilt with the police. I would've gone to them if I had to, but it was better this way: I wouldn't feel any gut level remorse for being the one to finger Ken; Archer and Buller would get the official credit for clearing up the case quickly; and Menske would likely get the best deal that the D.A. could offer.

I'd already written out the bulk of the story, so I did get a bit of a jump on the competition. And my inside dope on the relationship between Fitz and Menske made my story a better than average read. Sadly, the murders of Jack Willis and Dick Melvin, grisly as they were, had gotten little or no attention in the press, and I didn't dwell on them in my piece, as, from my point of view, the less said about Fitz's little kidnapping drama, the better.

Taking my advice about teaming up with Sid Rice worked out well for Ken. Rice was able to work some of his magic and got Ken a minimal sentence for manslaughter. He did a few years before obtaining an early release on parole due to ill health. I never tried to contact him. I thought about it but couldn't bring myself to do it. A while later I heard that he died somewhere up north within a year of his release.

After some effort the police finally did locate a mug shot of the hired shooter who had paid me a visit. He was a guy named John Harbach, a mid-level thug from Chicago with minor mob connections and several convictions for robbery and assault with intent, but interestingly, none for murder, or even attempted murder. "Either Mr. Harbach was an extremely careful assassin or a gifted amateur," Archer had said. "I guess the mob didn't want to waste any experienced resources on such a pennyante deal."

When they went to pick him up, the Chicago police found him dead in his room, a bullet hole in his chest and another in his head. Apparently, Paul Logan and his Chicago friends were big on tidying up after themselves.

Archer didn't seem too disappointed when he told me about it. He pointed out that all they really had on Harbach was my hearsay testimony of our conversation—the one when he was pointing an automatic at my vital organs. I had to admit that would've made me a less than objective witness. Archer figured the mob wasn't willing to take the chance that the police might have something more on him and that he might rat them out to save himself—after all, he probably really did know where the bodies were buried, some of them anyway.

The police never did say anything about Danny's kidnapping to the press. Since the whole thing had been a hoax and everyone involved with it was dead, Lt. Archer apparently decided to treat it as a non-event—albeit a "nonevent" that wound-up getting a couple of people killed.

With Menske's confession and conviction for manslaughter, the insurance investigators were satisfied and paid out on Fitz's policy. Archer, for reasons he scrupulously never discussed with me, had apparently neglected to mention Fitz's insurance scam to them. He may have *overlooked* that detail in his jubilation at having received the credit for solving four murders— Dr. Appel, his bludgeoned body having been discovered by a couple of rockhounds in the Mojavi where Cristiani had dumped him, constituting the fourth victim. Buller got some of the glory, if only because of my mentioning him by name in the newspapers. I suspected that he was probably less happy than Archer, due to his not being able to pin at least one of the murders on me. And I, if not exactly happy, was relieved to have the whole thing over and done with.

Pilar asked no questions when the police returned the $15,000 in ransom money. She probably considered it chump change, since Annie and I, with Charlie Stoke's help, had been able to close on a lucrative deal for *Watcher*, a deal that Ken Menske had all but finalized with Warner Bros.

About three months after everything had been resolved, rumors started to circulate in the gossip columns that Pilar Fuertes and Charlie Stoke were seen to be "keeping company"—a Tinseltown euphemism for sleeping together. I knew for a fact that a full-blown affair had started a lot earlier, being as Annie and I were frequently commanded guests of young Master Daniel Fitzgerald at the Fuertes-Fitzgerald mansion and had observed the romance developing.

It took only another three months before Pilar and Charlie tied the knot—mourning apparently being on a tight time schedule in Hollywood. But it was okay with me, as I expected Fitz would've been happy to know that someone who cared about them as much as Stoke did was looking out for Pilar and Danny.

Annie got the job that she'd been interviewing for on the evening that I'd spent being shot at by Lou Cristiani, chasing down the long-legged, less than demurely attired Agnes Miller, and confronting a remorseful Ken Menske. The position was as the assistant to some talented writers at MGM, not exactly the semi-executive level, close relationship that she'd had with Fitz, but potentially interesting and enjoyable work. The way that I liked to put it was, "She found it almost as pleasant a way to spend her daytime hours as she did the evenings and weekends of our continued flourishing relationship."

I didn't 'go south' with Danny's trust money, as Sgt. Buller had predicted I would. However, I did receive what Charlie Stoke might refer to as "something of a perquisite" in the form of long, gratifying tête-à-tête lunches twice a year with the person I'd asked to join me as a co-trustee for Danny's trust fund: Joan Blondell.